XENO XOO

REASSEMBLY BOOK 4

C.P. JAMES

XENO XOO: REASSEMBLY BOOK 4

For Ecuador, for being so nice to us aliens.

CHAPTER ONE

TARGET PRACTICE

Fifteen Screvari Scythe GL-11e fighters appeared on the scopes as though space itself had gathered into a formation of ships. There was no blinding flash of light, no shimmer, no jumpgate. They weren't there, and then they were. Geddy didn't know how to fight this way, but he figured he'd better learn. Any other ship would be toast, but the *Armstrong*, the Alliance gunship Commander Verveik called a Berzerker, had the same Zelnad tech.

It enveloped the ship in a bubble universe, whatever the hell that was, and delivered it instantly to any point in charted space. No jarring quantum compression, no time dilation, no nothing. Blink and you'd miss it. The device itself was little more than a chunky tablet loaded with star charts.

Geddy cracked his knuckles and spoke the command. "Phantoms, deploy."

The *Armstrong's* bag of tricks was deep, and he'd been working his way up to this one. Should he ever find himself in a pinch, three drones about the size of a standard escape pod would deploy from the top and sides to aid in its defense.

Even from up close, like his first breathless sight of her back in Verveik's hidden silo, you couldn't tell they were tiny ships. Such a clever design. Cooler still was the hologram tech that could make them seem full size.

Even so, it was fifteen against four.

— *There are too many.*

— I'll decide when there's too many, Eli.

— *Have you not yet slaked your thirst for blood?*

— Impossible.

— *I know this is a difficult time, but—*

— Hold that thought. I need to shoot something.

They were about as far from any civilized worlds as it was possible to get. They'd been monitoring the so-called band of thieves, the untraceable subspace frequency that Jeledine and her sketchy extended network used, for more than two weeks. Any chatter about a salvage trawler and its crew or a gorgeous Temerurian woman would've set off literal alarms.

Until they knew who took Oz and why, they had to be very careful. Jel put out feelers about the beam that yanked Oz into the clouds back on Verdithea without really saying what it was. She'd never heard of a gravity beam powerful enough to do that. Her hope was that someone, somewhere, had run across it. That, too, hadn't yielded any results.

Geddy's initial panic over Oz and the *Fizmo's* disappearance soon rebounded into buoyant optimism. *Of course* he would find his girl and his crew. But as the days stretched on, that morphed into rage. How long before it dissolved into despair?

Meanwhile, his urgency about the Zelnad threat had continued to build. Verveik and the Committee were supposedly maneuvering to rebuild the Alliance, but it didn't seem like enough. The sense that the Zelnads were racing unimpeded toward their endgame never left his mind.

The metallic sound of releasing clamps came from the rear of the ship as the phantoms detached. They positioned themselves around the nose, one to each side and one directly above. Even from up close, the size illusion was utterly convincing.

— *I still do not think this is healthy.*

— Yeah, well, I can only scream into a pillow so much.

Eli, the ancient Sagacean in his head, had grown increasingly concerned about Geddy's deteriorating mental state. Maybe war games weren't healthy, but he needed the distraction. Besides, it did serve a clear tactical purpose.

The light around the front screen flashed an urgent red, and the launch alarm blared like a klaxon.

"Missile launches detected," said Cherie, his AI copilot. "Evasive action recommended."

"Countermeasures," Geddy said.

A staccato string of *doonk, doonk, doonks* came from overhead as mushroom-shaped charges deployed and fanned out in front of the approaching missiles, splitting over and over into a sparkling curtain of chaff. The projectiles burst ineffectually into reddish orange puffs instantly squelched by the vacuum.

"That the best you got, fuckers?" Geddy growled.

These old-ass Screvari ships, relics from a long-decimated army called the Triad, were just the fish in a barrel of anger and spite. Someone took Oz from him, and they would pay dearly. But until that someone was identified, he had only his feeble rage and a simulated Screvari squadron. They'd seen Zelnad fighters once over Temeruria, but they were only escorts. There just wasn't enough data to guess at their capabilities. Besides, those ships had conventional jump tech, and he suspected there were newer ones.

"My turn. Phantoms, weapons free."

The drones scattered, drawing fire away from the *Armstrong* as the fighters unleashed a torrent of red disruptor bolts.

— You know what I've always wanted to try?

— *Do I even want to know?*

Geddy tapped a few buttons on the large holoscreen and disabled his shields, a small grin tugging at the corners of his mouth. This ship was just awesome. Disabling the shields on the *Fiz* would've taken ... actually, he didn't know, because you'd be insane to disable the *Fiz's* shields. Anything bigger than a fist would go right through it like an aluminum can.

— *Did you just do what I think you did?*

— You mean charge ahead without protection? I've done that before.

— *I'm almost afraid to ask why.*

— I want to make sure this is really tukrium.

The big gunship was clad in the galaxy's toughest metal, which had a reputation for being as immune to disruptor fire as any shield.

He winced and closed one eye as the volley approached. The first bolt struck the ship's starboard wing, slicing it clean off. Geddy looked out the side in time to see the red-hot end of the neatly severed wing go dark.

— Umm ...

His head swiveled back to the screen a millisecond before the main cluster of bolts tore through the bridge, rupturing the delicate barrier between him and the void. Instinctively, he blew the air from his lungs, closed his eyes, and waited for the cold to take him.

"Mission failed," Cherie intoned. Even now, she managed to sound encouraging.

He heaved a sigh. "Yeah, no shit, Cherie. Review mission parameters."

The screen switched to Simulation Mode settings. Under the Enemies heading, Disruptor Power was set to 124 percent.

"A hundred twenty-four percent?" Geddy's face pinched in confusion. "How is that even possible?"

— Morpho changed the code to allow physically impossible values.

— Why in hell would he–

The settings screen blinked away, and the ship's actual scopes took its place. A single ship, Afolosian by the looks of it, was closing in on their position as a bright purple fargate closed behind it. The *Armstrong's* database hadn't been updated since it was created more than eighty years ago, so it didn't recognize the model, but Geddy did. It was a small merchant vessel with limited armaments. Not a threat by any stretch.

He activated the comm. "Jel, we've got company."

Jeledine, his former partner and booty call, had been working on something in the ship's small, but well-equipped maintenance bay ever since they left Doxx-Mora. She'd been cagey about what it was.

Metallic footsteps heralded her approach. She felt badly that her extensive network hadn't come through yet, but she was every bit as anxious for a clue as he was.

The safest way to deliver anything valuable, be it goods or

information, was still in-person. Whatever tech was behind the gravity beam that snatched Oz away, in atmosphere no less, suggested Zelnad involvement. Now that the whole galaxy had seen what they were capable of, it seemed almost no one was willing to stick their necks out.

Jel plunked down beside him and squinted up at the ship's image.

"Friend of yours?" Geddy asked.

She gave a slow shake of her head. "I don't recognize it."

A ripple of nerves and adrenaline shot through him. Could this be the lead they'd been hoping for? He hailed the vessel, and the pilot came on screen. As expected, he was Afolosian, a race mostly known for asteroid mining.

His pale green face studied them a few moments before responding. He bore the hardened look of a mercenary or a thief. A ragged scar began at the corner of his small, round mouth and disappeared beneath the collar of his jacket, which made his neck appear preternaturally long.

His dark orange eyes narrowed at Jel. "Are you the in-and-out girl?"

Jel whispered to Geddy, "Y'know, I've never been crazy about that handle." She turned back to the screen. "Yeah, that's me."

"What sort of ship is that?" the Afolosian's voice interrupted. "I've never seen anything like it."

"It's the S.S. *None Of Your Business*," Geddy replied gruffly. "Who are you?"

"I see no reason to bring names into this ... transaction, do you?"

"Suit yourself," Jel said. "Whatcha got?"

The pilot's posture softened, and he sank deeper into his

chair. The ship hovered a kilometer away, still in line with the vector it followed here to facilitate a fast escape. Now that the price of novaspheres was solidly into five figures, getting here and back represented a significant investment. He wouldn't have come unless he thought he had a shot at the reward, which they'd set at half a million credits. Thanks to his old friend Smegmo Eilgars, who had inherited an inconceivable fortune, they didn't have to worry about money. That's why he was on the Committee along with Geddy, Verveik and all the others.

"A prominent scientist named Krezek recently disappeared from the University of Braaphis. A student claimed he was pulled into the clouds as you described. The authorities dismissed her account of events. I didn't."

Jel exchanged a significant look with Geddy. "How long ago?"

"Three weeks."

"How's that supposed to help us?" Geddy asked.

"I happened to be on my way back to Afolos that day. My scopes detected an illegal jumpgate well inside the markers. Based on the gate's orientation, there's only one place it could've been headed."

"Don't keep us in suspense," said Geddy.

"What about the half million?"

"It's yours. Assuming we believe you."

"That might be a problem, because it's hard to believe," the Afolosian said.

"Try us."

The pilot paused a moment for dramatic effect. "Stemir."

CHAPTER TWO

LEAD, FOLLOW, OR FOLLOW THE LEAD

JEL'S DELICATE FEATURES HARDENED, and her olive complexion blanched to nearly match her silky white hair. She was from Stemir, a small planet known for producing some of the galaxy's most alluring women. It had its criminal elements like any place, but if Geddy were to list the most likely spots for Oz to be, Stemir would've been near the very bottom.

"Stemir? You're sure?" Geddy asked. Jel remained too stunned to speak.

Jumpgates were square to the vector they opened, so if you got a decent measurement, you could narrow down the potential destinations. But it was an inexact science, and the further you went, the more of a crapshoot it was, especially if they had to make more than one jump.

"Since there are no other worlds within a parsec of Stemir, I'd say I am. Now, about the reward ..."

Jel hadn't been back to Stemir in a long time. Geddy had tried to learn why but was loath to press her about it. The size of her reaction was curious.

"Give us a sec, would ya?" said Geddy, and paused the channel. He turned to Jel. "Are you okay?"

She gave her head a cleansing shake. "Yeah, yeah, I'm ... I wasn't expecting that."

"You think this guy's on the level?"

"Long trip just to lie."

"It's not much to go on. You still have friends there?"

Her sparkling blue eyes drifted down to her lap. "A few. Whether they'll help us or not ... I dunno."

Geddy didn't care about the money, largely because it wasn't his. If they failed to stop the Zelnads, everything would cease to exist. This might be the only lead they got.

He reopened the channel. "Transmit your information."

The informant tapped a few buttons. As soon as the info appeared on Geddy's screen, he authenticated and then transferred half a million credits from the *Fizmo's* newly augmented account.

A smile crept across the man's thin lips as he noted the receipt of the funds. "Pleasure doing business with you. Good luck finding your friend."

He spun around and launched a novasphere. It exploded into a massive, shimmering purple slit. A second after the ship entered, it vanished into a pinpoint of light, and the jumpgate collapsed behind it.

Geddy turned to Jel. "Did I just blow half a million credits on bogus info?"

She shook her head ruefully. "I don't think so."

"Then what's going on?"

"Nothing," she demurred. "It's just ... any time I think of home, I think of ..."

"Oraisa," he finished.

Jeledine's little sister got turned into a Zelnad about a year ago and hadn't been heard from since. It was why she joined Geddy in this fight.

"We used to be so close. It's my fault we drifted apart. Maybe if I'd reached out sooner, I–"

"Jel, don't ..."

Tears filled her eyes. She let them come unashamed of her emotions. "No, no, it's true. Ori had a brittle soul. Like she was always under a shadow. I knew that, and I left anyway."

— Need some help here, bud. This ain't exactly my department.

— *She's regretful. Just empathize.*

"Listen, we all wish we could go back and make different choices. Like running product for the Double A. But as a great band once said, yesterday's gone."

She wiped her tears and allowed a sheepish grin. "And we need to give tomorrow a fighting chance."

"Close enough."

GEDDY HADN'T BEEN to Stemir in about a decade. It wasn't close to anything and didn't lie on any major trade routes. It had decent weather if you didn't mind the occasional acid rainstorm, but the food was marginal, and it didn't look like much from space.

Its women, however, straddled the line between myth and legend.

Eons ago, Stemirans were like any other humanoid race in terms of sexual reproduction. Females were subjugated, and that was the way of things for millennia until evolution seemingly started working in reverse. The males became increasingly primitive in thought and deed, retreating deeper into their lizard brains while the females sought knowledge and growth.

Eventually, the females took over and offered money in exchange for sperm, collecting all they would ever need to perpetuate their species. The men continued to devolve and retreated to the hills. Meanwhile, women bio-engineered their eggs to ensure each new baby was female.

But some still missed having men around, as young Geddy Starheart gleefully discovered. Now, he only cared about finding Oz. What a difference a few years made.

Geddy had mounted the jump device on the console. Looking at it again made him think about Commander Verveik. Supposedly, he'd arranged for every ship in the New Alliance fleet to be retrofitted with the magical tech. Until then, this would have to do. He entered the coordinates for Stemir and chose a point outside the markers. *EXECUTE POINT-TO-POINT?* appeared on the small screen.

He turned to Jel, who was chewing on her lip. "You good?"

"Yeah," she forced a thin smile. "Let's find Oz."

He tapped YES and space shifted around them like a filmic dissolve. The stars were different, and a brilliant yellow and red nebula bisected the void. As though by magic, they'd been transported near the galaxy's outer edge, almost two parsecs away.

A marbled tan planet, dotted with green, hung innocuously ahead of them. His heart rate quickened as he thought of Oz, pushing away any worry that she might not be there.

Jel shook her head in disbelief. To that point, she'd only experienced one bubble jump, from Doxx-Mora where they'd left her ship to the rendezvous. "Man, that is some serious voodoo shit. How does that thing work again?"

"You're asking *me*?"

"Good point."

Geddy clapped his hands. "Well, we've maybe narrowed down Oz's location to an entire planet. Which hemisphere do you want to take?"

Her eyes darkened again, and she heaved a big sigh. "Look, Ged, I ... uh ..."

His sarcastic smile flattened. "What?"

"I think I might know where she is."

He sucked in a short breath. Had she been withholding information? "Okay ..."

"A while back, I took this job. Sometimes these things get bounced around between middlemen, so I don't always know who made the—"

"Spit it out, Jel."

"Somebody was looking for an introduction on Stemir. A person who could help hide a crew and a ship."

"Who?"

"Her name's Pinka Polvo. She runs a bar on the outskirts of Derving. It's what you might call a ... reverse brothel."

Geddy knew a lot of things that started with the word "reverse" and had to do with sex, but this was a new one. "Go on ..."

"I don't think Stemir's like you remember it. From what I hear, the High Cabinet clamped down on the number of men coming in, so Pinka's been running them on the sly. Sex slaves to older women who miss the good ol' days."

He could only assume these "older women" were from the generation whose company he used to enjoy when he visited.

— *Geddy, I need you to remain objective.*

— Yeah, but—

— *Objective.*

"Those poor, poor men."

Jel rolled her eyes and continued. "The point is, I think the people I introduced to Pinka might be the ones who took Oz."

"Where's Derving?"

"In the northern desert."

He hadn't heard of it, but that didn't mean much. Back in the day, you barely took one step out of the spaceport in Bragos and eager young "personal concierges" would give you a brief tour of the area between the gates and the nearest hotel. Apparently, that was no longer the case.

"So, what's our play?"

Her face pinched in confusion. "Geddy, I just told you I might've had a role in Oz's abduction. You should want to wring my neck."

"It's not like you did it knowingly. You really think you're gonna get judgment from me? Hell, half the shit I used to run for Tretiak went to warlords and criminals. I don't even want to know what I had a hand in. All I care about is putting the band back together, starting with her."

A playful grin came to her lips. "Does that mean I'm in the band?"

"We'll see. The bar is high, as you know."

Jel's smile broadened. "I guess this is as good a time as

any to give you this, then." She reached into her jacket pocket and removed a small metal bracelet.

"What's this?"

"A gift from me to you. You *and* Eli, really."

— *Aww.*

"Oh wow." He took it and turned it over in his hands. It flared out in one spot but was otherwise uniformly smooth. "Is this what you've been working on?"

She nodded. "Ever since you told me about this 'Zelnad harmonic,' it got me thinking. What if we could make it so the Nads couldn't detect Eli?"

"Like noise canceling," Geddy said, running his fingers over the bracelet.

"Exactly."

Dr. Dennimore, the scientist working for Verveik on Verdithea, had isolated the Zelnads' unique electromagnetic signature so they could be detected. When he first encountered Geddy, he figured him for one because Eli emitted the same specific waves. All his research was now accessible through the *Armstrong's* computer.

She showed him how to work the hidden clasp and put it on his right wrist. It fit nicely.

"Jewelry with a purpose," he said, admiring the look of it. "What a concept. Thank you."

Jel's cheeks flushed a bit, and she smiled warmly. "You're welcome."

He pushed forward on the thrusters, and they shot like a cannon toward Stemir, the stick lively and comforting in his hand. It had been a while since he had done this manually. "Hey, whaddya say we do this the hard way?"

She pulled back doubtfully. "You want to raw-dog the entry?"

His eyebrows flared suggestively. "Ain't nothing like the real thing, baby."

A big, toothy smile lit up Jel's face and she tightened her restraints. "Then go for it. The world might be ending soon."

CHAPTER THREE

PINKA

GEDDY SET the *Armstrong* down in an arroyo at the edge of the isolated little town and engaged stealth. No sooner had he shut down the engines than Morpho came swinging across the ceiling and plopped down on his shoulder. Hughey Twoey, Jel's shapeshifting robot companion, followed closely behind. Morpho claimed to be learning his way around every junction and bolt on the ship, but Geddy suspected he and Hughey were shagging, or whatever version of it took place between a synthetic organism and a bot.

"Well, look who showed up," Geddy said, giving him a little pat, then wiped his hand on his pants. "Is it my imagination, or are you stickier than usual?"

Morpho slung a tendril out and pasted himself against the screen, surveying the darkened scene outside. There wasn't much to see besides the eroding walls of the long-empty river.

Geddy unbuckled himself and joined Jel at the back of the bridge, where she'd pulled their jackets out of a skinny locker. "Watch the ship, Morph. Keep comms open and don't let yourself get ... distracted."

The sticky black blob rolled down the screen onto the console and wrapped himself around the control stick. Not until he and Oz almost died battling skysnakes on Verdithea did he even realize Morpho could pilot a ship.

Geddy strapped on his old Exeter D6 and donned his trusty NASA jacket, the one made from an old spacesuit. It needed a wash, which was probably appropriate for the seedy establishment they were going to visit.

"Same goes for you, Hughey." Jel fluffed her pale locks out over the back of her short-waisted gray leather jacket and wrapped a scarf around her face. "Best behavior."

The bot, which most frequently took the shape of a cylinder, bent toward her in a little bow.

"All right," said Geddy. "Let's go find Oz."

The moment they climbed over the lip of the arroyo, the wind hit like a sandblaster, and Geddy immediately felt the grit on his teeth. He spat it out and flipped up his collar.

"Not the face shot you had in mind?" Jel teased

This was not the Stemir he'd come to know and love. He'd only ever been to the city. "Very funny."

The town might as well have dropped out of the sky like a movie set. There were no roads per se, just a haphazard grid of nondescript buildings. Pinka's Place was the same dull taupe color as the sand, suggesting it was made of the stuff. It was little more than three connected hollowed-out hemispheres, the largest of which was in the center with the eponymous sign fixed over the door. Had the days of hedonistic abandon really been reduced to this?

About a dozen small craft, presumably shuttles or taxis

hired in Bragos, were scattered behind the building. Geddy couldn't help but wonder if his younger self would've gone to so much trouble only to service some horned-out, desperate Stemiran cougar.

Eh, probably.

Jel paused to unwrap her scarf. The *thump-thump* of dance music pounded against the door, a strange contrast to its crude appearance.

"Please let me do most of the talking," Jel implored. "I don't know what the climate is in here, but I know how to read a room."

"You don't think I do?"

— *You don't.*

— Whose side are you on?

— *Oz's.*

Jel pushed through the door, and terrible music assaulted their ears. A busy bar hugged the curved wall to their left. Strobe lights pulsed in time with the music, purples and whites and oranges, illuminating a cluster of Stemiran revelers at the center. Wide steps led up to an exposed second level of ten closed doors that overlooked the circular dance floor. Giant glowing arrows directed the flow of traffic up one set of stairs and down the other. Closed doors behind the bar and to the right presumably led to the smaller domes.

Ordinarily, Geddy would've expected to see young girls dressed in clingy skirts, dolled up and vying for the males' attention. Here, the aesthetic was the opposite. Young men who looked like they needed the money lined the back wall in form-fitting T-shirts and shorts, waiting to be selected by older women.

One of the gyrating Stemiran MILFs wandered over and ran a finger thoughtfully across the young men's chests and stomachs. A ripped young Zorran man stood motionless while she inspected his entire body like the judge at a dog show. His excitement was as evident as his dedication to exercise.

The woman waved her hand at the bartender, a wiry and much older woman with short-cropped pink hair. She tapped something into a glowing terminal and nodded, and the grateful man was led upstairs.

— *Is this what they call a meat market?*

— Heavy on the meat.

"Couples' night is Wednesday," growled a woman to their right. She sat behind a little table just inside the door and held a p-shaped device Geddy recognized as a DiagnoStik, presumably to check for STDs. "Beat it."

Jel, who seemed as troubled by this scene as him and Eli, ignored her. "We're here to see Pinka."

"Is she expecting you?"

"Definitely not."

The woman looked past them at the bartender, who glanced up from her labors just long enough to recognize Jel. She motioned them over.

Jel lifted her chin in greeting and started off toward her with Geddy in tow. Everyone there was female except for him and the smorgasbord of men along the wall. More than a few paused their conversations as Geddy passed, several licking their lips with predatory relish. They were all beautiful, of course, but the power dynamic was inverted here, and it made Geddy uncomfortable.

"Not many humans come out this way," said one.

"They're selfish lovers," declared her friend. "I doubt this one's any different."

— For the record, nobody's more generous in bed than me. Nobody. You'll see.

— *I can hardly wait.*

Pinka wiped her hands on a towel and jerked her head toward the end of the bar. After they squeezed through a gap at the end, she led them into to a small office. Geddy pulled the door closed behind them, barely muffling the migraine-inducing music.

The woman was tall and lean with fierce eyes and spiky pink hair that flopped to one side whenever she moved, exposing the buzzcut underneath. Unlike the others, she didn't size him up at all. After feeling like a parade float out in the bar, it was hard not take it personally.

— I don't think this one's into me.

— *She's a businesswoman.*

— But clearly a lesbian, right?

Eli paused.

— *Sometimes, I wonder if civilization shouldn't end after all.*

The office was nicely appointed, with two sofas along the wall that resembled parentheses and an ornate handmade desk in between. Pinka leaned against it, crossing her arms and her feet. Her eyes locked on Jeledine.

"Been a while, Jelly."

— Aw, why didn't I ever think of that? What a great nickname.

— *You could go by Jelly.*

— Huh? Why?

— *Have you stood in front of a mirror lately?*

— Are you seriously body shaming me right now?

She finally looked Geddy up and down. "Who's your friend?"

He stuck out his hand. "Geddy Starheart."

Pinka's eyes lingered on him only a moment before pivoting back to Jel, her arms tightening across her chest. "What can I do for you?"

"A few months ago, I referred someone to you. They needed a place to lay low."

Pinka shrugged. "I remember. They paid well. But something tells me you didn't just come looking for your cut."

"We need to know who and where they are," Geddy blurted.

Irritation flashed in Pinka's eyes as they darted between him and Jel. Her expression turned patronizing. "Oh, Jelly. That's not how this works, and you know it."

Jel squared her jaw. "They took our friend."

"Not my problem."

Geddy took a step forward. She didn't flinch. "How much?"

She stared him down, making him feel very small. "I'm sorry?"

"Who and where. Name your price."

Her brow furrowed. "You think my integrity's for sale?"

"How about half a million?"

Pinka cocked her head and smirked, her shoulders visibly relaxing, then slid her eyes back to Jel. "Is he for real?"

"Look, I know it's a big ask, but we have to find her."

"A million, then," Geddy said, happy to have ample bribe money from Smegmo. Saving the universe required greasing some palms.

Her eyebrows flared impressively at the offer. "A million. Now that'll loosen a gal's principles right up. So, what's her name?"

"What's who's name?"

"The girl you're looking for." Noting Geddy's surprised expression, she rolled her eyes. "You think I don't know love when I see it? Please."

"It won't come back to you," Jel asserted, bringing them back on topic.

"Like hell it won't. I'm the only one who knows where they are."

"Please." There was no point hiding his desperation.

Pinka chewed her lip for a moment, then took a breath. "One million it is, Loverboy. They're pirates. At least, that's the vibe I got."

"How many?" asked Geddy.

She shrugged. "Couldn't say."

"Where?"

"The Harmeres. In the caves."

Geddy's head whirled to Jel. "You know it?"

Jel nodded. "It's a mountain range to the east. As remote as you can get."

"Fine. Let's get the coordinates and blaze."

"No." Her eyes returned to Pinka. "For that kind of money, we get a personal escort."

Pinka gave a sly grin. "Make the transfer. Then we'll see how generous I'm feeling."

— *Can you trust her?*

— I don't know. Are reverse-brothel owners trustworthy?

Geddy sighed and raised his left wrist, which bore his comm device. Pinka's self-assured smile continued to trouble him as she did likewise, opening the data link. It felt dirty, and not in a good way. He'd bribed hundreds of people in his day, but it was usually a few hundred here, a thousand there. Was this how things were done now?

He transferred the funds, and Pinka's shit-eating grin widened further. She lowered her arm and grabbed her own dusty leather bomber jacket before heading for the door.

She glanced over her shoulder at Geddy. "You sure you don't want me to introduce you to some of the ladies? I think you'd be a real hit."

"Rain check."

CHAPTER FOUR

YO-HO-HO

WHILE THEY WALKED to Pinka's sandskimmer, Geddy sent a short message to Morpho back on the *Armstrong* via UDC, or universal distress code. It was the easiest and most reliable way for them to communicate.

HEADED EAST, he messaged. FOLLOW IN STEALTH.

K, came Morpho's one-letter reply.

Her skimmer was about what he expected for a woman who wanted to stay below the radar. An off-the-shelf four-seater with a single Kemik AL-414 engine, only a couple generations newer than the ones he installed on his beloved *Penetrator*. She probably used it for supply runs to Bragos, about five hundred clicks southwest.

He anxiously watched Pinka's scopes as they flew to make sure the *Armstrong* didn't show up, but her basic scanners remained free of signals. It was hard not to notice her objectively terrible flying. Pinka didn't have much feel for the stick, which wasn't overly surprising.

"So, pirates," he said, making note of how far they'd gone.

The remoteness of this place was further eroding his sugar-coated memories of Stemir.

"Like I said, it was just a vibe I got. The woman was Ceonian."

"Ceonian? You sure about that?"

"Oh, you know what they sound like." Pinka gave a dismissive wave of her hand. "Like they're talking underwater."

It had a note of derision, but she wasn't wrong. Smegmo Eilgars was Ceonian and he had the same bubbly tone, like he was lightly gargling.

"I don't suppose she gave her name."

Pinka barked a laugh, as though the question was ridiculous. "Again ... not how it works."

That Pinka would hide some pirates and not ask questions didn't confound the imagination. Hell, he probably would've done the same back in the day. But her willingness to betray their trust, even for a million credits, made him a bit uneasy.

The faint orange light of Stemir's lone moon did little to illuminate the utterly flat expanse of desert and scrub brush. The ship's lights only penetrated a couple hundred meters into the inky night, yet Pinka skimmed the ground at six hundred kilometers per hour, seemingly confident in her scopes and object-avoidance system.

"I guess Stemir's been through some ... cultural changes," he observed, trying to get Pinka talking.

Pinka grimaced and shook her head, making a lazy detour around a low hill, its outline merely a starless void against the sky. "Hmph. The High Cabinet's been cracking down on all vice. Most men aren't even allowed out of the spaceport now."

"Too bad you're not in the vibrator business." Geddy grinned at his own wit while Jeledine closed her eyes and expelled air through her nose. "So, how do men get to you?"

"If they want it bad enough, they find me. The Cabinet doesn't give two shits what happens out here. But it's only a matter of time before they shut me down, too."

Geddy eyed Jel, who appeared nearly as uncomfortable as he was. "What'll you do then?"

"Oh, don't you worry about ol' Pinka. She's got her fingers in many pies." She threw her head back and cackled at her own joke. "We're almost there."

While Pinka flew, Geddy unconsciously ran his fingers down the handle of his Exeter. He surreptitiously tapped out a quick UDC message to Morpho.

STILL THERE?

YES, came the reply.

Relief washed over him. Having Morph and Hughey nearby in the gunship made him feel better about being this isolated. If shit went down, the *Armstrong* could turn just about anything into rubble, but until then, its origins needed to be kept as secret as possible. They weren't ready for people to learn about the New Alliance.

Pinka finally reduced her speed and skirted the edge of an unremarkable stretch of mountains. They were close enough that the ship's landing lights picked up jagged formations of volcanic rock.

Swinging wide around a finger of pumice, Pinka extended the skids and settled down in a semicircular cove with few clear details. There could've been an army waiting in ambush, and they wouldn't have seen it.

— I had no idea it got this dark.

— *I don't like this.*

— Me neither, but what's our other option?

— *Do you believe she is here?*

— I have to.

Once they were on the ground, Pinka powered down the engines. As their powerful whine faded, she opened a locker at the rear of the cabin and handed each of them a flashlight before affixing a headlamp to herself.

"Where the hell are we?" Geddy asked. "I don't see any cave."

"I figured you'd want to do some recon," she replied.

"I THINK I'M HAVING A ... heart attack."

Geddy had been panting for a solid fifteen minutes as they climbed, never quite catching his breath. The rarefied air chafed his lungs. Was he really that out of shape?

They were climbing up the side of what might once have been a lava dome. It was utterly bereft of vegetation, and bits of basalt under their feet crumbled away like ball bearings. They may as well have been wading through quicksand.

Neither Jel nor Pinka were remotely winded. Pinka turned around and smirked, her face at the very edge of his flashlight's throw. "Stemir's atmosphere has less oxygen than you're used to. Maybe that's why humans are lousy lovers."

"Are we there yet?" Geddy asked, ignoring the jab.

Pinka turned around again with a finger to her lips.

Twenty meters ahead, a faint sliver of yellow artificial light protruded from the darkness. It was a natural chimney and a welcome sign of life. Hopefully Oz's life. As impossible as it seemed, his heart made double time.

Muffled voices sounded as they neared the opening.

Pinka got down on all fours for the final five meters and crawled toward it like a stalking panther. Geddy and Jel followed suit. Spreading out around the opening, they eased their eyes over the edge.

What they could see of the chamber was quite large but irregular, with fins of rock that obscured much of it from view. A no-frills encampment had been erected, comprising a large tent and a ring of stacked terraformer crates encircled by lights. It reminded him of Verveik's improvised camp on Verdithea.

"Jel," Geddy whispered. "Do you see her?"

Jel shook her head. "I don't see anyone."

"Hey, Loverboy," said Pinka. "Come have a look."

She eased herself away from her vantage point on the other side of the chimney, and Geddy carefully took her place. From there, he could discern the translucent green wall of a force-field cell, and through it, a shock of red locks tumbling over a lilywhite shoulder.

Oz.

"She's here!" Geddy raised his eyes excitedly to Jel, a broad smile decorating his face. "Holy shit, she's really here!"

"You're sure it's her?" Jel asked.

"Yeah, but she's in a cell."

Still no sign of pirates, but the number of cots and quantity of supplies suggested a handful, maybe more.

Geddy rolled onto his side and met Pinka's eyes. "How do we get in?"

Pinka couldn't help but return his smile. She jutted her head over her shoulder. "This way."

They followed Pinka across the top of the lava dome to the other side. The first stirrings of dawn draped the horizon in an orange-blue gradient. Geddy turned back just before they headed down the other side in hopes he might discern the *Armstrong's* outline or the imprint of its skids in the sand, but no such luck.

As Pinka descended the slippery rock, Geddy hung back and sent Morpho another quick message.

FOUND HER. GOING IN. LEAVING MIC OPEN.

When he looked up, he found Pinka had stopped and was looking straight at him. "Is there a problem?"

"Just a quick selfie," he said. "Just wait 'til my friends see I'm in a godforsaken desert."

So far, Pinka had been as good as her word, but that didn't mean he trusted her.

Here the dome was steeper yet, making it that much more treacherous. They descended in zigzagging switchbacks until they reached the bottom. By then, his thighs were on fire and the sun had climbed higher, revealing far more topography than he expected. They were basically at the point where the Northern Desert bled out into faintly green hills.

A ship large enough to hold all this gear should've been obvious, but he saw nothing of the sort.

Pinka hugged the edge of the lava dome until they rounded a finger of rock jutting into the sand. She pointed across to a narrow crack from which the same diffuse light emanated.

"There it is. Good luck." She turned on her heels to leave.

"Where are you going?" Jel asked.

"You wanted me to show you where they were. I showed you."

"But how are we supposed to–"

"Their ship must be somewhere." Geddy cut her off. "We'll take it back to Derving."

She didn't know yet that Morpho had followed them in the *Armstrong*. He'd tell her once Pinka was gone.

"Pleasure doing business."

Pinka gave a dismissive wave and continued across the hard-packed sand.

"Thanks for everything!" Geddy called sarcastically after her.

They watched until she disappeared.

"So ... where's this ship you plan to steal?" Jel asked.

"Relax. I had Morph follow us."

She scowled. "When were you gonna tell me??"

"I just did."

CHAPTER FIVE

SPELUNKING

THE TRIANGULAR CRACK was in the middle of a bulge of basalt, the ground strewn with rocks. At some point, eons ago, the whole side of the formation must have exploded violently outward, tearing a vertical rip in the dome's thick shell that widened as it neared the ground.

After listening for voices, Geddy and Jel inched their way through the passage, which was so narrow at shoulder height that they had to crawl. The warm desert air soon gave way to the cool and musty smell of the cave. Fine, silica-rich dust immediately filled the air as they kicked it up.

"Sorry about the view," he muttered over his shoulder. "You should've gone first."

"Aren't you sweet?" Jel retorted. "At least you'll be shot first."

His impulse was to laugh, but there was no guarantee it wouldn't happen. They were literally coming through the front door of a pirate hideout, which sounded more like an Old West epitaph than an idea.

— *What if one of them decided to leave right now?*

— Banish that thought.

Muffled voices drifted into his ears, a male and a female. He couldn't make out what they were saying. As the crack flared out enough to return to a crouch, he and Jel drew their blasters.

The entry into the chamber was thick with shadows that hid their approach as they emerged into the dimly lit cavern. Electric lights mounted on telescoping stands were aimed at the walls, bathing the scene in a dim yellow glow. Geddy and Jel tiptoed between the battlement of crates and ducked behind a stack near the corner of the empty tent.

The chamber's ceiling tapered toward the back and became nearly semicircular as it continued into the dark, following the ridge north. Thanks to mining shinium for seven years on The Deuce, Geddy knew all too well that a lava tube looked like a long, stone kwonset hut. It likely ran under the mountain for several kilometers.

A man's voice, low and irritated, echoed through the cave. "They're late."

"They'll be here," the woman replied.

"You shouldn't have made this deal."

The lady pirate gave an incredulous *tut*. "Relax, Horschus. We still have leverage."

"What leverage? You counted on extorting that Temerurian bitch's family, only they don't want her."

"Just let me do the talking."

Geddy and Jel raised their eyes just over the crates. The woman's back was to them, but between her voice and her lobster-like features, it was clear she was the Ceonian leader Pinka mentioned. But upon seeing her, a wave of familiarity crashed over Geddy. His eyes narrowed as they drifted down to the custom-made Screvari blaster that hung on her exoskeletal leg.

The gun that once belonged to him.

He pulled Jel back down behind the crates. "Holy shit, I *know* her."

"You do?"

"Look at her blaster."

Jel stole another peek as the pirates' conversation grew more heated. She'd seen it on his hip many times in the past. "Is that ...?"

"The PDQ. Hel-lo, beautiful."

— *I am lost.*

— Before your time, pal. Your time in my head, anyway.

On Geddy's twenty-fifth birthday, Tretiak Bouche, his old boss at the Double A Auction on Kigantu, gave him the PDQ as a gift. It was made of tukrium, exceedingly rare for a ranged weapon, and treated with a secret Screvari process that turned it jet black. It was light, accurate, and unbelievably powerful. Screvari weapons were given names by their makers like swords of myth. His was called Black Sigel. He added PDQ — pretty damn quick — himself, and later had *Property of Geddy Muthafuckin' Starheart* etched into the underside of the barrel.

The lady pirate called herself Queen Tymeri. He and Smegmo had a run-in with her a decade earlier on Ceonus, when she was an ambitious madam who owned a piece of the castanea drug trade. Geddy destroyed her brothel to facilitate their escape, but she came away with the PDQ. He hadn't seen it since.

"Where are the others?" asked Jel.

That was a good question. There had to be more than

two pirates guarding Oz, but he didn't see anyone else. The far side of the cavern was obstructed by the tent. To know she was just on the other side but not be able to see her was torture.

To their right, from the direction of the entrance, came the shuffling of feet. Two diminutive Nichuan men, quite possibly twins, came running right through the crack, panting. They hurried over to where Tymeri and her minion were still arguing.

"What're you two so worked up about?" Tymeri demanded.

"They're here," said one of the twins.

— *Who's here?*

— Cable installers, maybe? I'm not good at guessing.

Geddy could practically feel Eli shake his head.

Tymeri gave her lieutenant a smug grin. "Ye of little faith." Returning her attention to the Nichuan, she added, "Show them in."

The two Nichuans took off again, and Tymeri and her lieutenant took a few steps closer to the entrance. It brought them both fully into view.

The one she called Horschus was a big Screvari, fully two meters tall and wearing an old Triad-era hat that made him appear even taller. Knives were tucked all around his black leather outfit, and a blaster rifle was slung across his back. He towered over Tymeri, who was even shorter than Jel.

The remains of her spiny exoskeleton had become darker and more mottled over the years, making her crustacean-like features that much more severe. Ceonians' bodies betrayed a great deal of their formerly aquatic existence, most obviously their hands and faces, which called to mind a bipedal jumbo shrimp.

Once the Nichuans were gone, the Screvari pirate adjusted the straps of his thick vest. Tymeri stepped around him and continued toward the opaque lava tube where it continued under the mountain.

— Where are they going?

— *There must be another entrance through that tube.*

The two pirates turned on headlamps as they neared the edge of the available light, then stood with their backs to Geddy and Jel, fixed on the void.

"What're they doing?" Jel asked.

"Eli thinks they're coming in through that lava tube. C'mon, this is our shot."

Still crouching, they stole across the camp, keeping the tent between them and the rear of the chamber. On the far side of the tent, where shadows were fewer, the crates felt like scant cover. The pirates need only glance over their right shoulder to see them.

Geddy peered out from the edge of the crate and discovered not one, but two improvised force-field cells that used the chamber as their back wall. For a glorious moment, time stood still, and nothing remained between him and Oz but a crackling, translucent wall of energy a few atoms thick. His whole body flushed with joy. He dashed over to the edge of the force field, as close as he dared. She was slumped against the rock wall, asleep, but stirred at his approach and gasped. Her fleshy locks, which had been a dull reddish-brown, brightened with her mood.

"Geddy! Jel!" Reflexively, she lunged across the sandy floor and reached for him, but the field stung her hand, and she yanked it away, sucking air through her teeth as she shook it. "Shit, I hate it when I do that!"

"Boy, am I ever glad to see you." Geddy whispered, checking nervously to his left where the pirates had their backs to them. Jel, on her hands and knees, was inspecting the chunky metal devices producing the field. Geddy brought his attention back to Oz. "Are you okay? Did they hurt you?"

"I'm fine. How did you find me?"

"Long story. Did they really take you for ransom?"

"Clearly, they don't know my family. Where's the crew? Voprot's gotta be itching to ..." She trailed off, reading his dark expression. "Oh god, what happened?"

"The Fiz disappeared. I don't know where they are."

"What?!"

His index finger flew to his lips as his head swiveled to see if they'd been heard.

"Shhh. I'll explain later."

"But—"

Jel remove a small roll of tools from within her jacket. "Can you shut them off?"

"Yep, just need a minute ..."

Oz looked anxiously past Geddy at the pirates. "Hurry."

Geddy nodded toward the faint cones of light by the dark tunnel, at the edge of what Oz could see. "I don't suppose you know who they're expecting."

"It's the Zelnads! The scientist is making something for them." She nodded to her right, where the corner of another cell poked out from behind one of the rock fins.

"Why?"

Oz shook her head. "I dunno. They force him to work. They won't let me talk to him."

A faint glow drew Geddy's attention back to the rear of the cave. Bluish light heralded the approach of a distant ship.

He leaned over to get a better look at the nearby cell. A makeshift laboratory was set up, and a man stood near the force field to see what was happening in the lava tube.

But the scientist wasn't Geddy's concern. He checked nervously on Jel, whose squinting left eye couldn't have been more than a centimeter from the field generator's delicate inner wiring.

"Jel?"

Jel bit hard on her lower lip, painstaking effort creasing her brow, but then there was a tiny *click* and the wall of energy dissolved. "Boom."

Geddy and Oz dove at each other through the ozone-smelling air, embracing like they hadn't seen each other in years.

"Boom," he whispered in her ear.

CHAPTER SIX

A BAD BARGAIN

A LOW RUMBLE built in the lava tube as the Zelnad ship approached. Now that they had Oz, the logical thing was to take her and bolt in the opposite direction. But the poor Afolosian scientist looked so desperate. If the Zelnads wanted him, Geddy needed to know why.

"Enough with the mushy stuff," Jel said as Geddy and Oz embraced. "Let's bounce."

"We can't," Geddy and Oz replied in unison.

"Huh?"

Oz dropped to all fours and crawled behind the crates to listen in on the proceedings. Geddy followed right behind, and Jel expelled a heavy sigh as she joined them.

Bright lights blazed out of the darkness, carving silhouettes of the pirates as they shielded their eyes from the approaching ship. It glided slowly on account of the very tight quarters, but not so slowly that Geddy didn't recognize immediately it as Pinka's sandskimmer.

The bitch double-crossed them.

"Change of plans," Geddy said. "Let's–"

The cold barrel of a blaster pressed into the back of his head, and he winced.

Thanks to Pinks, the two Nichuans had the drop on them. The other one took their weapons while the barrel bored deeper into his skull.

Nichuans resembled sturdy goblins, with long, pointy noses and ears that, appropriately, drooped as they aged. Their skin ranged from pale green to gray, and their teeth were as crooked as a Basoan politician. The tallest Nichuan wouldn't have reached Geddy's shoulder, barely taller than Durandians. But they were absurdly strong for their size. When he was seventeen, he watched a Nichuan pirate shake some poor bastard's hand, then rip his arm clean off.

Pinka's face was visible through the front of her ship. When a second set of lights appeared behind her, Geddy realized she was only an escort. The ship that followed her in was one of the brand-new Hovensbys that stole the show at IASS.

"Get up," commanded the Nichuan.

The three of them obeyed, Geddy stealing a glance at his wrist to ensure the voice channel back to the *Armstrong* was still open. With any luck, Morpho would be listening.

Tymeri came swaggering up wearing a self-satisfied sneer. "Well, well, well. I guess the universe has a sense of humor after all."

"Well, it did spawn *you*," Geddy said.

Sensing their familiarity, Oz frowned, her eyes darting back and forth between them. "Hold up ... you two *know each other?*"

"He destroyed my whorehouse and crushed three of my girls."

"What??" Oz said.

Geddy held up his hands in denial. "She's making it sound worse than it was. Or maybe better. The point is–"

Her hand flashed to her waist in a blur, and she leveled the PDQ at him. "I'd stop talking if I were you," she hissed.

"What're we doing with them?" asked one of the twins.

Tymeri glanced over her shoulder at the approaching ships. "Nothing yet. Watch out for this one, though. He's slippery."

"You used to be slippery, too, I'd imagine," Geddy said, an eyebrow raised as he looked from Oz to Jel. "Of course, that was a long, *long* time ago."

"Just keep them quiet." Her dark eyes met the Nichuans' in turn. "If they so much as fart, put them down."

"With pleasure," the twin behind him intoned as Tymeri turned on her heels.

Pinka's ship gently touched down, followed by the Hovensby. The belly of her ship opened, and she climbed down the ladder, throwing a smirking wave as she approached Tymeri and Horschus.

— I knew she was bad news.

— *And yet, she still brought us to Oz.*

The belly of the Hovensby opened, and an unseen force lowered the two passengers gently to the ground. One was Ornean, same as Dr. Tardigan, but shorter and plumper. The other made Geddy gasp in surprise.

It was Colonel Pritchard himself, presumed leader of the Zelnads and the man who had delivered news of his parents' deaths. Geddy only remembered him as the stoic, square-jawed military man to whom his old man reported. Now, he was just an evil spore in a Pritchard skinsuit.

Oz looked up anxiously at Geddy, her yellow eyes wide and bright.

"I must say, Tymeri, at least you know how to hide." Pritchard's eyes roamed over the cavern. He wore casual pants and a sport coat, which weren't exactly deep-space travel clothes. Then again, with the Hovensby bubble drive, your time in space was short.

"Can't be too careful these days," returned Tymeri, eyeing them warily.

Geddy glared at Pinka, kicking himself for trusting her. Technically, she'd done what she promised, but he'd made a devil's bargain. Was she part of Tymeri's crew or just an opportunist?

Pritchard looked past her to where Geddy and the girls were being held at gunpoint. He headed in their direction. "Who are your friends?"

— *Will he recognize you?*

— I'm more worried about him sensing you.

— *Let's hope Jel's device works.*

"Interlopers," Tymeri said. "Come to rescue the princess."

To that point, nothing about Pritchard's manner suggested he could sense Eli.

"Princess?" Pritchard regarded Oz in a way Geddy didn't appreciate, like she was chattel. "Ah, yes. Your golden goose."

"Only her family doesn't want her." Tymeri glared at Oz, who stared back murderously. "I was counting on that money."

He gave an indifferent shrug. "I fail to see how that is our problem. You made your bargain."

"Getting Krezek wasn't cheap. I owe people," she said through clenched teeth.

"No money *or* revenge? *Tsk tsk*," returned Pritchard with mock sympathy. "Bad day for a pirate."

"Revenge?" Geddy asked. "Revenge for what?"

Oz answered through her tight-lipped stare. "She blames me for the Star Guard blowing up her ship."

Geddy shook his head. "What are you—"

He cut himself off and gasped as the Tymeri-shaped piece of the puzzle finally slid into place. A couple months earlier, they'd failed to outrun an old Gundrun warship flown by pirates. They almost punched their way into the *Fizmo* when the Temerurian Star Guard blasted it to smithereens. That was an unusually forceful response from a pacifistic planet, so Tymeri must have figured out that a royal was on board.

"Oh, *shit*. That was you?!" He threw his head back and laughed. "You're right. The universe has some solid material."

- *True, but it is mostly space and gases.*
- Good one!

Tymeri took a quick step forward, bringing her arthropodic facial features uncomfortably close. Geddy's left eye twitched at the stench of her breath. Like shrimp cocktail left out in the sun.

"Can I offer you a mint?"

"It should never have happened," Tymeri growled.

"Enough prattling!" Pritchard said, silencing both of them.

His focus quickly shifted from Oz to Geddy, his eyes narrowing in faint recognition. Geddy could almost hear the bastard saying to his 12-year-old self, *Eddie, it's about your parents. There's been an accident ...*

Zelnad Pritchard replied, "My host's memories often manifest as déjà vu. Do we know each other?"

"I was in the crowd at your big speech," Geddy replied. "You signed my Hovensby T-shirt."

Zelnad Pritchard gave an appreciative smirk but shook his head with syrupy slowness. "No, that's not it. It's from ... before. Earth 2. He *did* know you."

The way he said it sent a chill down his back.

"Sorry, Pritchard, or King Zelnad, or whoever the hell you are — I just worked the geo tunnels. Maybe I've got one of those faces."

Pritchard pursed his lips as though considering this. "It will come to me."

"Like she said, I'm just here to rescue the princess. We're seeing each other. It's serious." He gave Oz a wink.

The old man squinted down his nose at Geddy in the same imperious way he remembered seeing as a kid, like he had to make a little show of sizing everyone up. "A hero."

"Not yet."

— Are you sure he's not reading my mind? Or yours?

— *I don't think so.*

Pritchard flared his eyebrows and returned his focus to Tymeri. "Where is the pheromone?"

"I can't walk away with nothing!" Tymeri insisted.

Unamused by her demand, his arm shot out and grabbed her roughly by her neck. Horschus reached for one of his knives, but as he did, something seized him in an invisible field, paralyzing him. He lifted free of the ground.

Geddy's eyes shot to the Ornean, who held a small rectangular device in his fingers. Whatever it was had paralyzed the big Screvari.

"How about your life?" Pritchard hissed. "Or is it as worthless to you as it seems?"

Tymeri's eyes darted between Pritchard and her hapless lieutenant for a few seconds. So much for leverage.

"Right this way," she croaked.

Pritchard released her, and the Ornean set Horschus back down. He immediately fell to one knee, his hand over his heart as he caught his breath. Tymeri rubbed her neck as she led Pritchard and the Ornean over to the scientist's cell.

"Dr. Ehrmut Krezek." She gestured at him.

The moment he got a good look at the Ornean, the Afolosian scientist gasped and sprang to his feet, eyes wide. Tymeri and Pritchard ceased to exist. "Milbart, my god, is it really you??"

"It *is* me, Ehrmut ... in some ways."

Zelnads spoke in the same calm, menacing tone. Krezek seemed to understand at once what it meant. Milbart was no more, but his knowledge remained. The Nads were using it like a library.

He fell to his knees and heaved sobs. The kind you didn't cry for just any colleague. "Oh, Milbart, not you!"

Geddy's heart broke for them. How many times had this scene played out across the universe? His eyes turned unexpectedly glassy. This easily could've happened to Oz.

— *Stay strong, Geddy. This is what we are trying to prevent.*

The Ornean formerly known as Milbart knelt as close as he dared to the charged wall of his cell and calmly asked, "Where is the pheromone?"

Krezek swept his hand across the sand and threw it at Milbart's face. "To hell with you!" The sand bounced harmlessly off the force field, tendrils of wispy smoke accompanying the crackle.

Milbart didn't flinch. "I hope for your sake you have completed it."

"You gave me no choice!" Krezek spat.

"Hurry up," said Pritchard. "We have much to do."

Dr. Krezek got back on his feet and shuffled like a zombie to a small storage unit behind him. He opened it, and cold air crept down the side, tendrils of fog spreading across the metal table. A finger-sized cryotube slid out of a tray, and Krezek picked it up with a set of tongs.

Milbart withdrew both a pair of silver gloves and a small diagnostic device from his jacket. Something on his wrist allowed his hand to pass through the force field, and he opened his palm expectantly.

Just before Krezek passed him the tube, he hesitated. "What's to stop me from smashing this against the wall?"

Again, Milbart didn't move. "You know what."

Krezek's determined expression fell, and his shoulders sagged. "Please. She's the only family I have left."

"Then I suggest you comply."

He resignedly dropped the little tube into Milbart's hand. When he withdrew it, the field instantly re-closed.

Milbart placed the tube in his little handheld device and waited as an assay was run. After a few seconds, a chime indicated it was complete.

He turned to Pritchard. "It's clean."

"Then our business is concluded." Pritchard turned to leave.

While Tymeri fumed, Geddy stole a glance over his shoulder at the Nichuan twins covering them, but they weren't that close. Making a move now was risky. Someone would get shot. And there was still Tymeri and Horschus.

But greasing them wouldn't matter. All Zelnads were basically of the same mind, like a hydra with a million heads.

"That's it?" Tymeri's voice had an edge of irritation. "What're we supposed to do with the chemist?"

Pritchard shrugged. "Whatever suits you." He pinched off a smirk and continued toward the Hovensby. Two steps later, he abruptly stopped and pointed a finger at Geddy as he about-faced. "Kepler."

Adrenaline flooded through Geddy as his heart kicked into high gear.

"You're the son of Major Lucas Kepler of the Planetary Defense Force — the *late* Lucas Kepler. Eddie, if I'm not mistaken."

"Good memory," Geddy said quickly, before either of the girls could react.

"Enjoy your princess, hero."

Geddy lifted his chin. "I do like a happy ending."

CHAPTER SEVEN

THE NEW DEAL

GEDDY's and Tymeri's respective crews watched the Hovensby lift from the cave floor, pivot, and glide silently away down the lava tube. As soon as it rounded a gentle curve to the right, Tymeri stomped her foot in the sand and screamed.

"Fuuuuuck!!" Her voice echoed down the tube after the ship.

"I knew this would happen," sneered Horschus. "Now we have nothing!"

"Hold up, now," said Pinka, taking a step closer. "Loverboy here's got money to spare."

— Where the hell is Morpho?

— *The signal must not reach outside.*

Tymeri perked up, shifting her attention from Oz to Geddy. "Is that right?"

"He paid a cool million just to find her. Imagine what he'd pay to save her life."

Oz spun her head toward Geddy, her expression a mix of shock, anger, and adoration.

"A million?" Tymeri mused. "Now how does a washed-up trawler captain come up with that kind of scratch? Unless ..." A self-satisfied grin decorated her face.

"What?" asked Horschus, who was keenly interested. "You think he has more?"

Her beady, protruding eyes locked with Geddy's. "No. But his sugar daddy, Smegmo Eilgars, does."

"Who?" asked Horschus.

"A Ceonian trillionaire. I wonder what he'd pay to save his old pal, Geddy Starheart."

"He has nothing to do with this," Geddy said. "And he's not my sugar daddy." Although he kind of was.

"We'll see."

A nod from her, and the Nichuans shuffled behind them, giving their blasters a rattle to remind them they were there.

Geddy rolled his eyes. She knew so little about him. What he'd done and seen. He didn't intimidate easily and neither did Oz or Jel.

"Sorry, sweetheart, but I've had almost as many guns in my face as you've had dicks."

"What did you just say?" she hissed.

The whole scene played out in his mind. Tymeri would hem and haw about squeezing money out of Smegmo, then shake him down even more. Improbably, she had axes to grind for him and Oz, and now she'd be committed enough to hold them here until somebody broke. But there wasn't time for that.

What did Commander Verveik say? You can't rebuild the Alliance without alliances. Maybe he could turn Tymeri from foe to friend.

"Just let us go, Tymeri. This is a waste of everyone's time."

Tymeri flared the ridges that passed for eyebrows. "Oh, I'm sorry. Have we inconvenienced you?"

"The Zelnads want to destroy civilization, and you're helping them."

Her expression became pained. "Oh, don't tell me you're one of those Zelnad-conspiracy wackos."

"It's true! I– er, *we* want to stop them, and you're in the way. You want a payout, fine. I'll get you your precious money and we can part company. Or ..."

Her ball-bearing eyes crinkled. "Or what?"

"Or you can choose a new side."

"I'm not on anyone's side," Tymeri declared. "Just mine."

"Don't be naïve. What did they want the scientist for?" he asked.

"Some chemical. It's none of my business." She clung to her ignorance like a life preserver.

"A pheromone." A heavy voice came from behind. Krezek was still in his cell slumped down against the cavern wall with his head between his knees.

"A what?" Pinka asked.

"Pheromone. Biochemicals that influence animal behavior. It's the focus of my research."

Geddy's head spun to Oz and Jel, his eyes wide. The subject of Zelnads and animals was of immense interest to them. Tatiana Semenov, his ex, revealed to the Committee that the Zelnads tried to acquire mogorodons, the massive and destructive sea monsters that bedeviled Earth 3. They also suspected that the *Sirwin*, a Xellaran vessel the *Fiz* discovered months earlier, had been transporting a pair of deadly ranses to Myadan.

If their theory was correct, the Zelnads were trying to acquire breeding pairs of at least two deadly species. What better way to expedite the end of civilization than to unleash scores of rampaging beasts on unsuspecting worlds?

"What animals?" Geddy asked.

Krezek shook his head. He'd perked up a bit, perhaps just happy to be talking to a fellow captive. "I don't know. I was only provided with DNA profiles. I made them a broad-spectrum sex pheromone to stimulate mating. Frenzied, unnatural mating. Such a thing should not exist."

So that's how they were going to do it. Send breeding pairs out into the universe and make them horny as hell. Sure, it might take centuries, but the Nads had been at this for eons. How many other galaxies had they already stripped of intelligent life? For all they knew, theirs might be the last.

Geddy's eyes swung back to Tymeri. "What're you gonna do with him?"

The equivocation on her face suggested she had yet to decide. "Y'know, I'd be more concerned with what I'm going to do with *you*. We have a score to settle, remember?"

"Screw that! All this business with the Coalition, Gundrun, the Triad ... it's bullshit. They want to end all civilization in the universe. These hormones are–"

"Pheromones," corrected Krezek. He rose and took a step closer to the force field.

"These *pheromones* are meant for dangerous creatures. We're talking ranses, mogorodons, and who knows what else. They want to spread them like a plague and wipe everyone out ... including their own home world."

Pinka and Tymeri exchanged a dubious look. "Is that why they saved Gundrun? Because they want to destroy it?" Pinka asked sarcastically. "He's lying."

"That was a stunt to convince everyone they're good guys, but they're not," Oz pointed out.

"I see." Tymeri's tone dripped with derision. "So, only Geddy Starheart and his teeny, tiny circle of friends know what's *really* going on?"

Pinka and Horschus sniggered, and that put Geddy over the edge. It was time to end this. He exchanged a furtive glance with Jel and Oz as if to say, *be ready*. It was hard to see this ending well either way. To his surprise, however, Jel wore a tiny knowing smirk and gave her head a small shake that said, *Don't*.

— *Does she know something we do not?*

— Apparently, but that's not saying much.

From somewhere behind them came a faint *whoosh* like a zephyr had rushed in through the crack. No one else seemed to notice, but Jel's eyes swung briefly in that direction.

— I need to get us out of this.

— *Buy a little time. Trust her.*

"Join us," Geddy said. "Or watch the world end knowing you did nothing to stop it."

Tymeri's expression briefly softened as though she was considering it, but she sneered at Oz before returning her gaze to Geddy. "I should've gotten ten million for her, but since I'm feeling charitable, I'll let you walk away for half that."

Geddy couldn't help but laugh at her audacity. "Pound sand, Bubba Gump."

Again, the wind let forth a sinister whistle, sharp and

loud as an approaching storm. This time, it got everyone's attention.

Tymeri nodded at the Nichuans. "Check it out." They trotted off, and Tymeri pointed the PDQ at him again. "What's that?"

"How should I know? We came with her." He nodded at Pinka, who could only shrug in agreement. "It's got nice balance, doesn't it?"

"Yeah, but that's not its best feature."

"Then what is?" he asked.

"That it used to belong to y–"

A bloodcurdling scream from the direction of the entrance cut her off. Everybody sucked in a collective breath.

A moment later, one of the Nichuan guards stumbled into view holding what remained of his right hand up in front of him. Everything above his first knuckles was intact, but the rest resembled a coarse-bristled brush dripping red paint.

Behind him, the sand billowed as though an industrial fan had been activated. A whirling funnel of sand raced across the cave floor.

Hughey Twoey, Jeledine's shape-shifting bot, had turned himself into a mini tornado. That meant the Armstrong couldn't be far away.

The injured Nichuan renewed his pained shrieks and scrambled away from the whirlwind. Hughey's tiny metal nanobots had shredded his hand. It turned toward Tymeri and her remaining crew, and their eyes widened in fear.

"What the hell is that?" Horschus asked, firing two useless blaster shots into it.

Geddy instinctively stepped back, but Jel's hand on his back stopped him.

"It's just my robot," she said, beaming with pride.

Tymeri and the others unleashed a volley of bolts at the Hughey-nado as they ran away into the dark and empty lava tube. But just as they reached the edge of the light, they skidded to a stop and backed up. Three small, unmanned ships crept out of the tube in front of them. Wingtip to wingtip, they spanned nearly the full girth of the tunnel itself, the tips of their rotary disruptors glowing yellow. The pirates were trapped between Hughey and the *Armstrong's* phantoms, their outlines made ghostly by the dust.

Morpho!

"What the hell are those?" Oz asked, thoroughly confused.

"Say hello to my little friends," Geddy replied with a wink.

Now that no one was covering them, Jel started walking toward the *Armstrong*, and Geddy and Oz followed. "C'mon. Let's renegotiate."

The Nichuan guard with the bloody hand lay on the ground, the ragged wound caked with powdery sand. In their haste to escape, Horschus had dropped his weapon. Geddy snatched it out of the sand and leveled it at his face. As they approached the pirates, the Hughey-nado spun to a stop and reformed into his typical cylindrical shape. The nanobots vibrated to shake off the dust, making a sound like a drunk kazooist aiming for an F sharp.

"Drop your weapons," Geddy ordered, stopping Tymeri before she could raise the PDQ. "Or reap the whirlwind."

— Did that sound as cool as it felt to say?

— *Meh.*

"Nice," Oz gave Geddy a high-five before smugly

relieving Tymeri of the PDQ. She cast a pitying look at the whimpering amputee, who clutched the wrist of his injured hand and shook with agony.

A cathartic smile split Oz's face as she returned to him holding the long pistol. "Nice gun. You'd almost think it was compensating for something."

Geddy took it, savoring the exquisite balance. How perfectly his fingers curled around the custom handle. He examined it in the faint light, a weirdly beautiful clash of black and yellow that caught the Screvari-made weapon just so.

With surprising relish, he yanked his old Exeter D6 from its holster and tossed it in the air, then, with his left hand, shot it right at the apex. A spray of cheap steel and dusty capacitors tinkled against the wall of the tube.

Barely any kick, and accurate as ever. At best, the Exeter was accurate across an uguinok table.

"Here's what's gonna happen, mateys ..." Geddy leveled the weapon at the center of Tymeri's murderous expression. "... I'm going to tell you the truth, and you're going to listen. Otherwise, this cave becomes a mausoleum. Understand?"

They all looked to Tymeri, who knew she'd been beaten. She gave a tiny nod. "Fine, Starheart. We're all ears."

Geddy lowered the PDQ and took a deep breath.

"Once upon a time, I heard this little voice in my head ..."

CHAPTER EIGHT

BREAKING THROUGH

By the time Geddy finished telling Tymeri about the Zelnad threat to everything and everyone, her expression had morphed from anger to skepticism to something like resignation. She was a prime example of why they wanted it all gone, or so he imagined. A criminal entrepreneur who was both the product and cause of a deeply broken world.

"That's it?" she asked.

"Isn't that enough?"

"It's a lot to swallow," Tymeri said.

— *Geddy, this is not the time for a—*

"Yeah, well, I figured if anyone could handle it ..."

"I believe you."

The rest of her crew appeared shocked by the admission, none more so than Horschus.

"You do?"

She let out a long exhale. "I almost didn't take this job, but when those Temerurian pricks blew up my ship and crew," again, she looked askance at Oz, "it left me in a lurch. The only way I could figure to get the professor and get out fast was something that didn't exist. A terrestrial tractor beam. So, I went to Basoa and started asking around. One name kept coming up over and over. Lestiko."

If you needed something made, Basoa was the place to go. It was as skeezy a place as any in the galaxy, but full of exceptional engineers who could be bought.

"They've been trying to figure out gravity guns since I was a kid," Geddy remarked. "You're telling me some Basoan nerd made you one?"

"This dude wasn't just any Basoan. He had a workshop full of tech you can't even imagine. Next-level stuff. I told him what I wanted, we settled on a price, and he told me to come back in two weeks. Obviously, I was skeptical, but when I came back, there it was. I watched it pull a bird right out of the sky."

Oz gave her an incredulous look. "How is that possible?"

"I asked the same thing. He said he used to be a Zelnad. That he 'broke through.' Does that make any sense to you?"

Back on Aku, when he was at the mercy of the Zelnad called the Metallurgist, Eli briefly commandeered Geddy's body. Instead of Eli sharing his headspace, he took over, forcing Geddy to become a passenger in some distant back seat. It gave him a taste of what it was like for a Zelnad host. But what if a host became strong enough to retake control?

The thought gave him a thrill. If hosts were still in there somewhere, maybe they, too, could "break through."

"It might," Geddy replied. "Were there others like him?"

Tymeri shrugged. "I don't know. But after the beam worked so well on the scientist, I decided to renegotiate. The princess' location in exchange for the pheromone. Somehow,

Pritchard knew she was on Xellara, so I jumped there and followed the Darkstars through the wormhole."

That explained a lot. Oz's old flame, Rader, was revealed to be a Zelnad while they were at the IASS show. That's how they knew where she was.

"I didn't know what planet that was or what you and the Xellarans wanted with it, but I didn't care. I just waited until she was out in the open and took her." Tymeri locked eyes with Oz, sneering. "I never imagined her family wouldn't want her."

"All the more reason to join us," Geddy said.

Tymeri crossed her arms defiantly, exchanging a dubious look with her crew. "And what does this 'New Alliance' of yours pay?"

Now it was Oz's turn to step in. "I don't think you get it, Tymeri. If the Zelnads win, there won't be any money. There won't be any *anything*."

She gave her head a slow shake. "So fucking what?"

- *You're wasting your time.*
- Maybe.

"This isn't a negotiation," Geddy said. "It's an offer."

"Then consider your *offer* rejected."

Oz and Jel had already been sending furtive looks his way. He'd hoped that, with nothing left and nowhere to turn, Tymeri would see the writing on the wall. But knowing the truth about the Zelnads didn't change her mind about anything, and the chip on her shoulder was still there.

After a moment, he gave an indifferent shrug. "Suit yourself, Tymeri." He looked from Oz to Jel. "Let's bounce."

"What're we gonna do with them?" Jel asked.

The smart thing to do was take them all out. That was the only way to ensure they didn't come back to haunt them, and nobody would miss a handful of desperate pirates. But it also wasn't an option. He'd killed people from the controls of a starship, but executing prisoners wasn't his style.

"You want to hide in a cave while the grown-ups save the universe, be my guest," he told Tymeri. "Just stay the hell out of our way."

He started backing up, and the girls followed, his and Jel's blasters still trained on the pirates.

"Where are my blades?" Oz asked, referring to her energy katanas.

"In the tent." Oz ran off to retrieve them.

"What about the scientist?" Jel asked Geddy.

"Let him out. He's coming with us."

Jel hurried over to Krezek's cell to disable the walls. Geddy kept the PDQ leveled at Tymeri.

"You know what your problem is, Starheart?" Tymeri's gravelly voice was low.

- *Oh, wow. Where to begin?*
- Nobody asked you.

"You still think civilization deserves saving."

His gut reaction was to reject this statement, but she had a point. He'd been where she was, and not that long ago.

Oz returned with her blades and scabbards as Jel deactivated the walls of Krezek's cell. He shuffled along beside her in a daze. Behind the pirates, the phantoms still hovered, ready to cut them in half if they made a move.

Tymeri talked a tough game, but for all her pirate postur-ing, hearing what the Zelnads were up to had rattled her. Worse, her only assets were about to walk out the door. But if she wanted to live out the rest of her days robbing merchant ships and trawlers, there wasn't much he could do about it.

"Then I guess we're both on our own again."

"Looks that way," said Tymeri flatly.

Geddy kept his blaster trained on them, backing toward Jel and Oz as they headed toward the exit.

"If you change your mind ..." he offered.

"I won't," she assured him.

With a thin-lipped nod, he turned fully around and followed the others through the camp and toward the crack in the cave wall.

A couple of minutes later, the unforgiving Stemiran sun blazed down on them. Geddy shielded his eyes and squinted. The *Armstrong* was nowhere to be seen.

Jel's eyes drifted down to Hughey. "Where's Morpho?"

In lieu of a reply, he cast himself end over end across the dust like a flock of tiny birds in the shape of a slinky. He was barely five meters away when the ship materialized in front of them, large enough to block the still-climbing sun. Oz took a few steps back as it appeared, her mouth hanging open at the sight of the unfamiliar ship. The ramp lowered to the ground.

"What ... the ... hell?" she muttered.

Geddy put a comforting arm around her shoulders. "Wel-come to the *Armstrong*. Come on, let's b."

CHAPTER NINE

FINALLY!

AFTER Oz's grand tour of the *Armstrong*, the three of them enjoyed a replicator-printed dinner that tasted eighty percent real. Dr. Krezek, still traumatized by the encounter with his former colleague, took his dinner in his room. The ship had berths for up to eight crew members, which technically made it even more accommodating than the *Fizmo* even though it was much smaller.

Jel caught Geddy and Oz making eyes at each other and abruptly announced she was going to bed, leaving them alone. Since they had nowhere to jump to yet, Geddy had simply pointed them toward the core systems and set her on autopilot. They returned together to the empty bridge, where the front row of seats were the perfect distance apart for holding each other's feet in their laps.

Having her hands on him at all, even over the top of his socked feet, felt luxurious.

"What're we gonna do now, Ged? Where's the *Fiz*?"

"I wish I knew."

"What could've been so urgent that they jumped away without us?"

Her pleading expression was hard to watch. At that moment, he shared her hopeless confusion. Geddy's device was working, but he hadn't received a single message from them. The *Fiz's* comms couldn't have penetrated Verdithea's metal-infused jungle canopy, so whatever happened, Denk would've known he'd be leaving them in the dark. But as far as they knew, he was still in the *Dom*, the *Fizmo's* drop ship, in which Verveik had flown off.

"It must've been an emergency," he offered. "Family, maybe? I can't imagine anything else that would make them leave us."

"Denk wouldn't do anything dangerous, at least not on purpose. And even if he wanted to, Doc and Voprot wouldn't let him."

"I just wish I had a clue."

"About so many things ..." A twinkle shone in Oz's pale-yellow eyes.

Geddy couldn't help but laugh. "Tymeri's sunny disposition must've rubbed off on you."

Oz allowed an aw-shucks grin. "I just had a lot of time to think, y'know. About the mission, the Zelnads, the crew. You. I didn't know if I'd ever see any of you again, but I wouldn't let myself think that. If I did, it would've snowballed into despair."

If Geddy had gotten captured and held for ransom by pirates, he would've gone mad. He would've railed against his situation, analyzed and second-guessed every decision that led to it, and probably gotten himself shot from lobbing insults at his captors.

Oz, on the other hand, had a better mastery of herself. Sure, she'd acted rashly at times, but who didn't? It was one of the many reasons why he loved her.

- *Maybe she'll rub off on you someday.*
- How would that work?
- *I mean her fortitude.*
- Oh. Right.

"That's some ... real presence of mind," he said.

"I didn't know if you'd ever find me. All I knew was that you'd never stop looking. I held on to that."

Her slender fingers were rougher than usual. The dry cave air had taken a toll on her ordinarily buttery skin. He let his eyes drift down to their knotted fingers.

"Seeing you pulled into the clouds ... that was rough. I thought the Zelnads took you to be ..."

"... converted?"

He shrugged.

She twisted her lips doubtfully. "I don't think it works that way."

Geddy tilted his head. "What do you mean?"

"We still don't know how they decide who gets taken over and who doesn't."

— *Taking full control takes tremendous effort. I suspect it only happens when there is low psychological resistance.*

— What does that mean?

— *People who don't fly their own ship, so to speak.*

"What does Eli have to say about it?"

— *I love that she always asks after me. You can tell her that. I am—*

"He thinks they focus on people who won't put up much of a fight."

Her eyes drifted to the floor. "Hm. Guess it hardly matters now. So ... that whole time we were apart, you and Jeledine ...?"

It was a fair question. He and Jel did have a history. A decade earlier, she helped him break into a collector's house on Eicreon to retrieve an ancient suit of armor that had been sold to the Double A but not delivered. They hit it off. For about two years, they never missed an opportunity to share a hotel room or a card table. It was a bit more than friends with benefits, but not much. Mostly, they just had fun. It wasn't long after they parted company on good terms that he quit the auction, fled for Earth 2, and met Tatiana.

Jel was a kindred spirit, and a beautiful one, but they didn't have that spark. He and Tatiana did, but outside the bedroom, it didn't burn brightly. But Oz? Geddy had been waiting for her his whole life, but he hadn't realized it until she was gone.

"We're just friends," he replied flatly. "That's all we ever really were."

Her big, probing eyes traced a little pattern as she studied his face, then her mouth upturned into a heart-melting smile. "And Stemir? You didn't ... you know ...?"

"Ha! No, those days are long past." His fingers scratched absently at his ear. "Plus, none of them can hold a candle to you."

Oz's red locks flushed as brightly as he'd ever seen. Her hands worked their way under his right index finger and unfolded it, gently running lengthwise up and down his skin.

"So, you mean to tell me that it's still been more than seven years since you've ... been with anyone?"

Geddy cheeks flushed to match Oz's hair. "Unless you count a hologram named Cherie, but our relationship lacked ... substance."

Oz didn't own her sexuality like Tati, nor did she wear it with the same ease as the Stemirans. It lent her an innocence that had his entire body vibrating. Unless he said or did something monumentally stupid, this was going to happen. To this point, they'd only kissed and been sandwiched together in the Hell Well at the end of a Morpho-rope.

"Does that mean you think I'm ... substantial?"

— She's not asking if I think she's fat, right?

— *No!*

— Just making sure. I don't have the best track record.

"I very much do."

Oz dropped his finger and abruptly rose.

— Shit! What did I say?

— *Patience, Geddy.*

She slinked over to the bridge door and locked it. The pad flashed red, and she slowly turned around, her back pressed to the door, her hair brighter than he'd ever seen it. She reached behind her head and removed the band that usually gathered her locks together, allowing the warm, soft tendrils of fleshy hair to tumble over her shoulders.

All he could do was stare.

— *Are you waiting for an invitation? Come on, man!*

Geddy rose from the pilot's seat. "Activate stargazer mode."

All lights in the bridge faded away, and the tukrium collar protecting the nose retracted, revealing an ocean of nameless stars. There was just enough light to see Oz's lithe shape against the wall. He passed between the seats, and finally, there was nothing between them. Not the lingering sting of an argument or a life-or-death struggle. Not her family. Not the Zelnads. Nothing.

Well, almost nothing.

— *I trust you can take it from here.*

— What are you talking about?

— *I am going to detach from your consciousness for a while.*

— You can do that?

— *Yes, and I should.*

— Something tells me this won't take very long.

— *Even so, the next six or seven minutes should be yours alone.*

Geddy found himself oddly anxious about the idea. Hard to believe all this started with him wanting Eli out of his head. Life was funny sometimes.

— Don't be gone too long, okay?

Eli paused. — *I will miss you, too, Geddy. You deserve this.*

Oz cocked her head a little, as she so often did when she sensed Eli talking to him.

"What's he saying?" she asked.

Geddy came right up to her, their bodies just centimeters apart, and ran his fingers through her warm hair, gently pulsing with her quickening heartbeat.

He smirked. "He's not into threesomes. He's taking a little vacation."

"He can do that?"

"Apparently."

His fingertips drifted down to her face, tracing its smooth outline down to her neck. She leaned forward so he could slip her leather jacket off her shoulders. Just before it fell off her arms, he gave it a half twist, locking her arms behind her and pulling her forward as she gave a little gasp. Her eyes blazed up at him, her enormous pupils reflecting the stars overhead.

"I've always wondered. Is it true Temerurians mate for life?" he whispered.

The corners of her mouth teased into a grin. "That's an old story they ginned up to scare away men."

He flared his eyebrows. "It would've scared me away once."

"Why?"

"Because I didn't understand love then."

"Is that what this is? Love?"

"I hope so."

Oz's eyes bored right into his soul, searching it for something only she knew to look for. "You're a good man, Geddy Starheart. Someone should've told you that a long time ago."

The kiss he planted on Oz's lips was long, slow, and perfect. Jel and Dr. Krezek seemed parsecs away. Morpho and Hughey were doing whatever they did, and Eli was checked out. It was just the two of them in a practically indestructible ship surrounded by the Big Empty. They would find the *Fiz* or die trying. Same with the Zelnads. There were no guarantees. But for the first time in his weird and troubled life, he had something to fight for, and it felt good.

Really, *really* good.

CHAPTER TEN

A BIG HIT

HAVING THOROUGHLY CHRISTENED THE BRIDGE, Geddy walked Oz silently to her quarters, wishing they each had more than a sliver of mattress before returning to his own private space. Maybe once they were both caught up on sleep.

The *Armstrong* was such a treat to be in. Being a military vessel, the captain's quarters were smaller than the *Fiz*, but with far nicer appointments. The main crew compartments on the *Fiz* were designed by and for Ghruk. They'd been retrofitted over the years, but much more retro than fitted. Nothing was where you expected or worked like it should. You got used to it like you got used to a limp.

Geddy slept hard. When he awoke in the dark a few hours later, his thoughts were on the *Fiz*. Jel's network had delivered Oz to him, yet a missing trawler the size of a school gymnasium had vanished without a trace. Even now, it didn't seem possible.

"Are you there?" he whispered into the dark, not sure if Eli would answer.

— Yes.

"Where did you go?"

— I briefly detached from your consciousness.

"I do that all the time." Geddy chuckled at his own joke. "But where did you go?"

— Nowhere. I was simply alone.

"Well, I'm glad you're back."

— Did you tell her you loved her?

"I think so."

— I am glad. No news on the Fizmo?

"No."

— Perhaps they have tried to reach the Dominic.

"That occurred to me."

— Should you reach out to Commander Verveik?

That was the obvious play, but the ship's scopes were already set to alert him if the Dom's transponder was detected. The old Kailorian fighter's comms range was weak and didn't support narrow beam, so unless it came close, he had no way to reach Verveik directly. Either the old man would have to find them or Geddy would have to get in touch with Tretiak and the Committee. He didn't want to do that until he had his crew.

With sleep now out of reach, Geddy took a quick shower, dressed, and headed down to the galley. Surprisingly, Dr. Krezek was already up and struggling to use the recombinator to make coffee. The moment Geddy entered the room, Krezek gasped and whirled, his fright manifesting as nervous laughter.

"Captain Starheart, my goodness!" He gave his chest a comforting pat. "You gave me a start."

"Geddy is just fine, Dr. Krezek."

"Then you should call me Ehrmut," he corrected. "If we're being casual."

Krezek was about his height but very thin. To Geddy, Afolosians looked like they'd been squeezed from the sides, with long, vertically oriented features that made them appear taller and lankier than they were. By and large, they were a rough, hardworking people whose ancestors had fought a war against Gundrun two centuries earlier and lost badly. As a result, Afolos became a paranoid, rarely considered mining planet in the vicinity Gundrun and Zihnia. Nobody went there unless they had to.

Truth be told, Geddy never would've imagined there was a university in Braaphis, let alone a prominent researcher. His value to the Zelnads must have been great.

He crossed the room, anxious for a cup of coffee himself. "Having trouble?"

"I'm afraid so. On Afolos, we just pour hot water over grounds."

"Eh, why have the real thing when you can have it reproduced through a chemical process? May I?" Geddy placed a small cup in the box and closed the door, then indicated the controls on the side. "You just put in your plate or cup or whatever, then search for what you want here." He typed C-O-F into the display and chose *Coffee*. "How do you like it? I can't recommend the cream."

"Black is fine."

Black was the default setting, so Geddy hit start. The recombinator hummed, pulling water from the air and combining it with organic molecules it assembled from various food waste. About a minute later, a cheerful beep sounded, and Geddy opened the door to reveal the cup of piping-hot coffee. He handed it to Krezek with a smile as he took a seat.

"One black coffee."

He marveled at it, giving it a sniff. "Who could've imagined such a thing."

"Imagination is the secret ingredient."

Geddy popped his own cup into the machine and chose the same thing.

Krezek tasted it, a doubtful look on his face, but after tasting it, gave an appreciative nod. "You're right. I can almost imagine it's coffee."

Geddy removed his cup from the machine and lifted it to Krezek before taking a swallow, the bitter dark liquid searing his throat in the best way. "A generous appraisal."

"Listen, I haven't properly thanked you for saving me. I know I'm not who you came for."

He smirked and looked away. "Don't mention it. I'm sorry about your friend. You two seemed close."

His eyes turned glossy. "We were. But apparently, he's a Zelnad now."

Geddy gave Krezek's forearm a reassuring pat. "It's not his fault. It's none of their faults. They're hosts to a race of microscopic aliens as old as time."

His head tilted as though he hadn't heard Geddy right. "All that was real?"

He shook his head. "I'm afraid so. We're on a mission to help free your friend and every other Zelnad host from whatever spell they're under."

Krezek's eyes looked pleadingly at him. "Who's 'we?' Surely you don't mean just you and–"

"Hey!" Jel appeared breathlessly in the doorway, giving

both of them a minor heart attack and interrupting their conversation.

"Damn, Jel," Geddy said, running his fingers through his hair. "You sure know how to make an entrance."

"Sorry, but I think I might know where the *Fiz* went."

Geddy stood so quickly, it made him a bit dizzy. He placed his fingers on the table to steady himself. "How? I thought you were—"

"Sleeping? Yeah, right. I've been working on an algorithm to scan emergency channels from the crew's home worlds. See if maybe they picked something up ... a mayday, a recorded message, that sort of thing. Well, I finally got a hit."

"From where??" Geddy asked anxiously.

A wide grin formed on her lips, her smooth cheeks bulging out. "Durandia."

CHAPTER ELEVEN

A CRYP-TIC MESSAGE

AFTER GEDDY ASSEMBLED everyone in the galley, Jeledine asked Cherie, the ship's AI, to play the message she'd intercepted. He could feel the color drain from his face as he listened.

"Attention all vessels and governments. This is Norrin Napthar, Minister of Durandia. We need your help. Our city has been breached by crypsids."

Krezek's jaw dropped open, and he gasped. "No!"

"We have evacuated the city and sealed it off, but hundreds were lost in the attack. We are in emergency shelters on the surface but are quickly running out of food, water, and supplies. Please ... if you are in range of this message, send help. We are the last of our kind."

She stopped the playback. An aching silence hung in the air.

"Holy shit," Oz said. "You think Denk and the crew are there?"

"You got a better explanation?"

"Did they have enough novaspheres for that?"

He shrugged. "Something tells me that wouldn't stop him from trying to help his people."

"What the hell are crypsids?" Jel asked.

Krezek practically fell over himself answering. "Burrowing creatures. Like ants, but nearly a meter long. Once Durandia's surface became unlivable, the natives had to find a way to coexist with them. Over the centuries, they developed a sacred trust. The Durandians harvest light to grow their crops underground. Some of that food is shared with the crypsids, who in turn provide them with gamat, some of the richest fertilizer in the galaxy."

"By fertilizer ... you mean ...?"

"Their excrement, yes."

- *Seems like the crypsids got the better end of the deal.*

"You see, the crypsids live in a colony called a myre, separated from the city by a maze of tunnels. Years ago, the wardens discovered that—"

"Wardens?"' Geddy asked.

"Stewards of the crypsid relationship. They bring them food and return with gamat."

"Sounds dangerous," Oz said.

"It is. For decades, wardens relied on traditional plant oils to ward them off, but the protection it provided was insufficient. The Ministry heard about my work and commissioned me to develop a synthetic pheromone that imitated the queen crypsid's scent. Workers are not allowed near her, thus ..."

"... they avoid the wardens," Jel finished, nodding. "And it worked?"

"Very well, yes. Pheromones tap into deep biological imperatives. It's chemistry at its most primal."

"How long ago was this?"

"Oh, probably fourteen, fifteen years now. Shortly after Milbart and I ..."

"How did it happen?" Jel asked, her expression deeply sympathetic.

Krezek's mind had turned fully to his dear Milbart, and his eyes darkened. "He was my research assistant for many years. But he fell into profound despair, like a nosedive he couldn't quite pull out of. One day, he didn't show up for his lab. I never knew what happened to him until ..."

"My sister, too," Jel confessed. "She was in a really dark place for a while, then she was just ... gone. I never saw her again."

"I'm sorry," Krezek said. "I know it wasn't Milbart I saw in the cave, and yet, I got the sense he was in there somewhere."

Geddy knew this to be true. Zelnads took over a consciousness but didn't destroy it. They couldn't. Their hosts had knowledge and experience the Nads needed. But he also remembered how it felt to be in the backseat of his own body and mind. Eli had shown him back on Aku. If he wanted to do it again, he could, and Geddy couldn't stop him.

Almost no one truly understood what the Zelnads were. Even now, most people would've said they were a powerful cult or political movement. Recent events suggested the latter. But the truth was much harder to explain.

All Geddy knew about Durandia was that it was a desolate, lifeless, burned-out hellscape even harsher and hotter than Kigantu. But it had been that way for centuries, and its people had learned to live deep underground.

It pained him to know that he'd never talked to Denk much about it other than that day at the bar on Earth 3. Even then, all he really knew was that Denk refused to fight for the hand of a girl and fled in shame.

"What's the AI's name on this ship again?" Oz asked.

"Um ... Cherie." Geddy felt his cheeks flush, but the comely hologram at the Laguna Luxe Mall back on Earth 2 had helped keep him sane. It felt like keeping her alive in a way.

"Cherie, how far to Durandia?" Oz asked.

"One point three parsecs," cooed the sexy AI.

He'd painstakingly programmed her to sound like the hologram. When it was just him and the *Armstrong*, it was nice, but having Oz there to hear it was admittedly awkward.

Oz gave a hard roll of her eyes and turned to Geddy. "Seriously? You programmed the ship to sound like some floozy?"

"A floozy with a British lilt, thank you very much. Would you rather she sounded like you?"

"I was thinking more like Voprot."

He put up his hands in defeat. "Not in a thousand lifetimes."

Oz heaved a sigh. "All right, so we get Dr. Krezek back to Afolos, then–"

"I don't want to go back," Krezek declared.

Geddy and the girls exchanged a confused look.

"There's nothing for me there anymore. The university is failing, my longtime research assistant is a Zelnad, and my life's work has been co-opted to expedite the end of the world. Let me come with you to Durandia. I know Minister Napthar well. I can help."

Geddy hesitated to accept. Krezek seemed like a nice enough guy, but he didn't want or need to take on another crew member, especially not another academic. Doc Tardigan was plenty.

Still, he had a point. None of them knew a damn thing about Durandia. Like Afolos, you needed one helluva a reason to go there.

"Please," Krezek asked hopefully. "Let me help. I need this."

— *He is right, Geddy. He could be very useful.*

"Okay, Ehrmut. But as soon as we find my ship, we take you home. Fair enough?"

"Of course. Thank you, Geddy."

His eyes slid over to Oz to gauge her opinion on the matter. He didn't like the apologetic look on her face. The one she gets when she's about to rain on his parade.

"What?" Geddy asked.

"Durandia's hell and gone from here. Do you have blue balls?"

A wide grin split Geddy's face. He'd saved the best thing about the *Armstrong* for last. "Not anymore."

Oz REFUSED to believe the jump system worked like he said, which was understandable. He didn't believe it until he saw it, and neither had Jel. In lieu of a scientific explanation, he just entered Durandia's coordinates and executed the jump.

A blink later, they materialized just outside the markers. The outermost layer of its scorched and barren terrain was white as gypsum with ribbons of reddish brown and yellow. Relentless winds and searing heat had turned a massive ocean into a desert, leaving behind only its salts and a nearly flat plain dotted with crumbling plateaus and spires.

Oz stared with her mouth open, blinking, like it couldn't possibly be real. She had taken the seat beside him, with Jel and Krezek behind them. "Wait ... what just happened? Where are we?"

"Durandia." It was hard not to sound a little smug.

She shook her head, frowning. "But ... that's not possible."

"Yet here we are."

Krezek got out of his chair and leaned forward like his eyes were deceiving him. His hands made a tent over his mouth. "Are you saying we just crossed one point three parsecs in an *instant*? I didn't feel a thing!"

— *Didn't Oz say that last night?*

— Look at you with the burn! I'm so proud.

"It's the only way to travel," Jel said with a wink.

Geddy glanced over at Oz, whose incredulity remained. "I told you it'd be hard to wrap your head around."

Their approach vector took them through about five kilometers of the empty ocean basin as they approached Durandia's only spaceport, Wuntara Station. Carved into the face of a sharp cliff on the continental shelf, it wasn't much bigger than private spaceports he'd seen near the homes of wealthy Double A clients. Here and there, the petrified bones of ancient sea creatures jutted out of the rock.

A perfectly symmetrical half-dome had been carved out of the cliff, with lighted support ribs fanning out along its width like the ridges of a clamshell. It was maybe a hundred meters at its apex, making him wonder if the *Fiz* would even fit. The green force field over the opening made details difficult to discern.

Knowing the Durandians were not really spacefaring made it that much more improbable that a pilot as gifted as Denk came from here. He'd thought about the kid a lot since he and Oz decided to go down to Verdithea without him. It was the second time he'd put himself in harm's way instead of Denk, the first being the Ponley Point race. His head said it was the right call, but his heart wasn't so sure.

The spaceport's traffic control center should have contacted them by now to give them an approach vector, but the station was silent.

"Wuntara, this is the *Armstrong* on final approach. Do you copy?"

No response.

"Wuntara, this is the *Armstrong*. Is anyone there?"

Again, nothing.

Geddy turned to Oz. "You think they evacuated the *spaceport*?"

The green ring around the front screen lit up, and a haggard-looking Durandian man manically slid into the frame, wide-eyed and excited. "This is Wuntara. Tell me you have supplies!"

It broke Geddy's heart, but he had to say, "No, sorry."

The man's crestfallen expression was hard to watch. "Then you might as well turn around. There's nothing here."

"We're looking for a ship. The *For Sale Make Offer*. Have you seen it?"

"Seen it? I'm looking at it right now. Are you Captain Starheart?"

CHAPTER TWELVE

DURANDIA

As THE *ARMSTRONG* drew closer to the spaceport, Geddy could just make out the shape of the *Fizmo* parked in the largest bay but no other ships. Tourism probably wasn't a big focus.

"Yeah, that's me," Geddy said. "Is Denk Junt there?"

"He's at the camp with all the others. He told me to watch out for you. Do you think you could take some supplies with you? There aren't many left."

"Of course. We'll take as much as we can fit."

"Thank you. I'll meet you at pad 2A and get the pallets ready."

He blinked out, and they exchanged worried looks. Apparently, no one had come to Durandia's aid, and if they had, it wasn't nearly enough.

Geddy eased the ship through the green scrim of the shield. The *Fizmo* was on the upper level. It appeared intact, which brought no small measure of relief. At long last, he'd found his ship and his crew. Oz sighed, too, and gave his shoulder a squeeze.

"They're here, thank the stars."

The shield protected the spaceport from the harsh environment. What kind of protection did their emergency camp have, if any?

He spotted landing pad 2A on the lower level, where two loader bots were already moving pallets from along the back wall to the landing pad. Only a handful remained.

"How many people live here?" Oz asked Krezek.

"About ninety thousand. The young ones leave as soon as they come of age. There's nothing for them here. The population's been shrinking for decades."

"That's so sad," Jel said.

— *Those supplies won't last long.*

— No, indeed.

— *Do you think the Committee can help? Smegmo, maybe?*

— Maybe. Let's see what's going on first.

He set the ship down gently on the pad and powered down her engines, then opened the ramp to the ship's smallish hold. Two pallets would be a tight fit, but they'd manage. Stale, stifling air immediately filled the cabin. They unbuckled and made their way toward the back.

The man was there to greet them, his face a mask of despair. "Thank you. Our only cargo ship is currently serving as a hospital."

"Sorry to hear it. Geddy Starheart."

"Bartok. I'm the foreman here." They shook hands.

"We heard your emergency message," Oz said. "Is this really all you have left for supplies?"

"There was a flurry of shipments at first. Mostly from intergalactic aid organizations, plus some food from Zihnia and clothing from Eicreon, all of which is too big. We've gotten some money, but ..."

Durandia was a very small, self-sustaining planet that didn't participate in the galactic economy. No one in a position to help would truly care if they went extinct.

They stepped aside as the bots climbed the ramp and began maneuvering the pallets into position.

"So where is this camp?" Geddy asked.

Bartok pointed behind them toward the back of the spaceport. "Eight clicks north, in the shadow of the mountains. You can't miss it." His eyes narrowed in faint recognition at Dr. Krezek. "Have we met?"

"I believe so," Krezek said. "I was here many years ago."

Bartok brightened a bit and snapped his stubby fingers. "You're that scientist who created QP!"

"You have a fine memory, Mr. Bartok. If there's a way for me to help, I will."

"I hope you can. This is a much worse problem."

"What happened?" Krezek asked.

"A few weeks ago, the wardens were bringing food to the myre when a flood of crypsids just went berserk. They made it back to the wardengate but didn't get it closed in time. A moment later, they poured into the city like oil."

Geddy could already feel his blood pressure rising. Tunnels deep underground filled with rampaging giant ants? No thanks.

"My stars, that must've been terrifying," Jel said.

"We just weren't ready. There are protocols for this sort of thing, but in the moment, everyone panicked. They just dropped what they were doing and ran for the Spine."

"The only way in or out of the city," Krezek added, pointing at a massive, vault-like door behind the cargo area.

"Have you had a look inside?" Jel offered. "Maybe they've retreated."

Bartok gave his head a grim shake. "The Underground has food, warmth, light for crops, and it's much larger. Bigger myre, bigger colony."

"But the myre's a thousand years old at least. They'd never leave it unless ..." Krezek trailed off.

The bots had finished loading the pallets. They mutely descended the ramp, then dutifully returned to their docking stations, glancing impassively at Hughey as they went.

"What are you thinking?" Geddy asked Krezek.

"Crypsids conserve energy," he explained. "Unless they're feeding, tending to their young, or defending the myre, they don't move around much. The only reason they'd want to create a new myre is if theirs was overrun. Or ..." he trailed off.

"Or what?" Oz asked.

"Or if they *believed* it was. They're highly territorial, you see. An invasion would be highly unlikely, but if enough foreign pheromones were introduced, it could drive them to abandon the myre. The Underground would be a convenient option."

"How many myres are there?" Geddy asked.

Bartok shrugged. "Nobody knows for sure, but they're the dominant species here. Thousands, certainly."

— *Deep breaths, Geddy.*

— Whaddya mean? Thousands of underground nests full of crypsids? It's quite a calming thought.

— *What if this is the Zelnads?*

— What would they want with this hellhole?

— *Maybe they want the crypsids. We know they were looking for mogorodons and we know they were interested in ranses and maybe even skysnakes. That covers water, land, and sky.*

There were a handful of worlds where the populace lived underground other than Durandia, notably Aku. But there was Canus, Gethenia, Rastrides ...

"Well, I guess we'd better get moving. Thanks for the info, Bartok."

"Of course, Captain." He gestured at the *Armstrong.* "Some ship you've got there. That can't be tukrium, can it?" He stepped closer and ran his fingers over the surface.

It was, but the fewer people who knew that the better. Word of a fully tukrium-clad ship would travel as fast as the *Armstrong.*

"Yeah, right." He gave a convincing laugh, or so he hoped. "It's a krienium alloy. Looks and feels like tukrium, though, doesn't it?"

"I'll say. Well, good luck to you. And thanks again."

Geddy gave a tight nod. "We'll do what we can."

CHAPTER THIRTEEN

... AND IT FEELS SO GOOD

THE *ARMSTRONG* RACED low over the desert. Rolling hills of white sand, streaked here and there by contour lines of mineral deposits, stretched to the horizon in all directions. Lonely mesas and the desiccated ribcages of colossal, long-dead creatures were the only punctuation in a long and heart-breaking tale of environmental ruin.

He swung the ship in a wide circle over the bean-shaped Durandian encampment. It hugged the base of a mountain range, which likely spent the whole day in shadow. It was a haphazard affair, with silver geodesic emergency tents plunked down wherever the ground was relatively level. Seeing an entire race of people clustered together was both humbling and sad.

As Bartok had indicated, a small cargo ship was parked near the middle of the camp. A short line of people snaked halfway up the gentle grade, huddled under a reflective tarp. Otherwise, no one was outside.

"Look at all of them." Krezek leaned forward in his seat. "What's the outside temperature?"

Geddy switched the display to show a heat map. Anywhere not in shadow was in the orange-white spectrum, near 60C. The bright red areas in the ridge's shadow still approached 51C. Fifty was pretty much the threshold for needing envirosuits.

"Sixty in the sun, over fifty in the shade."

"Those aren't tents," Jel said, shaking her head. "They're ovens."

"How are we gonna find Denk in all this?" Oz asked.

"We don't have to find Denk." Geddy pointed out the window.

The vast, flat expanse of desert stretching west of the camp was featureless save for a lone figure whose shadow resembled a sliver embedded in porcelain skin. Taller than a stack of three Durandians, Voprot's prodigious tail swished along behind him like he was out for a Sunday stroll. The fleshy sacs in his neck were inflated to cool him, though it was hard to imagine how that worked in these temperatures.

— *Voprot! Oh, Geddy, you must be over the moon!*

— I'm ... weirdly happy to see him. What the hell's wrong with me?

A warm smile crept across Oz's lips. "I'll be damned. But what the hell's he doing outside?"

Each of Voprot's huge arms carried what appeared to be black spiky duffle bags. He had maybe half a kilometer to cover before reaching the camp. He stopped at the sight of their ship, squinting up into the sun. Then he lowered his head and quickened his pace.

"And what's he carrying?" Jel asked.

"They're crypsids," Krezek said anxiously. "He can't

enter camp with dead ones. The Durandians will lose their minds."

"What are you talking about?" Geddy asked.

"Durandians consider their relationship with crypsids to be sacred," Krezek replied, as though this was obvious.

"Oh, boy," Oz muttered.

Geddy lowered the skids and dropped the ship down, blocking Voprot's path. As he set it down on the very edge of the mountain shadow, Voprot dropped the crypsids and unfurled his electric whip as though expecting a fight. Geddy powered down the engines and turned to his crew. The external cameras showed Durandians at the edge of the camp poking their covered heads out of tents to see what was going on.

"All right, gang. Who wants to get baked?"

The *Armstrong* had state-of-the-art envirosuits with self-contained units that circulated cold gel through the material. They were rated at up to 80C, which was more than enough protection. It was probably even safe to go without helmets, at least in the shadows. Geddy handed them out, and they suited up.

Several minutes later, he lowered the ramp and stepped out onto the desiccated ground, long since swept clean of loose dirt. It might as well have been a concrete parking lot. He closed the ramp as soon as the others had joined him. Voprot again struck a defensive posture, the unimaginably strong sun beating on his scaly skin. He looked completely spent.

"Who are you?" he rasped. "What you want here?"

Their face shields were heavily mirrored, making it impossible for Voprot to recognize him. Geddy retracted his and took a couple steps forward, nearly to the edge of the ship's shadow. The sun felt like a blast furnace on his face, but it was tolerable.

"Hey, big guy."

Voprot gasped, new energy animating him. "Geddy!"

He dropped the dead crypsids, fell to all fours, and barreled toward Geddy with his giant mouth half open. If he didn't know the Kigantean like he did, it would've seemed like a violent attack was coming. He couldn't help but cringe.

Voprot wrapped him in a hug so tight that it forced the air from his lungs. Geddy's arms made it less than halfway around the big guy's thick torso. It was more like hanging on than hugging, because Voprot immediately lifted him from the ground like a toy with Geddy's face pressed to his chest.

"Can't … breathe," he managed.

"Sorry, Voprot forget how brittle you are!" His arms relaxed, but he continued to hold Geddy aloft. Then his head turned, and he gasped again. "Oz!"

He immediately dropped Geddy and brushed past him as he lunged for Oz. Geddy coughed to refill his lungs and turned to see Krezek and Jel take a couple of steps back.

"Hey V, what's goin' on?" came a familiar, but suspicious voice from the direction of the encampment. "These friends of y–"

A little Durandian, so completely wrapped in loose strips of cloth that he looked like he was made of them, came waddling up, a blaster hanging at his side. He cut himself off as soon as Geddy turned around.

"You look like an unlit torch," Geddy said, beaming at the sight of his plucky pilot.

"Cap?! Is it really you??" His pace quickened as he approached.

"You're a hard guy to find, Mr. Junt."

He dropped to one knee and opened his arms to receive Denk as he ran into him. They gave each other hearty pats on the back, though the layers of ragged cloth were so thick, Denk probably didn't feel it. Behind him, a crowd of curious, similarly dressed Durandian refugees began to gather.

"I knew you'd find us, Cap. I just knew it!"

They released each other and Geddy rose. "Jel picked up the emergency message. We figured this was where you had to be."

"What the heck kind of ship is this? Is that tukrium? Where's the *Dom*?"

Denk knew nothing about what happened on Verdithea, including Oz's abduction and the fact that Verveik had their old Kailorian dropship.

"I'll explain later. Where's Doc?"

"He's at the hospital with the minister. Where's ... Oz! Jeledine! Guy I don't know!" No sooner had Voprot released Oz than Denk wrapped his arms around her. Geddy gave the crowd a little wave and joined them as Denk and Oz embraced. She cackled with delight.

Only then did Denk notice the dead crypsids lying on the hard-baked ground. On closer inspection, they resembled a cross between crabs and ants.

"Uh, V, are those what I think they are?" Denk asked, breaking his hug with Oz.

"Voprot find food," the lizard declared proudly.

"Are you crazy?!" Denk's gloved hands flew to his head.

"You can't bring dead crypsids into camp! Where did you even find 'em?"

"Tunnel in mountains." Voprot gestured behind him. "Long way."

"Tunnel? What tunnel?"

"Big."

"Well, get them out of sight! Man, I tell ya ..." he shook his head. "You can't teach a lizard anything."

Voprot hurried over to retrieve the dead crypsids by their rear legs while Geddy and the others formed a little wall to hide them from view. He brought them back into the *Armstrong's* crisp shadow, making Geddy immensely glad to be in a suit with biohazard protection.

"Where Voprot put?"

Geddy reflexively searched the area around his feet, though he already knew there was literally nowhere to hide the damn things. "I guess digging a hole is out. Why didn't you just eat them on the way?"

"Voprot let ferment. Make meat tender."

Geddy threw up a bit in his mouth. "Well, big guy, I hate to do this to you, but ..." He drew the PDQ and glanced over his shoulder. A hundred Durandians, maybe more, were already shuffling closer to the ship. There wasn't a better option.

Voprot's eyes widened in panic. "No!"

"You heard Denk, pal. They can't see these. I'm really sorry."

The big lizard looked forlornly at the two smelly creatures in his claws and set them on the ground, then moved away. Geddy gave the PDQ two quick pulls of the trigger and turned them to dust.

"Voprot *so hungry* ..."

He gave his shoulder a comforting pat. "I know. Because you always are."

"It's getting bad here, Cap," Denk said. "We're down to quarter rations and we've maybe got a week's worth of water if we're lucky. Did Bartok send supplies with you? There was supposed to be a shipment coming from Kailoria."

He shook his head and heaved a sigh. "We brought what we could. I don't think the cavalry's coming, pal."

THE REFLECTIVE TENTS had no windows, making it impossible to tell how many Durandians were inside. A fine layer of dust had accumulated on the surface. They heard occasional muffled conversations as they walked toward Denk's tent, and a few heads poked out to see what the commotion was.

Denk shook his head in disbelief at Geddy and Oz's account of Verdithea. "Man, that's a wild story. I don't think I would've liked those skysnakes."

"That was no excuse to cut you guys out of the mission. I'm sorry."

"I'm sorry, too," Oz said heavily. "Although you would've died for sure."

"Instantly," Geddy agreed.

"Naw, it's okay." Denk gave a wave of his hand like all was forgiven. "Besides, I wouldn't have known Durandia was in trouble. Kinda sucks that no one else came."

The line of twenty or so people behind the converted cargo ship appeared ahead.

"Are they sick?" Oz asked.

"Some are. Mostly it's just dehydration. We started with a liter a day, but we're down to just two hundred milliliters now."

"That's nothing. Where does it come from?" Jel asked.

"There are storage tanks at the base of the mountain next to the air exchangers. The city's pretty much right under our feet"

When the people in line saw them in the envirosuits, they started to point and talk excitedly.

— *They think we are here to rescue them.*

— We'll do what we can, but that's not why we're here.

Denk bypassed the closed door of the hold and waddled around to the front of the ship, banging his fist on the underside of the ramp. After a few seconds, it opened and lowered to the ground. An older man with a prodigious braided beard ventured down the ramp, wincing a bit with each step. He, too, wore nomadic robes, but not nearly so thick as Denk's since he'd just been inside.

"Denk, my boy!" Geddy recognized the man's voice from the recorded message. It was Norrin Napthar, minister of the Underground. Once he descended further, he spotted them, and his hand flew to his chest. "My stars, you must be our surprise guests."

"Minister, this is my crew," Denk said proudly. "That there's Cap'n Starheart, First Officer Osmiya, Jeledine, and that fella's name is Dr.–"

"Krezek ..." Napthar finished, gleeful recognition playing across his hirsute face.

Krezek extended his hand. "I'm heartened to see you, old friend. It seems like yesterday."

"Speak for yourself, Ehrmut. You're the picture of health! Please, come in, come in."

He turned and shuffled up the ramp ahead of them. The ship was Zihnian and not very old, making Geddy wonder if Zihnians flew it here full and left it behind as part of their aid package. Napthar closed the ramp the moment they were all inside, and they removed their helmets.

Geddy ran his fingers through his hair and puffed out his cheeks while Napthar and Krezek embraced warmly.

The minister's face was even more drawn than Bartok's, as though the crisis had sucked the life out of him. And yet, his avuncular charm shone through. Geddy liked him right away.

"My goodness, it is wonderful to see your faces," he said, beaming. His eyes got a bit glassy. "Denk didn't tell me he finally reached you."

"He didn't. We intercepted your emergency message and took a chance he'd be here," Geddy said. "We got lucky was all."

Doc Tardigan appeared from the rear of the ship, looking sleep-deprived and wiping his hands on a towel. The biggest smile Geddy had ever seen on him split his face, and his eyes widened.

"Captain?! Osmiya?"

To Geddy's surprise, the stoic Doc marched straight toward them and gave the three of them an awkward, but sincere hug.

"It's good to see you, my friend." Geddy warmly patted Doc's shoulder.

"Likewise, Captain. Your timing is most fortuitous."

Geddy turned sideways to introduce Krezek. "Dr. Krons Tardigan, I'd like you to meet Dr. Ehrmut–"

"Krezek," Doc finished, eagerly extending his hand. "Of course. Who doesn't know his seminal work on the role of lipid-soluble aliphatic aldehydes in spignork reproduction?"

He gave an awkward, embarrassed giggle. "Oh, well, thank you."

"You had us all at seminal," Geddy said.

Ignoring him, Doc continued. "Are you aware of the situation in the Underground, Dr. Krezek? Do you think there is a biochemical solution?"

"Perhaps, but I'd like to have a look inside the city if that's possible. And please, call me Ehrmut."

Doc returned his smile.

"Denk said something about air exchangers?" Jel asked. "I assume those lead down to the city?"

"Yes, why?"

"Because I can get us eyes on the situation. See what we're dealing with."

Napthar shook his head as though that was out of the question. "If you mean a drone, I'm afraid the vent has several filters. Nothing much bigger than a pebble could get through."

Jel smiled. "That won't be a problem."

CHAPTER FOURTEEN

RECON

A RECTANGULAR OPENING the size of a small building had been carved into the black granite base of the mountain that loomed over the camp. At one end, a row of four colossal fans circulated outside air through the Underground. At the other, armed guards monitored water spigots protruding up from pipes in the ground. A long line of Durandians waited for their turns carrying small metal cups with numbers stamped on the sides. The guards checked every cup, ensuring they only took two hundred milliliters. A few begged for more.

Their haunted faces stared through narrow slits between their rags as they eased their way closer to their water rations.

"Once our water runs out, I don't know what we'll do," Napthar said, himself now a walking pile of laundry.

"What did you do for water in the city?" Geddy asked.

"It's built over an aquifer. Down there, we have all the water we could ever need. But the tanks are just below the surface. Filling them is unfortunately a manual process."

"Okay," Jel announced, now carrying a tablet she'd retrieved from the ship. Hughey Twoey glided along at her side. "Gather around. Hughey here's gonna check things out. Somebody tell me where I'm going."

Among the bot's diverse talents was the ability to get into small spaces and manipulate electronics. Geddy only recently learned he could do forward recon using its nanobot cloud like pixels to beam images wirelessly back to Jel's tablet.

Hughey swirled up into the air and let itself be sucked into one of the air intakes like a swarm of flies. It disappeared through the raised top of the exchanger.

Jel's screen remained black as Hughey picked his way through and around the series of filters.

"Hughey's Basoan-made, just like Original Hugh but more advanced.

"Original Hugh?" asked Napthar.

"My first shifter-bot. A custom job I paid for with my biggest-ever score," she recalled fondly. "Okay, looks like we are in business," Jel said, clearly pleased with herself.

The image on the tablet brightened as it fished for focus. The Durandian Underground slowly came into view.

Massive support columns had been strategically carved out of solid rock. A wide ledge wrapped around it in a corkscrew, now overgrown with untended crops. Rope bridges led to simple dwellings hollowed out of the walls. Light pipes conducted sunlight through myriad holes in the ceiling, bathing both the city and its crops in diffuse daylight.

It was quite spectacular, especially compared to the humanitarian crisis unfolding around them.

Denk sniffled. "Wow. I've never seen it from so high up."

"Looks empty," Oz said hopefully.

"They came in through the wardengate," Napthar reminded them. "On the other side of that pillar."

"You heard the man, Hughey. Let's get a closer look."

Hughey couldn't move that quickly and still retain a sharp image. It angled down and toward the gate in a slow arc around the pillars. As Oz noted, the place looked abandoned. If the crypsids had retreated to the myre, then they just needed to send in a team to close the gate and move everyone back inside.

Once Hughey passed the last pillar, the wardengate appeared along the ground where the cavern narrowed. It was essentially a smaller version of the vault-like door they'd seen at the spaceport, but it stood open. From a distance, it looked like black mold had grown around the gate and spread outward like a cancer. But as Hughey drew closer, the truth revealed itself to be far more horrific.

What looked like mold was actually a honeycomb of basket-shaped cells. At least a hundred of the giant digging insects flitted in and out of the gate, forming the structure with gooey abdominal secretions.

"Hughey, that's close enough." Jel paused to scratch at her little earpiece. "Damn."

"So much for retreating on their own," Oz said.

"It's not that many," Geddy said. "If we concentrated our fire, we should be able to close the ..." Krezek's and Napthar's horrified expressions stopped him short. "Sacred. Right. Sorry."

Krezek broke the uncomfortable silence. "There are thousands more in the tunnels, I assure you. Likely trying to make additional entrances. Even if we closed the wardengate, they would find a way in."

— *It is as Dr. Krezek feared. They are turning Durandia into a new myre.*

— Which means they're screwed.

— *Not necessarily.*

— What do you mean?

— *I suspect the Zelnads are behind this. It would explain Dr. Krezek's theory.*

"Hey Ehrmut, I know I'll regret asking this, but how do crypsids reproduce?" Geddy asked.

"At the center of the myre is an egg-laying queen. She is protected by a higher caste called the Elites who are the only ones allowed to mate with her. All the rest are Nurses, sterile females who tend to her young, or Diggers, who maintain the tunnel system."

"So, basically a reverse harem that's good with kids," Oz said. "I'm here for it."

Geddy pointed at his mirrored face shield. "You can't see it, but I'm proving that men can roll their eyes, too."

"Why do you ask, Captain?" Napthar asked.

"In theory, if you wanted to breed crypsids, you'd just need a queen and an Elite?"

"Or the queen and some sperm from one of the elites."

"It's a delicacy," Denk said. "My uncle gave it to me once as a kid."

— *Resist the urge, Geddy.*

— Why do you have to take all the fun away?

"Guys, I might know what's happening here," Geddy said. The others turned to face him. "I think the Zelnads want the queen."

"Zelnads?" Napthar asked. "I don't understand."

"They're not who you think. They're evil aliens from the

center of the universe who want to end civilization. We believe they're breeding deadly creatures to help do their dirty work."

Napthar couldn't have looked more confused. "But ... the Zelnads saved Gundrun."

"That was a manufactured crisis to gain support. They purposely set the asteroid on a collision course with Gundrun so they could save the day and be heroes. Believe me, they're not on our side."

"It's true, Minister," Denk said. "They're the worst."

The minister's incredulity ebbed. "But how could they possibly take a queen? They would all die to protect her. And she's huge!"

"Pheromones," Krezek said. "If the Zelnads introduced pheromones from another myre, it would fool the colony into thinking it was lost." Krezek shook his head as if the idea was too terrible to let get stuck in his brain.

Napthar blinked away his disbelief. "You're saying the Zelnads drove the crypsids out of the myre in order to take the queen and ... breed them?"

"It makes sense," Geddy said.

Consternation pinched Napthar's face. "But the queen is fragile. Even if that was their goal, they'd have no way of getting her out."

— *They would find a way.*

— Something tells me they already have.

— *Where did Voprot find the crypsids?*

Voprot was leaned back against the cave wall with his tail stretched out and his legs splayed. He was still pouting about the crypsids he didn't get to eat.

"Voprot, you said you saw crypsids on your walk?"

"In tunnel," he muttered.

"What tunnel? Where?" the minister asked, stepping toward the giant resting lizard.

Pointing across the baked landscape in the direction of the distant mountains, Voprot said, "Over there. Long way for no meat."

"You walked to those mountains?" Incredulity filled Napthar's face. "Whatever for?"

"For solitude," Geddy hurriedly answered, eyeing Napthar nervously. "He needs his Voprot time or he gets grumpy."

"But that's got to be twenty kilometers!"

Voprot shrugged his wide shoulders, thankfully picking up the story Geddy was putting down. "Voprot at home in desert. Good to think."

— Not about pronouns, I guess.

— *Be nice. He covered pretty well.*

"What did this tunnel look like?" Geddy asked.

"Round." He stretched his arms out wide. "Dark. Big pile of rocks outside. And ship."

That little detail got everyone's attention.

"Ship?" Geddy asked. "What kind of ship?"

"Big ship."

"You didn't consider that an important detail??"

"Holy shit," Oz said. "They must be drilling their way in!"

Napthar looked like a light breeze might blow him over.

"Well, that's it then, Cap. We've gotta stop 'em," Denk declared. "We *can* stop 'em, right?"

Geddy gulped, again grateful for the mirrored shield. The thought of crawling around in the dark with those things made him queasy. Getting eaten alive by frantic crypsids wasn't high on his list.

"Ehrmut, could queen pheromone be used to draw the crypsids back to the myre?"

Krezek wrinkled his nose. "I don't think so. To return to a myre they thought was overrun would take something far more powerful."

"Like what?" Geddy asked.

Krezek façade grew solemn. "Fear. When threatened, the queen secretes a hormone that draws all the workers to her. Like a chemical panic button. If we could somehow fabricate that and force it into the tunnels, they would rush to her, but ..."

Geddy's mouth turned to cotton. "But what?"

"But someone would have to physically collect it from the underside of the queen."

A seething mass of man-eating insects and glistening eggs played through Geddy's mind, while his intestines tied themselves into a Prusik knot. Meanwhile, Denk drew himself up to his full height, roughly even with Geddy's navel, and squared his jaw.

"I'll do it."

CHAPTER FIFTEEN

VOPROT'S BIG HOLE

THE *ARMSTRONG* BANKED STEEPLY to the left as it climbed to surveillance height. Napthar and Doc had returned to the hospital, but not before they made a show of unloading the two pallets from the cargo hold. Napthar assured Geddy he would be tight-lipped about the mission. Hope would spread like wildfire throughout the camp, and sometimes that was dangerous.

After they took off, they circled back to the spaceport for a pair of industrial fans, which Bartok helped them jury-rig to run on batteries. He also gave them some small oxygen masks, just in case. All he knew was that Krezek thought he could get the crypsids to return to the myre where they belonged — an effort he was delighted to support.

If the plan didn't work, Geddy would reach out directly to Smegmo for help. This wasn't the kind of problem money alone could solve, but he could buy them more time at least. He couldn't go to the Committee yet, though. Tretiak and Verveik weren't remotely convinced about the killer-creature theory, but they might be if they had proof. Proof that Geddy and the crew were in a position to obtain.

He leveled the ship out. The parallel mountain ranges with the flats in between resembled the ridged backs of titans rising from the sand. But one of these things was not like the other. An unnaturally conical hillock, invisible from the encampment, was set apart from the ridge where it clearly didn't belong. Nearby, a black circular void was cut into the rock.

"Well, V, there's your pile of rocks," Geddy said. "And your perfectly round tunnel."

"Voprot not lie."

— Which is why he's so fun at parties.

"I don't see a ship." Jel's brow furrowed as she studied the *Armstrong's* scanners.

A red oval shape appeared on the far side of the rock pile, and Geddy zoomed in. It was of regular design and painted in a dusty red pattern. He judged it to be a Knetosian cargo vessel, which didn't make sense until he remembered that Knetos' main industry was terraforming.

"That's a conventional starship," Oz asked, her tone suggesting she already knew the answer. "Definitely not Zelnad."

"It's Knetosian," Geddy said. "A planet with enough big drills to hollow out a moon."

"Any signs of life?" Jel asked.

He switched to IR, which showed no life aboard the ship. "Nope."

Oz smiled broadly. "Which means they're all still in there. What's the plan?"

"Pretty simple... we head down the tunnel and stop the

Zelnads. Denk scrapes some lady jizz off the queen, then we flip on the fans and skedaddle before we're eaten alive."

"Actually, crypsids prefer rotten meat. You'd have to be dead for weeks before they ate you," Denk said.

Geddy gave him a thin-lipped smile. "Thank you for that detailed information, Denk." He turned to Krezek. "Ehrmut, you sure you're up for this? We don't know what we're getting into."

"I understand the risks."

This seemed way more dangerous and terrifying than Ponley Point, but if Denk wanted to get down and dirty with the crypsid queen, Geddy wouldn't stand in his way.

"Want me to send Hughey down ahead?" Jel asked. "Check things out before we go in?"

"Something tells me we don't have that kind of time. We'll put him and Morph on point," Geddy said.

Geddy engaged stealth mode, making it all but invisible. They probably weren't watching the skies, but you never know with the Nads. He chose a spot tight to the mountains but hidden from view of the other ship, less than half a kilometer from the perfectly circular hole at the base.

As they touched down onto the parched earth, Voprot pointed at the tunnel. "That where Voprot found lunch he not get to eat."

CHAPTER SIXTEEN

MYRED

THE FRESHLY DRILLED tunnel descended in the general direction of the city and the spaceport. It was fully three meters across. How freaking big was this queen Denk planned to molest?

Geddy and Oz carried survival packs from the *Armstrong,* which included rescue gear. Denk and Voprot carried the borrowed oxygen masks, weapons, and the fans. Krezek chose not to carry a weapon, but as captain, Geddy insisted he take a blaster pistol from the closet. Now, as they walked the ramrod-straight highway to hell, he seemed glad to have it.

The headlamps threw light a good fifty meters down the smooth-sided tunnel, but that wouldn't stop a few thousand skittering, snapping crypsids from pouring out of the dark beyond. It was Hughey and Morpho's job to ensure that didn't happen, in addition to watching out for the Zelnads.

Jel had switched to a special contact lens in her right eye that displayed Hughey's feed. Morpho swung along a short distance behind. The rest of them crept along at a distance, weapons at the ready.

Nearly an hour later, Jel stopped cold. "Hold up. There's something up here."

The hair on the back of Geddy's neck bristled. Taking a shallow breath, he clicked the safety off his PDQ.

"It's the horde, isn't it?" Geddy whispered.

— *You need to remain calm.*

— I'm in a dark tunnel on my way to a crypsid hive. It's not exactly calming.

— *But you're the captain.*

"No, it's something on the roof of the tunnel. Hughey, can you throw a little light on that for me?"

A minute later, they reached the deformity in the tunnel, an oval-shaped hole.

"Looks like part of another tunnel," Jel said, an uncertain look on her face. "I think they drilled right through a section of the myre."

"It's a crypsid tunnel," Denk said as he studied it. "It looks old."

A pile of dirt and pebbles stood directly below it. The pile had been disturbed, presumably by the unfortunate crypsids who had fallen through and become lunch for Voprot. But there were also a couple of footprints.

"Must where Voprot's lunch came from," Oz offered.

"But Voprot not get to—"

"We know!" Geddy said. "Morph, check it out." Geddy watched as Morpho dutifully slung his way up into oblong hole.

A couple minutes later, he heard Morpho slither back

toward him before he dropped out and landed on his shoulder. He plugged a tendril into Geddy's ear without asking.

— **The tunnel is empty and seldom used. I do not believe it poses a threat.**

— Where does it go?

— **I did not follow it to its terminus.**

— All I want to know is that crypsids aren't gonna fill this damn tunnel behind us.

— **Unlikely. The two crypsids Voprot found must have sensed outside air and became curious.**

— Let's hope so.

— *Hi, Morpho!*

— **Hello, Eli.**

Morpho unplugged from his ear with a little *pop* and flung himself back down toward Hughey.

"He thinks we're good," Geddy announced. "Let's keep trucking."

Meanwhile, Krezek took out the little bottle of queen pheromone Napthar had placed in his care.

"Guess we'd better slather up." He lifted the bottle into the light. It only lasted about an hour. "Geddy, you want to go first?"

Geddy holstered the PDQ and stepped forward, wrinkling his nose at the amber liquid. He uncapped it and took a hesitant whiff from a distance, followed by a full inhale with the bottle nearly touching his nose. Surprisingly, it didn't smell like anything at all. "You sure this is the stuff?"

"To you, it's odorless. To them, it's the overpowering odor of a superior caste."

Krezek instructed him to dab the oily substance around his collar, his elbows, his knees, and his boots. It didn't seem like enough, but Geddy wasn't about to second-guess him on pheromone dosage.

The others followed suit, ending with Denk. "My dad was a warden for a few years. I begged him to take me into the tunnels with him, but he always said I wasn't allowed." He dabbed the stuff on his ragged clothes, a few of which he'd shed before leaving the *Armstrong*.

"One night, he handed me a bottle of QP and said, 'Rub this all over yourself. Every centimeter you can until it's gone.' Afterward, he walked me down to the wardengate and took me all the way to the myre."

— And to think my old man only shared a beer with me.

— *I think it's sweet.*

— Of course you do.

"Any crypsid run-ins along the way?" Krezek asked.

"Not a single one." Denk gave an impish grin. "But I saw plenty from the ledge where the tunnel meets the myre. Crypsids as far as you could see. It was like a moving carpet." He knelt to apply the QP to his own boots. "Only problem was, I smelled so much like the queen that some near the ledge got confused. Anyway, next thing I knew, all those glassy eyes are looking straight at us. Dad grabbed my hand, and we ran out of there as fast as we could. They got the gate closed behind us just in time."

"Holy shit," Oz said, sharing a wide-eyed look with Jel.

Denk rose and handed the bottle back to Krezek not even half empty.

"Guys, Hughey's got something up here," Jel said. "It might be the myre."

Geddy's pulse quickened. They hadn't seen shit so far, but that might be about to change. He found himself hoping the bugs were still in the city so he wouldn't have to see any.

Weapons drawn, they continued down. Soon, a faint blue glow that reminded him of moonlight replaced the darkness. Geddy could just make out Hughey's glimmering outline at the edge of a void.

"What's making that light?"

Denk answered, "The myre glows. It's the bacteria that feed on their dung."

"Denk's exactly right," Krezek confirmed. "The myre floor teems with bioluminescent microorganisms."

"Kill your headlamps," Geddy said, and they continued with the faint blue glow lighting the way.

They emerged at the tunnel opening, and the sight took Geddy's breath away.

To his eyes, the myre appeared to be a colossal bubble formed as the planet's molten surface solidified long ago. Everything was smooth and rounded, with deep pockets set into the walls and roof where other, smaller bubbles once formed. The furthest point was at least two hundred meters away. The roof was comparatively low, however, maybe twenty meters at its highest, making it feel like was pressing in from above.

Coming down the tunnel was bad enough, but now they were hundreds of meters down and completely out of their element. His claustrophobia, which had largely settled into the background, dug its cruel claws into his heart and squeezed. The only thing that worked in this situation was to close his eyes and take deep breaths. The acrid scent of guano invaded his nostrils, limiting how much oxygen he could take in. His lungs screamed for more air.

"You okay?" Oz asked.

"Just revisiting my life choices. Why does it smell like we're standing in the world's largest litter box?"

Krezek inhaled deeply. "Ammonia vapor. That explains the low ceiling. This chamber was much taller once. The brightness of the organisms on the ground suggests a layer of gamat several meters deep."

"In other words, it's full of shit. You should feel right at home," Oz said, giving him a wink.

"Cute," Geddy said through a pained expression.

Geddy checked the envirosuit's readout on his forearm. O_2 was about eighty percent what it had been on the surface and NH_3, ammonia, was off the charts.

He shrugged the pack off his shoulders and unzipped it, then handed Denk and Voprot their oxygen masks. "Time to go on oxygen."

No one disputed the need. He, Oz, and Krezek put their helmets back on while Denk and Voprot donned the masks. Voprot put his on upside-down, and it only covered about half his snout.

"Here, lemme help you with that," Geddy said, flipping it back upright and lengthening the straps. It looked ridiculous, and it probably wouldn't do much, but it was better than nothing. He sighed. "Try to breathe through your nose. If you start to feel woozy, go back to the tunnel, okay?"

Voprot nodded okay. Geddy opened the valve of his own mask just as his face shield began to fog, and delicious O_2 filled his lungs.

"Where's the queen?" Jel asked beside him.

"There's a depression near the middle like a cradle," Denk said. "You basically can't see her until you're right on top of it."

"What about the Elites?" Geddy's eyes remained closed, his heart rate finally slowing a bit.

Krezek got on his hands and knees and eased himself out on the edge where the drill had broken through. "Oh, no," Krezek whispered. "Look."

Geddy reluctantly joined him, then followed his shaking finger down to the myre floor below. A ragged semicircle of enormous, tangled corpses lay as though a bomb had detonated. They were fully ten times the size of the Diggers and shaped like oblong spiders. Limbs and cracked shards of exoskeletons were strewn everywhere, two or three deep in places.

Next to them, half-buried in the powdery-looking floor ten meters below was the drill, poking up like a lawn dart.

"Found the drill," Geddy said.

"They must've attacked when it broke through," Oz said next to him.

"Yeah, and it didn't end well." The sight of the massacre made him strangely sad, and more than a little angry. Not even creatures that lived deep underground could escape the Zelnads' reach. "Who's gonna mate with her now?"

"You would be worried about that," Oz said.

"No, no," Krezek said. "It's a good question. In fact, a handful of Diggers will evolve into Elites."

"In other words, they'll change for their queen." She shot a look at Geddy, who also left his mirrored shield up so everyone could see his face. "Must be nice."

"See there?" Denk pointed straight across to a ledge

where another, much smaller tunnel came into the myre. "That's the tunnel back to Durandia."

"You're sure?" Geddy asked. "How long has it been since you were down here?"

"I'm sure," he replied with finality.

He checked over his shoulder at Voprot, who had crouched behind Denk. "Then that's where we'll set up the fans. Once Denk collects the sample, we need to move fast. V, you up for some running?"

"Yes, Geddy! Voprot ready!"

Distant voices met their ears. Their heads spun in unison toward the sound. A single helmet briefly appeared over wavelike undulations in the chamber floor, then disappeared just as quickly.

"It's the Nads, I'm sure of it," Geddy said. "They must be extracting the queen as we speak."

"She must be heavily sedated," Krezek said gravely. "She cannot be harmed. If she is, the whole colony will come flooding in."

"Jel, Hughey, let's see what we're dealing with," Geddy said.

"You heard the man, Hughey."

The shimmering cloud of nanobots floated up toward the ceiling and quickly disappeared among the rocks. Faint images played across the contact lens in Jel's right eye.

"Okay, coming up on the cradle now ..." She blinked. "Damn, she's big."

"How big?" Geddy asked.

"Six, seven meters long at least. Like a giant tick about to pop."

"Thanks for that horrifying description. How many Nads?"

After seeing what happened to the Elites, Geddy was very concerned about their weapons. The PDQ might hold its own, but if it came to a gunfight, they'd lose.

She shook her head. "A handful, maybe more. They're just talking right now. We've got the drop on them."

— *Remember what Tymeri said about the Basoan named Lestiko.*

— What about him?

— *If he was able to retake control, maybe others can, too.*

Hiding in the bodies of ordinary people was a dastardly tactic. The only difference between them and Geddy was the intention of the Sagacean inside. But killing a Zelnad meant killing its host. They were bound, just like him and Eli.

"These are regular people who got hijacked. Nobody kills anybody unless they have to. We clear?"

Reluctant nods all around. "Then what's our play?" Oz asked.

— *You could force them to comply through nonviolent means.*

— How?

— *Very few species can breathe ammonia for long.*

— That right?

— *It may be in even higher concentrations along the floor. It depends on the humidity.*

He checked the wrist computer again. Humidity was eighty-three percent.

"Ehrmut, you think eighty-three percent humidity's enough to concentrate that ammonia along the ground?"

"Quite possibly," he admitted. "Why?"

"Because I might now how to stop this fight before it can start."

Oz cocked an eyebrow and gave him an *Oh really?* look. Of course, she knew he'd gotten a prompt from Eli. "Just popped into your head, did it?"

He winked. "Call it a flash of inspiration."

CHAPTER SEVENTEEN

KILLER QUEEN

GEDDY'S BOOT sank surprisingly deep into the powdery, spongy floor of the myre, pausing to let his eyes sweep over the pile of dead elites and the buried drill. His gauge confirmed Krezek's suspicions. Ammonia was a good deal higher down here, which demanded a richer mixture of O_2. They'd have to work fast or risk blowing through their supply.

Oz climbed down the rope ladder after him, followed by Denk and Krezek. Voprot jumped from the edge of the tunnel and immediately sunk to his knees in ancient crypsid shit. Only his massive tail kept him from going deeper still.

"Agh! Voprot stuck!"

While he figured out how to extract himself, they advanced on the large boulder of volcanic rock that kept them out of view.

Staying tight to it, Geddy edged around to where he could see the Zelnads. They'd moved away from the cradle and stood around a metal box nearby, talking and seemingly oblivious to their presence. Morpho hopped up to his shoulder, his small body tensed and ready.

"Okay, Morph, you're up. They're close together right now. Once Hughey cuts their O2, you grab their weapons. Oz and I'll start moving in while Voprot ..." He turned around to find the lizard loping across to him with his mask half hanging off his face, useless. If the ammonia troubled him, he didn't show it. "... blocks their escape. Denk, Krezek, watch both the tunnels so we don't get surprised. Got it?"

He checked each of them for understanding, finally looking to Oz. "You ready?"

"I'm sure this will work perfectly."

"That's the spirit. Morph, make me proud. Don't let them see you."

Morpho gave his customary salute and hopped off his shoulder. In midair, he transformed into a thin spider shape and flattened his points of contact like duck feet, crawling off toward the Zelnads while barely leaving any prints. The darkness swallowed him instantly.

A couple minutes passed, during which one of the Zelnads bent down and removed something like a short rifle from the box. If it was a weapon, it was unlike any he'd ever seen. It was short and chunky, with two handles and a business end that resembled the cap of a big white mushroom.

"What the hell's that?" Geddy whispered to Oz.

Her eyes peeled wide. "I've seen something like that."

"You have? Where?"

"On the nose of Tymeri's ship."

Of course! Watching this little operation, he couldn't help but wonder how the hell they were going to extract this giant creature from her dimple in the cave floor. He figured bots would carry her up through the tunnel like the ones back at the spaceport, but no. They were going to use the same gravity tech that snatched Oz away and push it up the tunnel like a frictionless shopping cart.

The other Zelnads fanned out to either side of the one carrying the gravity gun. He pointed it down at the depression, and a low, pulsating hum echoed through the cavern, worrying Geddy that the crypsids would hear it and burst back into the myre at any moment.

"C'mon, Morph. Any day now ..."

A shiny, pillowy form rose into view. It looked so much like a small starship at first that he wondered if this might be a huge mix-up. But as the Nads trained their helmet lights on it, its details came into focus.

The queen was similar in shape to a snail, but wider and entirely soft. The widening coil of her abdomen towered behind her relatively small thorax. It was a translucent, faintly purple sac that apparently churned out eggs all day.

"Like moving a waterbed," Geddy said.

"She's so fragile," Krezek muttered to no one in particular, "Please be careful."

One of the Nads quickly drew their weapon, a short rifle, and aimed off to his left. Had Morpho given himself away?

A second later, their hands flew to their helmets. Hughey had cut their air.

"Now!" Geddy said.

Their helmet lights spun around wildly in the dark as they flailed about, yet the one with the gravity beam continued lifting the queen free of the cradle. Geddy and Oz raced across the mushy ground as fast as they could, but it was like running through fluffy sand.

"Leave him to me," Geddy said. "If he drops her, we're in a world of hurt."

"So, I get six, you get one?"

"I'm a feminist."

Geddy leveled the PDQ and Oz drew her energy blades, the red light playing across the glowing blue ground as they ran. The very surprised Nads reached for their weapons, but they were already gone. Morpho was the best pickpocket in the galaxy. He reappeared after a moment and dropped the rifles in a pile at Geddy's feet.

"Good boy."

He turned his attention to the man with the gravity gun as Oz came around behind them. They eyed an escape back toward the tunnel, but when Voprot's electric whip turned on, glowing nearly the same blue as the cavern, they realized they were boxed in.

"I'm gonna need you to lower that bug back down. Gently."

"I will not." He was Afolosian, like Krezek.

— Do I have to ask?

— Yes, they are all Zelnad.

"Then you'll die of asphyxiation. Or choking on ammonia fumes. Which I guess is also asphyxiation. You get the gist. Just set her down and we'll turn your O2 back on."

Geddy glanced down at the pile of weapons. Morpho was gone. A couple Nads fell to their knees in the soft ground, gasping for air. They pulled off their helmets and threw them aside, inhaling deeply the poisoned air. An Eicrean and a Zorran.

"Put her down gently."

He tilted his head. "You know what happens if I drop her."

"I do."

"Then you should've seen this coming."

"No!"

He released the controls, and the queen started to fall as though in slow motion. It was only half a meter or so, but in that split second, Morpho shot a sticky tendril out and yanked the device away before she hit the floor. She stopped centimeters from the ground and hovered, her gelatinous body rippling from the sudden shift. The Zelnad lurched for the device once it left his hands, but the moment he did, Hughey's nanobots covered his face shield, blinding him.

He flailed about, stumbled, and fell into the cradle. Bouncing hard off the side of the floating queen, he rolled to a stop half under her. Geddy and Oz gasped and dashed over to the edge.

There wasn't enough space to get off a shot. The choking Zelnad clawed helplessly at his face trying to get Hughey off.

Denk, Jel, and Krezek came up beside them. One of the other Nads got up and ran, wild-eyed, back toward the tunnel. Voprot casually stiff-armed him.

"Keep her right there, Morph. Jel, I think Hughey's work is done for now."

Hughey removed himself from the Zelnad's face shield. Geddy knelt at the edge of the cradle, and their eyes met.

"Looks like you're between a rock and a soft place," Geddy said.

"It doesn't matter what you do to me, *human*." His lips curled distastefully around the word. "Nothing you do matters at all."

"Probably not. But I've already got a guilty conscience, so ..."

Geddy extended his hand. The man's eyes narrowed suspiciously. "You wish to ... help me?"

"Only 'cuz everyone's watching."

The queen's pulsing body was only a few centimeters from Geddy's face. Being that close was more thrilling than threatening. In her helplessness, she radiated a weirdly calming energy.

Reluctantly, the Zelnad clasped Geddy's wrist, right over the bracelet that protected him from detection. Geddy hauled him out from under the queen and helped him crawl over the edge.

"See? We're not so bad," Geddy offered. "Now go join your little Zelnad friends. We've got work to do."

CHAPTER EIGHTEEN

WE'RE BIG FANS

GEDDY TURNED the gravity gun over in his hands, marveling at its shockingly light weight. The mushroom-cap end pointed up and away. The controls were minimal but clever. His right hand fit neatly around a rubberized handle at the back. When he squeezed it, the fluttering hum started up, and he flinched.

"Found the 'on' switch," he said to Krezek over his right shoulder.

The handle moved smoothly in and out and could twist as well. When moving it in and out didn't do anything, he gave it a small twist to the right. When he did, a chunk of rock broke off from the ceiling, but didn't fall.

"Careful, Ged," Oz warned.

Lowering the gun made the rock follow.

— Okay, twist for power. How about the old in and out?

— *Just point it away from everyone.*

He slowly pulled the handle back, and the rock drifted closer.

"Cool," he muttered. "This should work."

He shoved the handle forward as he relaxed his grip, and the rock sailed away, smashing back into the ceiling and exploding into bits that rained down around them on the mushy ground.

Hughey had reactivated the remaining six Zelnads' air supply. Without their weapons, they didn't pose much of a threat. He'd deal with them when the job was done. For now, having Oz and Jel standing guard was enough. None of the others had uttered a word.

"I'd been wondering about the best way to frighten her," Krezek said excitedly. "This device is the solution."

"Wait — *frighten* her?"

"It's the only way to collect enough of her fear pheromone. But we must only lift her enough for Denk to access the gland near her cloaca. A drop could kill her."

"And I've gotta get the lid on the jar right away," Denk confirmed.

"Yes, immediately. A few parts per million in the air could bring the whole colony rushing back."

"Perfect," Geddy said, failing to slow his racing pulse. "As soon as Denk gets the sample and gets clear, I'll gently lower her while Voprot takes Denk to the city tunnel as fast as he can. They set up the fans, open the sample, and we all haul ass out of here."

"In the meantime, Jel and I will escort these guys back to the surface," Oz said.

"You think this will make any difference in the end?" taunted the Zelnad he'd just rescued. "You are drops of water. We are a flood."

"You should put that on a T-shirt," Geddy said.

"She's very agitated," Krezek said from the edge of the depression. "She should be producing the pheromone as we speak."

Geddy joined him and Denk. The queen's spindly front legs scratched absently at the ground, and her four glassy eyes rolled about as though finding focus.

"Okay, moment of truth. Oz?"

One by one, she hauled the Zelnad prisoners to their feet. "I'll meet you by the tunnel."

He gave her a tight nod, and she ordered them to move. Jel and Hughey walked beside them. He watched after them for a few seconds, then returned his attention to the queen.

"Okay, Denk, you ready to get intimate?"

"Ready, Cap."

"Voprot?"

"Ready, Geddy." He assumed a sprinter's stance.

"Okay, sweetheart. Time to get your juices flowing."

He pointed the gun at the queen and squeezed the handle. She gave a start, her heaving backside swaying like a rolling tide. Gently, Geddy lifted her up, and her motoring little legs made double time. A thin, high-pitched *scree* emerged from her shiny head. Krezek was down on all fours in the shitty soil trying to get a look underneath.

"That's far enough! Denk, go!"

Geddy froze. Morpho, who had been nearby while Hughey went back to recording mode, hopped up on his shoulder to watch.

Denk eased himself into the cradle, careful to avoid the queen's spiky legs as they scissored. He lay on his back and shuffled himself under her as her thin *scree* continued.

"You sure they can't hear that?" Geddy asked nervously.

"They're deaf and nearly blind. The pheromone is what we need to worry about," Krezek said. "Denk, do you see the gland? It should be a pale green color."

"Yeah, I see it!"

"Good. Now, express a small amount into the sample jar. Like I showed you."

"Okay, here goes ... Ugh, it's slimy! And it smells!"

Geddy believed Krezek when he said the others couldn't hear her, but it made him nervous, nonetheless. "You're doing great, buddy."

"Almost got it ... Just need to seal the jar."

The solid, regular hum coming from the device started to sputter, causing the queen to shake as the gravity field fluctuated.

"Hold her steady!" Krezek barked.

"I'm trying! Denk, get out of there now! This thing's on the fritz."

"Okay, I've got it!"

Denk pushed himself out from under the queen as the hum continued to waver. He rolled out of the way just before the beam gave out. Krezek gasped as she fell, but her fork-on-a-chalkboard protestations quickly faded as her weight settled back into the cradle.

Morpho left Geddy's shoulder to collect the sealed sample jar from Denk. He stickily crawled up the smooth sides while Geddy and Krezek extended their hands to Denk. Once again, Geddy was glad he couldn't smell anything, though he spotted a smear on his gloved hands.

"Stick your hands in the dirt! Quickly!"

They hauled Denk up and shoved their slimy hands into

the powdery soil, rubbing it all up and down their arms. But who knew how much of it was already in the air?

"Voprot, Denk, go fast!"

Denk took the jar back from Morpho as Voprot scooped him up onto his back and took off running toward the ledge.

———

VOPROT AND DENK vanished in a puff of shit-dust. Combined with the spongy earth, it made the silence as oppressive as the darkness.

Geddy and Krezek jogged back toward the boulder where they'd hidden earlier, intending to make sure Denk and Voprot had made it to the ledge. After the long journey down the tunnel, his legs were screaming. They'd closed about half the distance when they heard Denk cry out.

"V, I'm slipping ... Uf!"

They broke into a run, though the suits and soft ground made the going slow. After fifty meters, Geddy thought his heart was about to explode. He glanced down at his wrist, gasping.

He had twelve minutes of O_2 left, and it was dropping fast.

His arm stretched out to Krezek, who was in superior physical condition and unwittingly extending his lead.

"Ehrmut, slow down," he panted so hard the helmet's regulator couldn't quite keep up. Spots of fog appeared inside his helmet. Krezek slowed and frowned at the sight of him.

"What's wrong? You don't look so good."

"I'm running out of ... air ... and ... claustrophobic ..."

"Take long, deep breaths. Don't worry about the air right now. I'm still at fifty percent, so I can–"

"*Fifty?!* What are you, a free diver? I only have *twelve!* There must be a ... leak ..."

— I'm going to die. I'm dying. That means you are going to die, too. Sorry.

— *Stop saying die!*

— I'll pretend you said, 'Never say die.' It's more positive.

— *I'm here for you. I'm always here for you.*

"Afolos has less oxygen than Earth 2. I suppose I'm used to it."

"C'mon, let's ... keep moving. Denk, we're coming!"

"I'm okay, Cap!" His voice came faintly but distinctly through the helmet.

Twenty meters later, they found Denk standing upright in the dirt as Voprot clumsily brushed him off. He wasn't two paces away from the saw-toothed foreleg of a dead Elite. Any closer, and he would've been impaled.

Geddy hurried over to him. "What happened?"

Denk scrambled to his feet, wild-eyed with fear. "V dropped me, and I dropped the sample!"

"Voprot so sorry ..."

"Forget it!" Geddy said. "Let's find it and get this done!"

The four of them prodded around in the puffy ground looking for the little sample jar, a capped plastic cylinder maybe three centimeters wide. It seemed like a needle in a haystack.

"Everything okay over there?" came Oz's voice through Geddy's helmet.

He rose to his full height and about-faced toward the tunnel where they'd come in. Oz was about to climb the rope ladder. Jel stood guard at the back of the Zelnad prisoners. All helmets were turned in their direction.

"We dropped the sample," Geddy said. "Get out of here *now*."

His tone must have sounded urgent because Oz scrambled immediately up the ladder.

"Cap, over here!" Denk said.

Geddy whirled and ran back to where Krezek was inspecting the container. "Is it okay?"

In the full light of their helmets, it was plain to see the crack in the lid. A few drips of oily liquid glinted in the light. The city tunnel was practically right above them.

"Voprot!" Geddy barked. "Get him up there before we're swimming in crypsids!"

Voprot growled determinedly and picked Denk back up. Denk wrapped his arms around Voprot's thick neck and held on for dear life. Voprot bounded up the honeycombed wall and climbed onto the ledge. Geddy and Krezek backed up until they could see them working.

Denk unfastened the fan on Voprot's lower back, then Voprot returned the favor. They both crouched to set them up at the tunnel entrance.

Krezek wore an anxious expression. "This is taking too long."

Geddy checked his oxygen. Three minutes. He was about to reply when he heard a noise from the pile of dead elites. Just a small click, but to that point, the myre had been almost silent. It stood out.

Then it came again. And again.

Something in the pile wasn't dead.

He slapped Krezek's forearm and jutted his finger at it as

an injured Elite rose from the pile of carcasses like a Phoenix. Its body was an entirely different shape from the queen and the workers. It was flatter and sleeker, with six four-jointed legs and a set of scythe-like mandibles the size of machetes. How a Digger could turn into one defied all reason.

Purple blood oozed from a gash where its front right leg joined the thorax, and it was curled protectively underneath. Like the queen, four black eyes the size of his fist locked on to them. A set of long antennae unfolded from its back and swished about in the air.

"Oh, no," Krezek muttered. "The pheromone!"

"Voprot, Denk, we've got a live one!"

The elite's svelte body crouched to the ground, compressing its legs like springs before launching into the air. It landed halfway up the wall, and its injured rear legs struggled for purchase as it angled toward Voprot and Denk.

Geddy drew the PDQ and fired. The bug jumped sideways just before the blast cratered the wall. It clambered up and around the missing chunk and was nearly to the ledge when Voprot's whip shot out of nowhere and wrapped around one of its forelegs. He jerked it hard, and the creature's high-pitched *scree* echoed across the myre as it fell heavily back to the ground.

Geddy leveled the fully charged PDQ at the creature and turned it to dust before it could right itself.

"Let's go, guys!"

Voprot leapt out over the edge and landed on the ground in front of them, untroubled by the fifteen-meter drop. He whirled.

"Ready, Denk! Jump!"

"Look out belowww!" Denk flung himself into space, as absolute a show of faith as Geddy had ever seen.

Voprot caught Denk like a bale of hay and returned him to his back.

"Are the fans going?" Geddy demanded.

"Yeah, Cap."

"Then *run!*"

Voprot took off in the direction of the Zelnad tunnel across the way, still carrying Denk. It wasn't far — thirty meters at most — but Geddy was gassed by the time he caught up and couldn't seem to get enough air in his lungs. Voprot bounded up the wall and crouched at the top, his arm hanging down to help them up. Before Krezek started up the rope ladder, he turned back to check on Geddy. As he did, his eyes practically jumped out of their sockets.

Geddy spun his head around in time to see a river of crypsids explode from the city tunnel like black sludge from a hose.

— Holy shit, they're here already?!

— *Move, Geddy!*

The surprisingly spry Krezek scaled the ladder, then grabbed Voprot's claw to be hoisted up. Geddy reached the bottom just as Krezek disappeared from view. He took one more look back.

The angry Diggers spread in every direction from the tunnel, pouring over the ledge in a cascade before hitting the ground and finding their legs. Many made a beeline for the queen, but hundreds, maybe thousands more, were falling over themselves to get at him.

"Geddy, hurry!" Voprot urged.

The gauge on his arm flashed an angry red. His time was up. Whatever oxygen was left in his suit, that was it.

His muscles and lungs screaming, he scrambled up as the crypsids slammed into the wall at his feet. He swung his right arm up into Voprot's claw and felt his incredible power yank him up like a rag doll.

"Now we run!" Voprot said, taking off up the tunnel.

Geddy ripped off his helmet and took in a deep lungful of ammonia-tinged air. Krezek did likewise, and they both gave chase. Whether from the comparatively fresh air or adrenaline, energy surged into Geddy's legs, and he barreled up the tunnel, nearly keeping pace with Krezek. He was about to check over his shoulder again, but Eli stopped him.

— *Don't turn around. It slows you down!*

— They do it in movies!

— *This isn't a movie! If it was, you'd be Crewman Number Two who gets eaten alive.*

— Why Number Two?

Geddy didn't have to look anyway because he could feel them at his back like a foul wind. He briefly considered holding his ground, whipping out the PDQ and clogging the tunnel with dead crypsids, but his legs refused to stop. He'd done a pretty good job managing his fear, but it seized him now like an electric shock. One way or another, he was getting out of this godforsaken place.

Well ahead, he spotted the glow of Oz's blades as she urged on the prisoners. They closed fast, and Oz whirled, training her lights on them.

"They're right on our ass!" Geddy shouted.

Jel's lead on everyone had only extended, but not because she was especially fast. The prisoners were purposely slowing them down. Oz yelled at them, but they finally just stopped in the middle of the tunnel and formed a line across it.

"Oz, forget them!" Geddy urged.

"We are eternal," muttered the Afolosian. "You are not."

These people didn't deserve to die, but neither did Geddy and his crew.

"Screw this," Geddy said. "V clear the way!"

With Denk still on his back, Voprot lowered his shoulder and charged at the line of Nads like an all-star linebacker. They didn't flinch, but they should have. Voprot bowled them over with a sickening crunch. Geddy and Krezek charged through the pocket. Geddy dared a final glance over his shoulder as guilt washed over him. The Nads were going to die, and there was nothing he could do about it.

"I'm sorry."

He continued motoring toward the pinpoint of light that had appeared up ahead. The anguished screams of the Zelnads echoed down the tunnel as the horde consumed them. It made him wonder whose consciousness experienced death — the Zelnads or their hapless hosts. Or both?

As Geddy reached the end of the tunnel, he stumbled and fell, sprawling onto the parched earth. He immediately spun around, the PDQ at the ready as his chest heaved with effort. Two quick pulls of the trigger dropped a wall of rock into the tunnel opening, sealing it off.

Soon after, black legs shot between the cracks, scraping the rocks like tools as they sought a way through, but there would be none. Big as they were, they couldn't move that much weight.

He dropped the PDQ and flopped onto his back, panting

and grateful to be out of the planet's dark and alien plumbing. While he lay there, Oz marched over, picked up the PDQ, and with two pulls of the trigger turned the Knetosian ship to a smoking pile of metal. She dropped it onto his abdomen, making him wince.

"Hey, that's my pancreas! I totally need that! I think."

"You need to work on your core."

CHAPTER NINETEEN

THE SORT-OF COMMISSIONING

ONCE THEY WERE COMFORTABLY clear of Durandia's gravitational field, Denk opened the *Fizmo's* hold so Geddy could guide the *Armstrong* inside. Had her wings been just a meter longer, she wouldn't have fit, creating quite a conundrum. But it did fit, and per usual, there was nothing else in the hold. Jel and Oz rode with him while everyone else went up in the *Fiz*.

After the skids settled onto the deck, he powered her down and waited for Denk to re-pressurize the hold before getting out. His ears were already starting to pop, an unpleasant sensation which only yawning worked to reduce.

Oz hadn't spoken the entire trip back into space.

Taking the Zelnads prisoner was the right thing to do. In practical terms, they'd scored a huge win. They'd foiled a brazen Zelnad scheme to breed crypsids and unleash them on unsuspecting worlds. In so doing, they scored an immensely valuable piece of tech and saved Durandia.

Why didn't it feel better?

— I don't get it, E. There was nothing easy about what we did back there. We almost died. How could it seem ... too easy?

— *I know exactly what you mean.*

— Really?

— *It was as though they considered their mission immaterial somehow.*

— Right? Like their hearts weren't in it.

— *I do not believe they stopped in the tunnel in order to block our escape.*

Geddy gasped audibly. Oz lifted her eyes to his and studied him briefly. He smiled and waved it off, and she went back to staring listlessly out the front screen.

— You think they wanted to die?

— *Perhaps. Or the hosts did.*

Minister Napthar and the refugees were awaiting them when they returned to the camp. On learning it was safe to return to the Underground and shore up the wardengate, they cheered. That was nice, but it didn't last long.

They all knew this day would come. You couldn't kill a Zelnad without killing its host, too. Their hosts were sons and daughters, fathers and mothers who had the misfortune of being taken over. Jeledine's own sister was among them.

But there was a very real possibility, at least in Geddy's mind, that they didn't especially *want* to survive the encounter. The question of why offered tantalizing possibilities but no clear answers.

Geddy unbuckled his restraint and got up, but Oz remained where she was, a vacant look on her face. "You okay?" he asked.

"My whole time with the resistance, I killed four Xellarans. Every time, it was a case of me or them. That felt horrible enough, but this ..." She shook her head, her eyes glassy and unblinking. "Yeah, they were Zelnads, but they were *our* prisoners. *Our* responsibility."

He fell into a crouch and turned her chair so she faced him. Tears welled in her bottomless eyes. He took her hands and rubbed them reassuringly. "Oz, I get it. I really do. I feel shitty, too. But something about this doesn't add up, and I think you know it."

She raised her eyes from the floor. "What do you mean?"

"If Denk hadn't fumbled the pheromone on the three-yard line, we would've waltzed right into the endzone."

She cocked her head quizzically. "Huh?"

"Sorry. I'm trying to say that either that wasn't their A team, this wasn't that important a mission, or not all Zelnads are equally committed to the cause. Either way, they *chose* to stop in that tunnel. Maybe it was a willing sacrifice, or maybe–"

"They just wanted out," she finished.

He nodded. "Let's say crypsids really were part of the master plan. Why send half a dozen guys in a stolen Knetosian ship? Guys we easily got the best of?"

"I had the same thought," Jel said behind them. "It wasn't much of an op."

Geddy got back up and turned to her. "What's your take?"

"We know the Zelnads are smart, but we also know they use some of their hosts' knowledge. I gotta think they choose poorly sometimes."

— In fact, we do not choose at all.

— You sure as hell didn't choose me.

— Even so, I am glad we are friends.

— More than friends, amigo.

"It's not a choice at all," Geddy said. "Which makes it that much more likely that not all Zelnads are created equal." The light over the airlock door turned from red to green, indicating the hold had re-pressurized. He lowered the ramp, and the familiar smell of old metal met his nostrils.

"We'll noodle on it. In the meantime ..." his eyes sparkled. "Now that the band's back together, let's see if Verveik's tried to reach us."

Doc met them halfway across the hold, his arms folded behind his back.

"Any luck?" Geddy asked.

Doc pivoted and fell in with him and the girls as they entered the back of the bridge through the airlock door. "There was one contact on the frequency you mentioned, but the file seems corrupted."

Ships logged all comms traffic, from transponder pings to stray broadcasts. Doc led them to his terminal and pointed at the message. It was a large packet with unknown tracking data received a day earlier.

Doc attempted to open it, but the holoscreen displayed a warning: INVALID MARKER. UNABLE TO DECRYPT. "I attempted to run it through the usual protocols, but none will even recognize the file."

"May I?" Jel gestured at the chair.

"Be my guest," Doc said.

Jel's fingers flew across the screen as she swiped and pinched her way through a dizzying array of others.

"Older decryption protocols don't work on unsigned streams. We have to firewall it first ... like so."

She tapped the screen, and the stream was extracted. When it opened, Verveik's face appeared. The background wasn't the *Dom*, but it was too nondescript to identify. He looked beleaguered.

"Hello, Captain Starheart. I hope this finds you well, and that you've tracked down your crew. Sorry for the secrecy, but we can't be too careful right now.

"Since we parted company, I've met privately with a number of potential allies across the galaxy. The good news is, many are suspicious about the Zelnads' agenda. Unfortunately, without concrete proof of a conspiracy, no government will dare stand against them."

Geddy's heart sank, but he understood. Up until Gundrun's near-destruction they were the most feared and respected power in the galaxy. In saving them from complete destruction, the Zelnads bought a powerful ally, adding the former Triad planets for emphasis.

"The Committee has been working hard to build our case against them," Verveik continued. "Everett Hau's been working the PR angle, and people are starting to ask questions. Mr. Zirhof hired thousands of contractors to outfit the New Alliance ships with bubble tech as we speak.

"And finally, your ... associate, Miss Semenov, has been looking into the *Sirwin*, and it appears you're right. Something big is happening at the Myadan Xoo."

The *Sirwin* was the Myadan-bound derelict vessel they'd encountered months earlier. It was transporting at least two ranses, one of which punched a hole in the fuselage and killed everyone inside. Not exactly the kind of creatures you'd sell stuffed animals of in the Xoo gift shop.

"Miss Semenov is trying to find out exactly what that is. If they are breeding dangerous species as you suspect, Myadan's our best chance to prove it. We need to give her time."

— The one thing we don't have.

— *I agree.*

Jel's footage from the myre was compelling, but it only showed someone in envirosuits trying to take the queen. The footage from the *Armstrong* clearly showed a ship parked outside the tunnel, but it was Knetosian, and you couldn't really connect it to the Zelnads anyway. The gulf between *knowing* what was happening and *proving* it to powerful people had grown depressingly wide.

"In the meantime, I need you to investigate the origin of the asteroid. We know it came from the Elenian Belt, but not how it wound up on a collision course with Gundrun. If there is anything — and I mean *anything* — that directly implicates the Zelnads in knocking that rock out of orbit, I need you to find it."

Geddy's mind raced. Commander Verveik, his hero, needed his help. The Elenian Belt was where they'd encountered the *Sirwin*. It wasn't near any of the usual shipping routes or natural wormholes.

But it wasn't completely lifeless, either.

"See what you can learn and contact me through the Committee subfrequency. You have your orders. Good luck."

THE CREW, plus Jel and Dr. Krezek, were arranged in their usual spots around the workbench. Maybe it was being in his old bed or maybe it was just having his friends back, but Geddy felt great. The *Armstrong* was an awesome ship, but it was designed for armed escorts or terrestrial assaults, not for long hauls across space. Its quarters were functional but cramped, geared more toward young soldiers who might only be aboard for a week at a time.

He didn't know what to do with Krezek just yet. He said he felt much safer with them than he would back on Afolos, or just about anywhere else after what happened to him. You couldn't blame the guy for being skittish. They had much more to worry about than an extra mouth to feed, and besides, he was willing, even eager, to listen to Doc talk. That alone made him useful.

"Please tell me you're kidding."

"I'm not," Geddy said.

"Who are we talking about again?" Jel asked.

"Tev Joclen," Geddy said. "He's an old–"

"Asshole," Oz interjected.

"Fair enough. But he told me a mutual acquaintance of ours, a Soturian hustler named Sammo Yann, runs weapons out of a place in the Elenian Belt. I'm betting much of it is Zelnad tech."

Jel's white hair rippled as she shook her head. "*In* the Belt? As in, on an asteroid?"

"It's a perfect hiding place. All that iron and nickel? No scanner would ever find you, and even if it could, navigating it is damn near impossible."

Denk nodded. "It's gnarly all right. You wouldn't catch me in it, I'll tell ya that."

Oz rolled her eyes and held up her hands in deference. "Okay, I'll humor you. Let's say we do find your old pal Sammo in the Belt. You really think he had a role in the Gundrun event? He's not that big an operator."

"Maybe not, but if there's even a chance, our mission is to chase it down."

"Mission?" Denk asked hopefully.

"Verveik's orders. Our first official mission for the New Alliance."

Oz spun around on her chair and stopped to face him. "New Alliance, you say?"

"Yeah ..." he had no idea where this was going.

She exchanged a smile with the others in the crew. "How does one sign up for this ... *New Alliance*? Is there a recruiting office nearby?"

— Is she getting at what I think she is?

— *I think so.*

Geddy smirked. "You want me to make you ... soldiers? Can I do that?"

Oz smugly crossed her arms. "You tell me, *Captain*."

Denk hurried over beside her, followed by Voprot and Doc. A couple seconds later, Krezek and Jel did the same. They lined up shoulder to shoulder in front of the workbench wearing expectant looks.

— This is just ceremonial, right?

—*I say just roll with it.*

Geddy's eyes passed over all of them. They looked dead serious. He squared up to Oz and drew himself taller.

"Osmiya Nargonis, by the power *not* vested in me, I officially name you First Officer of the *For Sale Make Offer*. Welcome to the New Alliance."

A sly smile crept across her plump lips. She snapped a salute. "Sir, yes sir."

He moved to Denk. "Congratulations, Lieutenant Junt, on being the New Alliance's first commissioned pilot."

Denk's pudgy cheeks flushed red, and he saluted with his splinted hand. "Aw, man. Thanks, Cap. I won't let ya down."

He moved on to Voprot, craning his neck to look the enormous Kigantean in the eye. "Voprot ... er, do you have a last name? Nope, dumb question. Corporal Voprot, welcome to the New Alliance."

"Is corporal good?"

"It's near the top of the bottom," Geddy said.

"Voprot earn Geddy's trust?"

"That's a ... way of looking at it, sure."

Overcome with gratitude, Voprot pulled him tight to his tree-trunk body, pressing Geddy's face against his scaly skin. "Hey, big guy? The unsolicited hugging of a superior officer is sort of frowned upon in the New Alliance."

"Oh. Sorry."

Voprot relinquished him, and Geddy moved on to Doc. "Dr. Krons Tardigan, the New Alliance would like to offer you a position as Senior Science Officer."

Doc bowed low. "A position I humbly accept, Captain."

Geddy pointed to Jel and Krezek. "Part-timers. How does 'civilian contractor' sound?"

"Lucrative." Jel gave a wink. "And maybe fun."

Krezek lowered his head. "I remain at your service."

A smile split Geddy's face. Yeah, this was just for show, but also kinda not. It felt real in the moment, and that was good enough for him.

"All righty then. As captain of this vessel, my orders are to jump to Pretensia and pay ol' Tev a visit."

"That's a long way." Denk frowned and shook his head. "Do we have enough novaspheres?"

Geddy put a reassuring hand on his shoulder. "The days of blue balls are over, Lieutenant. There's a better way."

CHAPTER TWENTY

CHEWING THE FAT

TRUTHFULLY, Geddy wasn't remotely sure if the strange jump device Verveik left him with could handle a ship the size of the *Fiz*. If it hadn't, they would've had to park the ship on some remote moon and handle things with the *Armstrong*, which would've forced some tough decisions in terms of who should go and who should stay. However, when he activated the little tablet, the so-called "bubble universe" it created was able to envelop the *Fiz*.

With him in the captain's chair and Denk in the pilot's seat, he entered the coordinates for Pretensia. *EXECUTE POINT TO POINT?* appeared onscreen.

"Everyone ready?" he asked.

"R ... ready for what, exactly?" Denk asked nervously.

"This."

He tapped YES, and the space before them instantly changed. Hanging there in the stringy flux field between the gas giants Yedol and Lodey was the manmade moon *Pretensia*.

Denk checked himself over as though expecting to have

been turned inside-out by whatever voodoo enabled this. Doc Tardigan got up and shuffled to the front display.

"How in the name of the old gods ..." he muttered.

"Zirhof delivered a prototype to Verveik, who gave it to us. He's retrofitting the entire New Alliance fleet with it as we speak," Geddy said.

Tardigan's head gave a disbelieving shake. "The technology on the quantum cubes from Old Earth?"

"Hard to say."

Geddy hadn't told a soul about the potential connection to his parents, mainly because he wasn't sure whether to believe it. The day would come when he'd have to know for sure. For now, all that mattered was that it helped level the playing field against the Nads.

"I don't understand," Krezek said.

"Doc can fill you in. Lieutenant, hail the station, please."

For a few moments, Denk did nothing.

"Lieutenant Junt?"

"Oh, right, that's me!"

He opened a hailing frequency to the station, and a young female android came on-screen.

"Welcome back to Pretensia, *For Sale Make Offer*. How may I assist you today, Captain Starheart?"

Of course, their transponder and identities were already registered with the station. Apparently, that alone made them a bit nicer.

"We're back to see my old pal, Tev Joclen. Just looking for clearance to dock."

"I'd be glad to inquire. Just a moment." Her eyes unfocused briefly as she interacted with the database. "Unfortunately, Mr. Joclen cannot receive guests at this time."

Geddy frowned. "What does that mean?"

"That he cannot receive guests."

Oz gave him an *I told you so* look. "Like I said, asshole."

"Our newly remodeled lobby area is open to all, with exciting new retail shops to suit every taste. Would you like visitor docking clearance?"

"Uh, one moment, please," Geddy said.

He paused their conversation, muting her and cutting the camera feed.

"I told you this was a bad idea," Oz said.

"You have a better one?" Geddy challenged.

Jel piped up from the back of the bridge. "Tell we need some time."

After all the time they'd spent together, Geddy knew Jel wouldn't say anything unless she was pretty confident in her plan. He un-paused the conversation.

"We'll get back to you."

"Very well, Captain."

She blinked out, and Geddy swiveled his chair to face Jel. "What're you thinking?"

She marched over to where Doc was sitting. "Let's see what's up with this guy. Move."

Doc dutifully got up, having seen her work her magic earlier. Jel cracked her knuckles and went to work, again flying through menus with dizzying speed.

Geddy stood over her shoulder. "What're you doing?"

"Hacking into Pretensia's resident database."

Doc cleared his throat. "Respectfully, Jeledine, Pretensia Station has some of the galaxy's most advanced networking systems. I don't think it will be possible to simply–"

"All right, I'm in," Jel said, earning a surprised look from Doc. "It's Joclen with a J?"

"Yeah," Geddy confirmed.

She went straight to his record and expanded it. A picture appeared of him wearing his smarmiest expression.

"That's him? Ugh."

Oz pointed at her. "See? She can tell just by looking at him. Girls know these things."

"Let's see ... delinquent account to the tune of ..." she gave a low whistle. "Holy shit."

Geddy leaned over her shoulder. Tev's total debt to the station was 318,770 credits. "That's like a week's worth of lunches. Does it give his location?"

"Looks like ... some sort of onboard debtors' prison? He's on a work detail that cleans the liposuction tanks. Liposuction tanks?"

Geddy doubled over laughing. Tev was essentially a broker, and an unscrupulous one at that. As far as he knew, the man had never put in an honest day's work, so picturing him squeegeeing rich-prick fat off the walls of a big tank was comedy gold.

"Short of paying off his debts, how do we get him out?" Oz asked.

"That's pretty much the only way. Oh, but it says he put his ship up for collateral. We could settle his account, take his ship in payment, and sell it later for a profit."

Geddy glanced back at Oz, who at least seemed amenable to the idea. "What kind of ship?"

Tev's ship was the *Allegro*, a custom-built Kailorian racer with red and blue accents. It was almost laughably overpowered, with *three* Degarret 16R engines and stubby wings that made it almost unflyable in atmosphere. It was a four-seater, technically, but could maybe sleep two if they really enjoyed each other's company. It barely had any storage either, the third engine having taken up most of that space. Knowing Tev, he would rather die than let it go.

"Exactly the kind you'd expect."

She pursed her lips doubtfully. "Say we spring him. What then?"

Tev wouldn't go along with just any plan, even if it meant saving himself from liposuction duty. He'd need added incentive. And he was the last person in the galaxy who should know about the New Alliance and the Zelnad conspiracy. But that didn't mean he couldn't be useful.

"Okay, here's what we're gonna do ..."

It took several calls to several different people in *Pretensia's* back office, but Geddy was finally able to wrangle a face-to-face with Tev. First, he had to transfer a nonrefundable payment of a hundred thousand credits just to move his status up from "delinquent" to "probationary," which allowed him visitors. That galled Oz to no end, but they had little choice, and it wasn't their money anyway. The bigger issue would be getting Tev to agree to their deal. If he did, he would have to sign a legally binding document saying that he would never return to the station.

After docking the *Fiz*, Geddy bade the crew to stay, which they had no problem with. Two android guards met him on the other side of the airlock and led him through a service corridor behind the lobby. An elevator at the end plunged downward for a solid minute before opening into a dimly lit hallway with lights along the floor. Upon reaching an open door at the end, the guards motioned him inside.

"Ten minutes," said one.

"Ten minutes?" Geddy asked. "The tanks need that much cleaning?"

"You have no idea."

The androids about-faced in unison and marched to the end of the hall, where they posted up to wait.

— *I am a bit concerned about this.*

— You a better way to get close to Sammo?

— *Unfortunately, no.*

— We'll keep the reins tight, don't worry.

Geddy opened the door and found Tev seated behind a humming red force field. As soon as he saw Geddy, he popped out of his chair and grinned broadly. "Ho-ly shit. It *is* you! They wouldn't say who got me out of hock, but I had a feeling it was my old pal, Geddy Starheart."

"No one's getting sprung," Geddy said flatly. "Sit down."

Tev's smile melted away. He hadn't shaven in several weeks and had lost a good deal of weight. Only the latter looked good on him.

"Shoveling fat agrees with you."

Tev's downcast eyes flared mischievously. "Hey, it's cheaper than Pilates. And good for my skin."

Geddy pulled out the chair over to just in front of the force field and settled into it with a long exhale. "Listen, they only gave me ten minutes, so I'll cut to the chase. I need your help."

"Hmph. Like you needed my help last time? When you left me with those goons from accounting?"

Geddy slapped his thighs and got back up. "Well, this was fun. Guards!"

Tev held up his hands in contrition. "Okay, sorry. You know me, I run my mouth sometimes. Sit." Geddy reluctantly returned to his chair, and Tev gathered himself. "What can I do for you?"

- *I can't believe that worked.*
- Tev's as easy to play as a tambourine.

"I need to find Sammo Yann's hideout in the Elenian Belt."

"Didn't you find him last time?"

"More like he found me. This is about something else," replied Geddy. "Can you help me find him or not?"

He gave a noncommittal shrug. "Sure. Turn left at the big rock. You can't miss it."

— *Oz is right. He really is an asshole.*

— I'm painfully aware.

Geddy rolled his eyes and stood. "Forget it. Enjoy living large."

"All right, jeez." Tev stopped him, and Geddy pivoted back. "You used to have a better sense of humor."

"And you used to know an opportunity when you saw it." He paused and sat back.

"Yeah, I could probably find it again. What's the catch?"

"In exchange for settling your accounts, you give me the *Allegro* and come with us. Once we find Sammo, I'll drop you off at the nearest spaceport and we'll never see each other again."

His lips upturned into a creepy grin. "Does this 'we'

include that Temerurian smokeshow? That'd sure sweeten the pot."

Geddy gritted his teeth. "I'd be *very* careful, Tev."

Tev gave a soft whistle. "Ah, she's your girl now. Hats off, mate. Who ever imagined I'd be jealous of *you*?"

Anger flared in his gut, but he swallowed it down. "Are you in or not?"

"What're you planning to do with *Allie*?" he asked, referring to his ship.

"I'll sell it to some other entitled prick and pocket the difference."

Tev's lips downturned. "Pfft. Not a chance."

Geddy smirked. "What do they pay you here? Five hundred a week in the fat vat? At that rate, it should only take you ..."

— Help me out here.

— *About eight years, not counting expenses.*

"... eight years before you breathe fat-free air. And that's not even counting your lunchtime mogorodon polyps."

Tev's nostrils flared, his eyes steely. He knew he had no leverage. Geddy knew how miserable he had to be.

"I don't suppose there's a scenario where I keep my ship?"

Geddy shook his head. "Nope. But if you say yes now, I transfer the funds, load the *Allegro* into the dropship bay, and you're outta here in an hour or two." When Tev didn't react for several seconds, he continued. "This is the best offer you're gonna get."

Tev's brow furrowed as he considered the offer. "And all I gotta do is point you to Sammo's hideout?"

"For starters. And you don't ask questions."

Tev tapped his fingernails on the counter for a moment, swishing his lips back and forth as though it was a difficult choice.

"You drive a hard bargain, Starheart."

"Good." Geddy got up and turned for the door. Without looking back, he added, "Shave that ridiculous beard and get cleaned up. I'll see you shortly."

"One last ride, old friend," Tev said to his back.

"Sure, Tev. One last ride."

CHAPTER TWENTY-ONE

AN EFFECTIVE DEMONSTRATION

THE CREW'S buoyant optimism after Durandia ebbed noticeably with Tev on board. His characteristic bluster rubbed pretty much everyone the wrong way — none more than Oz, who couldn't stand to even be in the same room with him. The last thing Geddy needed was for Tev to know about the bubble tech, so he had Jel handle the jump to Elenia while he entertained Tev in the hold. He didn't even realize anything happened.

The *Allegro* was a bit longer than Geddy remembered, so much that it barely fit in the dropship bay left vacant by the *Dom*. His memory of it didn't quite align with how it struck him now, which was more of a midlife-crisis announcement than a practical ship. If you had to burn ass in a straight line, she was impressive, but maneuverability was poor, and its armaments were pathetic. In that sense, it was perfect for a guy like Tev, who vastly preferred running to fighting.

How they had ever been friends mystified Geddy. At one point, perhaps, his phony bravado and balding frat-boy aspect had a certain insouciant charm, but now, it was just grating.

"I tell ya, that place is such a racket. You have no idea." Tev's feet up were propped on the workbench as he pontificated about Pretensia.

"Oh, I think I kinda do."

"Didn't you fantasize about running out the clock there once?"

Geddy had, in truth, set his sights on an early retirement to Pretensia. But his notion of it was largely based on slick advertisements. The reality was just sad.

"I did. Then I saw it."

As they talked, Tev's eyes kept drifting to the *Armstrong*. But there was nothing to gain from telling him the truth.

"You're sure that's not tukrium?" Tev said.

"Positive."

"It looks military. Gundrun, maybe? How'd you come by it?"

"None of your business. Now listen, about Sammo ..."

He swatted the idea away with his hand. "Ah, we've got lots of time to worry about that. Gimme the dime tour."

"Sammo, Tev. Where is he?"

"What's the urgency? We must be two or three days from a jump vector."

— *He's stalling.*

— I know, but why?

"Tev, we made a bargain, and you're gonna honor it. Right now." He got up and started toward the bridge, motioning for Tev to follow. "The coordinates should be in the *Allegro's* memory, so let's just—"

Tev threw up his hands and rolled his eyes. "Listen, I don't have the *exact* location, okay, but I know how to get it. Why you got such a hard-on for this guy?"

Rage boiled up in Geddy's stomach, and his right hand curled into a fist. Through clenched teeth, he turned back and hissed, "You'd better be shitting me right now."

Only then did Tev slide off his stool. He gave an exasperated sigh and shrugged like it was no big deal. "What was I supposed to say? You gave me an out, and I took it. Anyone in my position would've done the same."

"You mean any *asshole*."

Tev approached, making a calming motion with his hands. "Hey, hey, it's not a problem. All's I need to do is contact him and arrange a meet. That's how we always did it."

Oz came striding through the airlock door. "We're ready. You got the coordinates?"

"No. In fact, Tev here was just telling me he doesn't actually know where Sammo's place is."

"What?!" Oz hissed, shooting daggers at him. "I knew this would happen! Didn't I tell you?"

"Relax, fancy pants. Everything's a negotiation."

Oz huffed and took an angry step toward Tev, but Geddy stopped her. "Hold up." He turned back to Tev. "Say what you want to say. If Oz doesn't like it, I'll let her have her way with you. And not in the way you're hoping."

Tev rolled his eyes. "Like I said, I just gotta reach out. There are backchannels, satellites, all that crap. It's gonna take some time."

"How much time?" Oz asked.

"I dunno. A day, maybe two. But look, I've been out of the game for a while now. He's gonna have questions. You gotta give me somethin' here."

"I'll give you something," muttered Oz, balling her hands into fists.

Geddy said to Tev, "Give us a sec," and pulled Oz back toward the *Armstrong* and out of earshot. "Oz, I'm as pissed as you are, believe me, but we need him."

"He's playing us. There's gotta be another way."

"Yeah, well, I'm all ears."

Oz fumed and sputtered but had no suggestions. They needed Tev, and that gave him leverage. He'd squeeze as much juice out of this situation as he possibly could.

Geddy continued. "Let's have him set up a meet. If he tries anything, I'll float him myself."

She bit her lip so hard, she winced, then raised her big yellow eyes to him. "I'm gonna hold you to that."

TEV'S BELLY barely fit between the controls and the pilot's seat of the *Allegro*, despite his weight loss. Of course, it had been custom-made for a younger and more svelte version of him. He powered up her systems as he talked. And boy, did he still like to talk.

"Remember when we were playing uguinok in a bar on Stemir and that cocky Zorran kid wanted to race me?"

Geddy gave a halfhearted smile. "How could I forget?"

"*Allie* left him in the dust, and we partied like friggin' rock stars. Man, those were good times. The girls there ... mmm, boy. What's the nerdy one's name, again?"

"Jeledine."

"I dunno how you do it, man. Two pieces of prime trim

parading around all the time? You oughta save your hard-on for them, not Sammo fucking Yann."

It was everything Geddy could do not to punch him in the throat. "Just make the damn call, Tev."

"I will. 'Soon as you tell me what the hell this is about."

Fortunately, he and Eli had worked out a plausible narrative to sell Tev that also would pique Sammo's interest. The crew was all in on the ruse.

"All right, but I have to warn you, it's juicy. Not to mention dangerous."

Tev's eyes sparkled. Geddy had used the magic word. "Dangerous, eh? You have my full attention."

"I assume you heard all about IASS."

He chuckled. "Heard about it? Hell, I might've even gone if I wasn't in lock-up. It sounded wild. What about it?"

"You know that new Hovensby drive they announced?"

"Oh yeah, that instant jump thing. Bubble-something or another."

"Bubble universe, that's right. Well, Dr. Tardigan reverse-engineered it. I've got a working prototype and full engineering schematics."

Tev's greedy eyes popped wide. "Bullshit."

Geddy held up the jump device. Jel had spent half the night replicating its interface on her own tablet.

"Here, I'll show you." He pulled up the ship's launch systems screen and remotely opened the door beneath the *Allegro*.

"You're serious."

"Buckle up. Let's take a ride."

Tev still looked doubtful, but he secured his restraint and released the dropouts. A puff of air from overhead pushed them out of the *Fizmo's* belly, and Tev activated the front display. Of course, they were already near the outer rim of the Elenian Belt, formed hundreds of years earlier when Elenia was shattered by some inner cataclysm. A bit less than half of it now remained, every bit as lifeless as the dense ring of rocks that orbited it. It used to be as green and perfect as Old Earth and Temeruria.

Tev frowned at the screen, his mouth hanging open. Geddy knew exactly what was running through his mind. *How did we just travel almost one point three parsecs without any of the normal jump effects? How did we even find a vector that fast?*

"Elenia? What the ...? How'd we get here?"

"How do you think?" Geddy assured him. "With this. Where do you want to go?"

Tev stared at him as though expecting to be let off the hook, but Geddy just stared right back. "You're serious."

"Name the place."

"All right, I'll play along. Nurithea. Other side of the galaxy. Two and a half parsecs, at least."

Geddy smiled and activated the bubble, which quickly formed around the *Allegro*. He pulled up the coordinates to Nurithea's nearest outer marker. *EXECUTE POINT TO POINT?* came up.

"You ready?"

"Sure," he said doubtfully.

Geddy tapped *YES*. In a blink, they were staring straight at Nurithea, a blue-green planet draped in swirling, piss-yellow clouds. Tev squinted at it as though it couldn't possibly be real.

"Here we are," Geddy said.

Tev's mouth went slack. "You gotta be kidding me."

He held up the tablet again. "It's portable, low-power, and works with practically any ship."

Incredulous, Tev turned to him. "Alright. If it's so easy, take us back."

Geddy swiped through the menu and tapped *YES* again when the screen said *RETURN TO PREVIOUS COORDI-NATES?* A blink later, they'd returned nearly to the same place, just a few hundred meters under the *Fiz*.

"See? Right where we left it."

Tev gave his head an incredulous shake. "Dude. You have *any idea* what this is worth?"

"I do," Geddy replied. "And so will Sammo. Now about that meeting ..."

CHAPTER TWENTY-TWO

THE MEET

WHEN TEV SAID he used back channels to contact Sammo, he wasn't kidding. He had to send a message via universal distress code to a dummy transponder, which was probably just a small relay satellite in geosync over a distant moon. The code would then be passed to a remote terminal on another world, which Sammo could access from just about anywhere.

Until they heard back, all they could do was wait. Denk busied himself building combat sims in the *Armstrong*. Doc and Krezek were trying to narrow down the Gundrun asteroid's likely origin in the Belt. Voprot mostly slept. Oz kept to her quarters so she didn't snap Tev's neck, which left Geddy, Tev, and Jeledine to pass the time in the galley.

It was all part of their plan to ensnare Sammo.

"Dude, this is huge," Tev mused. "Just cut me in. I still know people. We could start a bidding war and drive the price through the roof. We'd both walk away filthy rich."

Geddy gave Jel a conspiratorial look, then got up and closed the galley door. He returned to the table and whispered, "Look, I couldn't say it around Oz, but that's exactly what Jel and I had in mind."

A self-satisfied grin split Tev's face. "Now *there's* the Starheart I know! What're you thinking?"

"If Sammo even suspects I'm involved, the whole thing blows up. I need you to broker the deal. Do that, and you keep five percent."

"Ten," Tev quickly countered.

"Five."

Geddy held Tev's gaze, not giving an inch. Sweat beaded on Tev's reddening face. He was already on his third glass of Kailorian gin. "Alright. It's worth nine figures easy. Five still sets me up for life. How do you see this going down?"

Jel picked it up from there. "Assuming he agrees to the meet, you'll take the *Allegro* into the Belt. The account information you have will look legit, like it's just you, but it'll really be the ship's account."

"Once the transfer clears, hand over the tablet and hightail it back here," Geddy finished. "Only then do you get your cut."

His eyes darted nervously between them. "Isn't this Zelnad tech?"

"Supposedly," Geddy said. "Why?"

"Because I don't exactly want this coming back to me."

"It won't," Jel said with finality. "This bad boy is encrypted up the wazoo."

Tev nodded, staring at the tablet for several seconds as though convincing himself it would be worth it. But Geddy knew he missed the game. Longed for it, even. He couldn't possibly resist.

"All right. I'm in."

IN THE END, it only took Sammo three hours to agree to the meet. The coordinates were sent through the same untraceable relay as Tev's initial message, and the meeting was set for the next day. Geddy and Jel kept Tev distracted while the rest of the plan was set in motion.

Morpho and Hughey would stow away on the *Allegro*. While Tev met with Sammo, Hughey would infiltrate his hideout's systems in hopes of proving he had a role in the Gundrun event. Morpho would ensure everything went smoothly. The two of them purposely stayed out of sight while Tev was aboard.

Oz had been worried that Tev would simply rocket away in the *Allegro* and welch on their deal, but Geddy told her not to worry. He'd never walk away from such a big score.

Morpho and Hughey snuck aboard the *Allegro* while Jel walked Tev one more time through the jump interface she'd recreated on her own, nearly identical tablet. It wouldn't work, of course, but the point wasn't to actually sell Sammo anything. They were only buying time for Hughey to do his thing. By the time Sammo asked Tev for a demonstration, they'd be long gone and Tev would be left to talk his way out.

"Remember, if he wants a demonstration, you've gotta be well clear of the Belt or you might jump back into an asteroid," Jel reminded him.

He zipped it into the familiar black satchel he used to carry around and gave it a pat. "Yeah, yeah, I got it. That it, then?"

"Just keep your story straight," Geddy said. "We don't need him getting suspicious."

"Don't worry. Ol' Tev knows the score." He extended his hand. "Good to be back in the game with you, brother. I look forward to our celebratory toast."

It was hard not to feel a pang of guilt as they shook hands. They had been pretty good friends once, but that was a long time ago. Before Geddy could see who he really was.

Tev was practically floating as he opened the hatch down to the dropship bay. Poor bastard.

"Start at five hundred and don't go below four twenty-five," Geddy admonished. "You've got the account info?"

He gave an irritated look. "Come on, man. Have a little faith."

With that, he climbed down the ladder and gave a little wave. Geddy closed the hatch and locked it in place. Heaving a sigh, he rubbed his face as Oz came up beside him.

"You okay?" she asked.

"Yeah."

"He'll be fine. Guys like him always land on their feet."

"I know." He used to be viewed as one of those guys.

She gave his back a tender rub. "C'mon, Jel's already got the feeds pulled up. All we can do now is enjoy the show."

The front screen in the bridge split to show the two feeds, one from Hughey and the other from Jel's phony jump device. From under their feet came the chunky sound of the dropouts releasing. A couple seconds later, the *Allegro* zipped away toward its destination on the far side of the Belt. All Hughey's feed showed was a view of the floor and the heel of Tev's right foot.

Tardigan and Krezek stood at the back, watching with great interest. Geddy looked at Doc. "Any luck with the calculations?"

"I would say moderate luck, Captain," Doc replied. "The analysis was exceedingly complex, however we have narrowed down the asteroid's origins to a twenty-degree swath of the Belt."

"And Sammo's location?"

Doc's eyes darkened. "... is almost sixty degrees away from that."

It didn't mean Sammo didn't know something, but Geddy's shoulders sagged nonetheless.

Tev hummed to himself as he flew, clearly in a buoyant mood. Geddy figured it would take him half an hour to reach Sammo's location, but he arrived in just eighteen minutes. The *Allie* really was a speedster.

Jel was in Doc's usual spot at the navigator's station. Both screens were still black. She adjusted her earpiece. "Hughey, can you give us a visual yet?"

Hughey broke apart, turning the screen briefly black, then reformed behind and above Tev's seat. He was slowly descending toward the inner part of the belt, careful to avoid the seemingly infinite number of drifting rocks. Some were the size of basketballs while others were even bigger than the one that threatened Gundrun.

How Tev could maneuver that ship so delicately amazed Geddy. He still had a deft touch.

Out of nowhere, a transport-sized rock that drifted just in front of him.

"Whoa, Nelly," Tev muttered, just avoiding a collision.

Once it passed by, Sammo's hideout came into view.

From the outside, it appeared as a curiously symmetrical oval carved out of the pockmarked rock. It wouldn't have stood out at all except its orientation was fixed. Engines set into the rock fired every few seconds to keep it that way, and when another rock came flying toward it, a faint green shield flashed as it was deflected.

Tev slowed and lined up his entry into the small hangar. On his approach, hidden doors slid open and lights activated inside. He gave little taps on the stick to keep her lined up, slowly passing between the doors as he lowered the skids and touched down.

"All right, Hughey, lie low until he's gone," Jel said.

Hughey's virtual lens broke apart, and the screens went black again. They heard the hangar doors close behind them, followed by a hiss of air as it re-pressurized. There was a brief commotion as Tev exited the ship. A moment later, the microphone on Jel's tablet picked up the conversation.

"Long time, old friend." Sammo's voice came through loud and clear.

"Too long," agreed Tev. "You look like shit."

"So do you." They shared a laugh, then Sammo's voice dropped low. "You have it with you?"

"Right here." Everyone in the *Fiz* jumped as thunderclaps roared through the speakers.

"Sorry," Jel said while everyone rubbed their ears. "I think he patted his satchel."

"Is that the *Allegro*?" Sammo asked.

"The one and only. She still gets up and goes, too."

"You're certain you weren't followed?"

"No one can keep up with *Allie*."

"You won't mind if I give you a quick scan for trackers, then."

"Be my guest," said Tev.

The mic went quiet save for the swish of cloth as Tev shifted his position. Geddy's eyes shot to Jel.

"No worries." The look in her eye contradicted her words, but Geddy didn't push it.

A few seconds passed, and the scanner beeped. "All clear. Let's see it."

As Tev lifted the tablet out of the bag, the camera activated, and Sammo's face filled the screen. Geddy hadn't seen him since the Double A. At the time, he was clean-shaven with perfectly coiffed hair and a bespoke suit. Now, he sported a man-bun and a scraggly beard. His track suit completed the aging hippie look.

Geddy's fingernails dug into his palms. Sammo was a callous opportunist who stole his ship and was clearly in bed with the Zelnads. He couldn't want to nail the bastard to the wall.

Sammo pointed his scanner at the tablet. On camera, it had the effect of looking down a barrel. Geddy held his breath.

Satisfied, he turned the scanner off, and Geddy's entire body relaxed. Tev returned the tablet to the bag, taking their view away again.

"Sorry about all that," Sammo said. "Let's talk inside. Welcome to the outpost."

CHAPTER TWENTY-THREE

TEV'S PITCH

THE ENTIRE CREW gathered on the *Fiz's* bridge to eavesdrop on Tev and Sammo. Jeledine gave Hughey the all-clear to leave the *Allegro* and dig into the hideout's systems. Morpho would remain inside in case an intervention was required.

"I must admit, Tev, as surprised as I was to hear from you, I was more surprised by the reason. Suffice it to say, I'm skeptical."

"Can't say I blame you. Holy Hannah, this place looks different. Did you remodel?"

"Something like that. How's Pretensia?"

"Let's just say it was fun while it lasted."

While the two of them caught up, Hughey slipped through the open airlock. An entryway with tastefully lit stairs led up, framed by exotic-looking plants, white and green leaves twisting about each other as they tapered to a point.

This wasn't just some glorified storage unit for contraband. Sammo clearly spent a fair bit of time here. And it hadn't come cheaply.

Hughey turned to the left and caught the men's shadows as they disappeared around the corner. "All right, let's find an interface," Jel said into her headset. "Go right." The bot turned and progressed silently down the hallway to the right.

"Can I get you a drink?" The tablet was still in Tev's bag, so his feed remained black, but the microphone came through loud and clear.

"Thought you'd never ask," Tev replied. "Whatever you're having."

"Eicrean whisky it is," said Sammo. A few seconds later, they heard him pour two glasses. "So, how'd you come by this windfall?"

"A buddy of mine's an engineer for Hovensby. He'd just finished work on the bubble drive when the Zelnad deal was announced. They claimed it was their IP and fired him. That's when he came to me."

"He'll want a cut, obviously."

"Let me worry about him. It's just you and me here," Tev assured him.

Hughey passed the open door of one bedroom and proceeded to the next, which was closed. He slipped beneath it and reformed again, revealing a mini warehouse full of neatly stacked crates.

"Must be an extra cargo hold," Geddy said. "Can he access the systems from there?"

"That's what we're about to find out," Jel said. "Hughey look for an access panel around there somewhere, probably by the door."

Hughey stretched himself up and found a small screen beside the door. He broke apart to slip between the screen and the wall, but the feed remained active.

"Thank you, sir," Tev said, having received his drink. "To new opportunities."

"I'll drink to that," said Sammo, clinking his glass. "Now, let's have a closer look at this thing."

Tev again slipped the tablet free of his satchel, and Sammo's face appeared again. "I was expecting something bigger."

"I thought the same thing. But apparently, it works with any ship."

"Show me."

While Tev showed Sammo the real-looking interface, Hughey's screen morphed into dense lines of code.

Jel clapped her hands. "Yes! We're in."

"He's paranoid. He must have cameras all over the place," Geddy said. "We need recordings, logs, anything like that. Starting maybe a week before Gundrun and going back."

Jel nodded, typing feverishly into the terminal. "I'll look for log files first."

On the other screen, Sammo said, "It can't be that simple."

"I know," agreed Tev with a laugh. "But I've seen it work myself. Blink and you miss it."

"You said you have engineering schematics, too?"

"Yep."

"What schematics are those?" Geddy asked Jel, smirking.

"It's the wiring diagram for your tractor beam." She gave a wink. "Unless he's an engineer, he won't know the difference."

"Eh, it's all Basoan to me," Sammo joked. "I'll need a demonstration, of course."

"Obviously."

"Okay ..." Jel said, scrolling through the code. "We've got a flurry of sensor activity in the weeks leading up to Gundrun. I'll cross-reference the time stamps."

"Footage," Geddy emphasized. "We need footage."

"Maybe you'd prefer to swap places?" she asked drolly.

— *I do not think that would be a good idea.*

— She was being sarcastic.

— *It still would not be a good idea.*

Sammo set the tablet down so the camera pointed straight up at the ceiling. As soon as he turned his back, Tev stared into the screen as if trying to make sure they saw him.

"The asshole's going to give us away," Oz said what Geddy was thinking.

Sammo continued. "If this is the real deal, it's a gold mine. But of course, you already knew that. You got a number in mind?"

"It's worth at least a billion to someone."

Sammo let out a long whistle. "That's a big number."

"So's the market for something like this. It could mean the end of novaspheres, and not just for people who can afford a Hovensby," Tev said.

"Certain parties won't be too thrilled about that," Sammo noted.

"All the more reason to move fast. Imagine if this made it to the Double A. I guarantee Tretiak would set the opening bid at seven fifty, maybe even higher."

On Hughey's side of the screen, images of the Belt flashed by as video footage was matched with timestamps in the sensor logs.

"Okay," Jel said, cracking her knuckles. "We've got quite

a few potential clips here. Let's see ..." As she scrubbed through the footage, a clear pattern emerged. There were no ships or EVA activities whatsoever in any direction, however, someone in a spacesuit, presumably Sammo, passed in front of the camera on a regular cadence in the two weeks before Gundrun. Going, then returning every day at approximately the same time.

There wasn't a good angle on his face. The first several times, he passed just a few centimeters from the same wide-angle camera, then disappeared behind a jagged rock formation on the asteroid's surface. But then he'd reappear on another camera with a higher angle. In that image, he was always pulling an old starship engine and other gear on a huge gravity sled, full going out and empty coming in. Sometimes, it was only a couple hours between, and others, eight or ten. Whatever he was working on, he was diligent about it.

"What the hell's he doing?" Jel asked.

"Those are Belray C-92 engines," Geddy said. "He must have been attaching them to the rock."

"But we can't see him doing it," Oz noted.

Doc gasped and pointed at the screen as Jel was still on the high angle. "Wait! Freeze that!" He scooted up behind her and leaned close to get a better look.

"What do you see?" Geddy asked.

"Look at the view of Elenia. From this angle, you almost can't tell it was blown apart. See?"

Geddy noticed it immediately. He'd never seen it from that angle before. "Jel, can you overlay the view based on our projections? Right in the middle of Doc's twenty-degree arc."

"Hang on ..."

A few seconds later, Jel pulled it up and threw it on the front screen. It wasn't identical, but it lined up.

"It's pretty close," Oz said. "So what?"

"Sammo's *current* location is sixty degrees away from where this footage was taken," Doc said.

"Holy shit!" A thrilling realization washed over Geddy. "This footage isn't from his current hideout. It's from the old one!"

Abject shock fell over the bridge as they realized the implications. It wasn't proof, but it was strong evidence that Sammo sent his old hideout on a collision course for Gundrun.

But that theory quickly fell apart when you considered the number of engines needed to move that big a rock out of orbit and send it across the galaxy. Not to mention how long it would take. And it didn't explain how Gundrun's early warning satellites could've missed it until it was right on top of them.

"Yeah, but how?" Jel asked.

— *He jumped it.*

— He what?

— *He used the bubble tech to deliver it right to their doorstep.*

— Holy shit, you're right.

"He jumped it there," Geddy blurted, hopping out of his seat. "Most of the way, at least. Somewhere close enough that they wouldn't have time to react. Then he just needed to line it up with Gundrun, light the engines, and fly away."

"Seriously?" Jel asked.

Doc jumped in with the answer. "Geddy's right. Once he was close, he only needed a few engines to push it in the right direction. Their thrust and Gundrun's gravity would take care of the rest."

"Voprot have question," said the lizard from the back of the bridge.

They'd hit the jackpot. Sammo was responsible for the Gundrun event. Then he used the money they'd paid him to upgrade his secret pad. Apparently, he hadn't thought to delete the old footage.

"Even if you're right, it's not a smoking gun," Oz pointed out. "The footage supports our theory, but it doesn't prove anything."

"I agree with Oz," Doc said. "We need solid evidence."

"Voprot have question!" bellowed the lizard, stopping everyone cold.

"What is it, V?!" Geddy asked, irritated.

"If Sammo jump asteroid to Gundrun, why he want jump thing Tev have?"

Geddy's stomach dropped to his knees. Sammo didn't want what Tev was selling. He wanted to know where it came from.

CHAPTER TWENTY-FOUR

FOR THOSE ABOUT TO ROCK

AFTER DOWNLOADING THE FOOTAGE, Jel ordered Hughey to disable Sammo's comms and return to the *Allegro* immediately. Meanwhile, Tev and Sammo's conversation continued down its new and inevitable path.

— What do I do?!

— *Keep Sammo from escaping.*

As usual, Eli got there first. They had all the evidence they were going to get, but it wasn't enough. They needed Sammo to confess. And to do that, they needed him alive.

"Hughey, Morph, don't let Sammo leave!"

"What about Tev?" Oz asked.

Two synthetics. Two ships. Two guys. Even Geddy could do the math. Morph and Hughey could only deal with one.

"We get one shot at this," Geddy asserted. "Sammo's our priority."

Behind Oz's expressive eyes, a tussle played out between the side that despised Tev and the side that knew how much trouble he was in. Anyone with a conscience would've felt the same. But the same cold calculus applied. If they didn't have Sammo, they didn't have squat. Their first official mission for the New Alliance couldn't end in failure.

— I know this is the right call, but it doesn't feel that way.

— *It rarely does.*

"Well, old buddy ..." A tone of mock regret dripped from Sammo's voice, "... before we get too far ahead of ourselves, you're going to tell me how you *really* came by this technology."

Tev hesitated, then gave a nervous laugh. "I just told you I've got a guy–"

"At Hovensby, yes, I know. But we both know that's not true."

Geddy's mind raced. His carefully laid plan was falling apart because he'd underestimated Sammo. Tev's fate was out of their hands.

On the screen, Hughey had returned to the hangar and was heading for Sammo's ship to disable it. Morpho was still in the *Allegro.*

"Whaddya mean?" Tev was a smooth talker and was used to tight situations. Hearing the anxiety in his voice set Geddy even more on edge.

"After I heard from you, I did a little digging. The chief financial officer of Pretensia's an old friend of mine. He told me you were massively in debt to the station until you suddenly ... weren't. Who rescued you from such an unhappy retirement? I'm going to guess it's the same person who gave you this phony tablet."

Geddy locked eyes with Jel, his chest tightening. Hughey's feed had gone dark again. "What's happening?"

"He's disabling the fuel coupling."

"Forget that. We need to find his bubble drive," Geddy said. "We know he's got one. It's gotta be in his ship."

"You heard the man, H," Jel said. "Don't let him leave. Disable both ships!"

"Rescued me?" Tev stammered with fake indignation. "No, no, man, I just cashed in all my chips because I knew you and I would be getting very rich off this deal. Blew my whole nest egg to buy my freedom."

Hughey slipped in through the skid wells and angled for the console, then the image broke apart again as he searched for a bubble drive.

"You wanna know what I think?" Sammo's voice was cool and smooth. "I think you got bailed out. Shortly before you arrived, I got a look at Pretensia's visitor logs. Imagine my surprise when I saw the name Geddy Starheart."

Tev's voice shook as he replied. "Look, Sammo, I don't know where it came from. Geddy paid my bill in exchange for my help. But it's real! He jumped *Allie* to freakin' *Nurithea* and back to prove it, then had me come broker this deal with you. All's I care about is the money, man, I swear."

"For fuck's sake, Tev! He didn't even pressure you!" Geddy shouted at the screen, grabbing fistfuls of hair.

"Hughey found the drive," Jel said excitedly. "He's disabling it now."

"I've got one more question for you, Tev. Tell me the truth and you live. Where's Starheart now?"

A pregnant pause hung in the air, giving Geddy a sliver of hope that Tev would do the right thing.

"He's in that shitty trawler of his on the other side of Elenia."

- Damnit! I'm gonna wring his neck!
- *Yeah, this is bad.*

"Listening to us, no doubt." Sammo picked up the tablet and looked directly at it, giving his smarmiest smile and a little wave. "Hello, Starheart. I have to give it to you. This was a bold play. But to what end? You can't still be sore about your little ship, can you?"

— *He doesn't know what we really came for.*

— No, but that won't matter if he tells the Zelnads we have the bubble drive.

"You fucking set me up, Starheart!" Tev shouted, jabbing his finger at the camera. "I don't know what you're playing at, but I swear, I'm gonna make–"

Tev looked up and gasped. A flash of light lit up the screen and a blaster fired, so loud in the *Fiz'* bridge that they all gave a start. A sickening thud came through the speakers, echoing through the silent bridge.

THE CREW's stunned silence hung in the air. They'd used Tev, and he'd just been murdered.

Sammo set the tablet back on top of the table, giving them another view of the ceiling tiles. They heard the shuffling of clothes, and then Sammo grunted, presumably moving Tev's body.

"Sorry, Tevvy Baby. Guess it's off to the big swinger orgy in the sky." He grunted again. "As for you, Starheart, I hope you enjoyed the show."

Next, they heard drawers opening and closing. A few seconds later, Sammo's footsteps hurried out of the room.

"Hughey, Morph, he's coming!" Jel barked.

Hughey had already extracted himself from the guts of Sammo's ship into the cockpit. He retreated to the shadows behind the seat and peeked out the side. Through the cockpit, an image reformed of the small hangar.

It was empty, but Sammo would come charging through any moment. Only ... he didn't.

"Something's wrong," Geddy muttered.

"Cap, the scopes just picked up a ship from the far side of the asteroid at high speed."

"On screen!"

Denk swapped the view to the scopes. Whatever it was, it was hauling *ass*. At the same time, Sammo's asteroid began accelerating toward Elenia's remains, where it would soon be smashed to pebbles.

"He's got another damn ship!" Geddy said, anger flooding his body.

"And it appears he means to destroy his outpost," Doc said. "There must be engines on it, too."

Geddy strode out of the bridge toward the airlock. Oz jumped up and followed after him. "Jel, send Sammo's location to the *Armstrong*. And get Morpho and Hughey out of there."

"What're you doing?" Oz asked.

"I'm going after Sammo," Geddy said, quickening his pace.

"Are you sure that's a good idea?" she called after him.

"This can't be for nothing. We lose him, we're back to square one."

Geddy closed the airlock behind him and motored across the hold to the *Armstrong*. Once the ramp closed, he depressurized the hold, activating the doors just as Oz reached the airlock. She pressed her hand to the window, a tortured look on her face. She tapped the comm panel beside the door and her voice came through the *Armstrong's* comm.

"Can you catch him before he clears the Belt?" she asked.

He pulled back on the stick and this sleek ship lifted free of the deck. "I dunno, but we need to assume that ship's got the bubble drive, too."

"On it. And Geddy?"

"Yeah?" He took one last long look at her, hoping he'd get to wind his fingers through her long red locks again.

"Come back to me."

He smiled and gave a nod of his head as he backed the *Armstrong* out. As soon as he got clear of the *Fiz*, he punched it, the thrusters pinning him so hard to the seat that he struggled to breathe.

"Cap, his hideout just broke apart," came Denk's voice.

Geddy gritted his teeth. "Morpho and Hughey?"

"I don't know."

"Well, be ready to jump in front of him."

"You got it, Cap."

Geddy urged the *Armstrong* toward the far side of the Belt, passing as close to the shattered planet as he dared. The ring of rocks was dense and ten thousand kilometers thick. He just had to beat Sammo to his exit point.

He glanced to his right. When Elenia blew apart, its molten core hardened into city-sized crystals that reflected the stars, making it seem like it was made of them.

— *I wonder what really happened to it.*

"A good question for another time, pal."

At a full burn, it only took thirty seconds to get to the other side of the planet. He lined himself up with Sammo's current vector. The scanners had picked up his drive signature and was tracking his progress up through the disc of the Belt.

"Ged, he'll be clear of the Belt soon," came Oz's voice.

"I'm almost there."

Geddy targeted a skyscraper-sized asteroid at the upper edge of the Belt and launched two missiles at it. It exploded violently, turning a wide swath of rock into a curtain of debris. Sammo hit the brakes, coming to a complete stop as Geddy hailed him.

"Not so fast, dickhead."

Sammo's face came on screen wearing a cocky grin. "Starheart! I was starting to wonder where you were."

"You're outgunned, Sammo. I just want to talk."

"We just did."

As expected, he dove back into the Belt, so dense with metal-laden rock that even the *Armstrong's* exquisite scanners kept losing him. Geddy's fingers flew over the controls at nearly Jel-like speed.

"Denk, Jel ... I'm sending you coordinates. Get ready to jump on my mark."

"You're not goin' in there, are ya, Cap?"

"Just be ready to jump."

He whispered a wish to the universe before diving into the Belt just behind Sammo.

The space between rocks was tight, and the *Armstrong* was several times the size of Sammo's escape craft. Through his fingertips, he could feel the object avoidance system overriding his manual controls to avoid rocks he couldn't even see. Still, Sammo was opening more distance between them.

Countermeasures popped out of the back of Sammo's ship and exploded on the rocks, showering the *Armstrong* with debris, but they were no match for its tukrium armor. Geddy barreled right through, the spray of rock pinging harmlessly off the side.

"I've gotta say, I'm a little pissed you made me scuttle my new pad, Starheart. I just got it how I wanted it."

"You're welcome."

"Sorry about your old pal, Tev. He just wasn't much of a negotiator."

As boorish and annoying as Tev was, he deserved better than he got. Geddy put him in that situation, and now he was dead. Sammo had to pay, but killing him wasn't an option. Up ahead, Geddy saw him pitch upward and accelerate toward open space.

"Goodbye, Geddy."

Geddy toggled the channel back to the *Fiz*. "Denk, Jel ... jump now!"

But it was too late. Sammo was going to break free of the Belt and disappear.

Sammo broke into open space just as the *Fizmo* appeared right in front of him. The idea was to trap him between the two ships, but Geddy was still too far back and couldn't risk deploying the phantoms. Sammo immediately fired his retros and pivoted right, his momentum carrying him sideways into the *Fiz's* front shield. He bounced off, then his thrusters glowed bright blue and he rocketed away.

"No!" Geddy screamed, pounding his open palm on the console.

From his right peripheral vision came a flash of motion. He jerked his head toward it in time to see a slender gray projectile slice through the void and smash into Sammo's tail section, sending both into uncontrolled spins. Smoke and sparks vented into space as the two vehicles tumbled away from each other.

It was the *Allegro*.

"All right Morpho!" Geddy cried. "Denk, get in front of him!"

Denk brought the *Fiz* around on a course to intercept Sammo's disabled vessel as it tumbled through space. The last rocks disappeared as Geddy finally broke clear of the Belt. Meanwhile, the hold doors on the *Fiz* began to reopen.

— *He is moving too fast for the tractor beam.*

— Shit, you're right.

Their weak tractor beam couldn't handle anything that massive moving that quickly. If they didn't do something, it was going to smash into the front of the hold and destroy the airlock. But that wasn't the only problem. Zooming in on Sammo's ship revealed a crack in the front shield. It was venting air, accelerating its off-axis spin.

"Sammo, do you read me?" Nothing. "Sammo!" Still nothing. Hopefully he was unconscious and not dead.

"Denk, he's venting air. We need to get him inside now!"

As Geddy came shooting up behind Sammo's ship, his mind raced. If Denk didn't move right away, he'd have no choice but to blow it to bits.

"On it," said Oz.

She appeared from between the hold doors as Sammo's ship hurtled toward her. In her hands was the Zelnad gravity gun, which Doc and Krezek had somehow managed to fix. The ship tumbled straight at her.

"Are you crazy?!" shouted Geddy. "Shit. Denk, try to match the ship's velocity!"

He accelerated to catch up, pulling up even with them just as Oz hit Sammo's ship with the gravity gun. Its spin stopped almost immediately, and she eased it inside, backing up to make room. She maneuvered the ship over to the starboard side where the *Penetrator* was still parked and eased it down to the floor.

"Gotcha," Oz said, and Denk slowed down.

Geddy's tensed muscles relaxed and he folded forward, his head on the console as he allowed himself a laugh. "Well done, guys." Off comms, he muttered, "You're mine, you son of a bitch. And I'm gonna nail you to the fucking wall."

CHAPTER TWENTY-FIVE

SETTING THE STAGE

Sammo Yann sat in a chair between the workbench and the *Armstrong* in the *Fizmo's* hold, staring defiantly back at the crew. Thick straps were wrapped around his wrists and ankles. He had passed out, more from the G's he was pulling than from a lack of oxygen but came to shortly after Denk repressurized the hold.

They'd been at this for a few hours, asking pointed questions and only getting smirking non-answers.

"What were you doing on the asteroid?" Geddy asked.

He gave a casual shrug. "Planting charges, like I said."

"Charges, my ass. Why are you helping the Zelnads?"

"What makes you think I am?"

"You knew they were in the market for tukrium," Geddy said, anger rolling off him in waves. "That's why you took the *Penetrator*."

He rolled his eyes and gave his head a slow shake. "You still sore about that?" He nodded at Geddy's old ship in the aft starboard corner of the hold, which they'd recovered from Aku sans its shinium skin. "I'm happy you got it back. I only cared about the tukrium. Speaking of which, I've always wondered — why go to the trouble for a kit ship?"

Shinium, as Eli called it, was the only metal that could penetrate the barrier around Sagacea, Eli's home world, hence the ship's name. It was chemically identical to tukrium save for one key difference, revealed to him by the Metallurgist on Aku. It contained Sagacean spores that fell into the metal as it formed. Their presence was what made it special. The Nads were buying up all the tukrium to find it. But Geddy wasn't about to share that.

"Answer the question. Why are you working with the Zelnads?"

"You have no proof."

Geddy nodded to Voprot, who was on his haunches, staring murderously at Sammo. "Or we'll make you teach verb tenses to Voprot here."

Voprot unblinkingly cracked his lizardy knuckles. "Voprot very slow learner."

Sammo rolled his eyes. "Sorry, but you junior detectives are barking up the wrong tree. I'm not *helping* the Zelnads do anything. I'm only dealing some of their shit. In case you haven't noticed, they don't exactly need anyone's help."

"What's in it for you then? It can't just be money." Oz asked.

Before Sammo answered, Geddy noticed his lip twitch. A tell. What was he lying about?

"I hate to break it to you, sweetheart, but money's the only reason anyone does anything."

"Let's go back to why you took my ship," Geddy said. "I already know what you were doing on The Deuce."

A cocky grin crossed his lips. "Is that so?"

"It was part of your deal with Tatiana Semenov. She said you could take anything you wanted as payment. Payment for what?"

Sammo gave him a look of phony admonishment. "Oh, Geddy. You know how this works. I built my reputation on discretion. Just like you once did."

"You know what I think? I think she ran across your name in Ivan's records and thought you could help solve her cash-flow problems on Earth 3. You brokered some deal for her, and she offered up Earth 2. By then, the *Penetrator* was the most valuable thing on it. But you couldn't have found it without knowing I was there, which means you *knew* you were taking my only way off the planet."

Sammo gave an indifferent shrug. "That's an ... entertaining theory."

"What kind of deal did she make? A salvage contract? Something with the Temerurians?"

The self-assured Soturian chuckled, then shook his head. "You have quite the imagination. Maybe you huffed a little too much methane. Do you listen to the voices in your head, too?"

Geddy stiffened at the insult, but there was no way Sammo knew about Eli.

— *When you're smart, you do.*

— Which is roughly half the time.

"Just tell us the truth," Geddy said.

"I knew the salvage op on The Deuce was winding down. Ivan and I have a long history, so I reached out to his daughter and asked to sniff around. She said, 'Knock yourself out.'"

Geddy bit his lip. That did sound like her. But she'd told

Geddy that she contacted Sammo, not the other way around. One of them was lying, and he trusted Tots a whole lot more than this piece of cosmic crap.

"You expect me to believe you were willing to sift through scraps on The Deuce? Gimme some credit."

He daintily placed his hand over his heart. "I am but a humble merchant."

"I'll bet the Nads had him looking for tukrium," Oz declared. "Once the salvage op was done, Earth 2 would be fair game. The *Penetrator* wasn't a prize — it was evidence of shinium. They're probably mining it as we speak."

"Another fascinating theory. Only the Zelnads already have a reliable source of refined tukrium, don't they, Ms. Nargonis?"

— *This is not getting us anywhere.*

— I'm open to suggestions.

— *I have an idea.*

A LITTLE BEFORE three in the morning, the *Fizmo's* general alarm sounded, and Geddy eyes popped open.

Showtime.

He threw on some crew coveralls and pushed into the corridor. Oz came out at the same time, and he gave her a nod. As he passed, Geddy grabbed the front of her sleep shirt and pulled her into him, planting a long kiss on her tender lips.

"You still good with this?" he asked.

"I was about to ask you the same thing."

He nodded, unwilling to admit his hesitation. "You ready to play a Zelnad commander?"

"I was a theater nerd when I was younger. I've always had a flair for the dramatic."

He shouldn't have been surprised. Oz had many talents. A little improvisation was no problem. A voice filter would make it even easier.

At the direction of the Zelnads, Sammo sent that asteroid on its collision course with Gundrun. Now, Gundrun had joined the Zelnads in the so-called Coalition of Independent Worlds with the former Triad planets while the New Alliance struggled to take its first breath. The world needed to know the truth, and if that required a little sleight of hand, then so be it.

"We just need to make sure we sell it," he reminded her. "Otherwise, he'll never confess."

Geddy mussed his hair and dashed through the airlock doors as though in a panic. Voprot poked his giant head out of his nest in the subfloor like he'd just woken up, which was likely the case. Sammo, who was secured to the shelving unit, looked up from the makeshift bedroll where he'd been sleeping with passive curiosity.

"What's going on?" he asked. "Is your ship finally snapping in two?"

Geddy made a beeline for the *Armstrong*, barely glancing at Sammo as he stormed by. Jel, who preferred to sleep in her small berth, lowered the ramp and came down wearing only a very small pair of shorts and a camisole. To look her dead in the eye required his full concentration.

"What's going on?" she asked through a yawn.

"A Zelnad patrol just jumped in front of us." Geddy

jutted his chin at Sammo. "They want him."

"They can have him," she laughed, implying this was the obvious choice.

"That's not the point. They're gonna wonder about us, too."

She glanced furtively over at Sammo, who was listening intently. "So, what do we do?"

Geddy's head swung back and forth between the *Armstrong* and Sammo, scratching his chin as though it was some tough choice. "I'm gonna give 'em what they want."

"Geddy, no!" she protested. "I should be the one to do it."

"I got us into this mess, I'll get us out. Besides, I've dealt with these guys before."

She lunged forward and threw her arms around him. "Damnit, Geddy, you come back to us, you hear me?" With her head pressed to his chest, she whispered, "Too much?"

"You could dial it back a touch," he whispered back, then left her there and marched toward Sammo. "Get up. The Zelnads would like a word."

Sammo's face drained of color. His eyes narrowed as he sized them up. "With me?"

"That's what they said."

His voice quavered. "And you told them I was here?"

"Like I was gonna lie for an asshole like you." Geddy undid the plastic cuffs around his right wrist and ankle, roughly grabbed the crook of his left arm, and dragged him toward the *Armstrong* as Sammo resisted.

"What do they want with me?" Sammo asked.

"Damned if I know. Watch your head." He led Sammo up the ramp and shoved him into the copilot's seat. "Buckle up, buttercup. And don't touch anything."

Jel poked her head through the ramp opening. "Ged, I don't like this. Maybe we should just jump away."

"You should listen to her," Sammo said.

"Shut up," hissed Geddy, then returned his attention to Jel. "I would, but they already have our transponder. We have no choice."

"I hope you're right."

She descended the ramp, and he hit the close button, giving her a wink as the hatch folded back up. He took the pilot's seat and strapped in, vented the hold, and opened the door.

Sammo looked all around him. "Since we're both about to die, you might as well tell me what kind of hot rod this is."

"It's a Zihnian military prototype. That's all you get to know."

That wasn't actually a lie. The *Armstrong* was indeed a military ship, and its transponder said it was Zihnian. But its simulation mode also was indistinguishable from reality. Jel and Denk had worked through the night to set up this little scenario.

"Zihnian." Sammo gave a patronizing nod. "Sure."

Through the screen, they appeared to lift clear of the deck. Actuators in the skids simulated their movements. Geddy eased her through the hold doors, swung her around, and leveled her out right over the *Fizmo's* bridge. About five clicks in front of them was a colossal Zelnad destroyer flanked by two four-fighter squadrons.

In reality, there were no Zelnad ships, and they were still inside the hold, safe and sound. Even so, Geddy's chest tightened at the sight of them. Soon enough, it wouldn't be a simulation.

CHAPTER TWENTY-SIX

THE JIG IS UP

SAMMO'S HEAD snapped back and forth between the Zelnad ships and Geddy as though he didn't trust his eyes.

"Maybe you weren't bluffing," Sammo mumbled, squirming in his seat. Beads of sweat dotted his ridged forehead.

"I wish I was," Geddy said, adding a little shake to his voice.

— *Those ships look troublingly real.*

Acting afraid wasn't a big stretch. Jel and Denk liked programming sims, and they'd gotten really good at it. He glanced down at the little green simulation light on the console to reassure himself.

Sammo kept shaking his head. "This doesn't make any sense. How could they track me to you?"

"I dunno, but they did."

The warship dwarfed the *Fiz*. It was the same style they'd seen over Gundrun, a pyramid-shaped one he called a schnozz. It had joined ten others to form the supership the vaporized the asteroid and the chunk of moon it dislodged.

"That's it, then. We're both dead," Sammo said.

Geddy squinted at him. "What do they want with you?"

"How the hell should I know?"

"Just admit you've been helping them."

"I sell what they bring me, like anyone else."

"They're ... supplying the black market with their own tech?"

"Why do you think the Hovensby deal got so much attention?" Sammo asked. "They made sure everyone knew they made next-level tech."

Geddy eyed him doubtfully. "Sounds to me like you should have nothing to fear from them."

Sammo pretended to be calm, but the act was less believable by the second. Time to give the screw a little twist.

The front screen signaled a hail from the Zelnads. Geddy looked at Sammo. "I should probably answer that."

Sammo bit his lip but didn't respond. Geddy accepted the hail, and a stone-faced Ghruk appeared onscreen. Oz's cadence was similar to her real voice, but otherwise it sounded totally real.

"Sammo Yann. You are a difficult man to find."

"I don't know you," Sammo stammered. "Who are you?"

"You are to come with us."

Sammo gulped, his fingernails digging into the armrest as he glanced anxiously at Geddy. "Why?"

— *The trap is set. You are recording, right?*

—Just need to get him to say the words.

"To discuss our arrangement," said the Ghruk.

"Give us a quick sec." Geddy suspended the hail and locked eyes with Sammo.

White shown around his eyes, betraying his fear. "Are you insane?!"

"What's he talking about? What arrangement? And don't bullshit me."

Sammos eyes became glassy. "I already told you. I moved some product for them. That's it."

Geddy reached down by his seat and pulled out the jump terminal. "I said no bullshit! Come clean and I'll jump us out of here right now."

"What about your ship?"

"Don't worry about them. What arrangement?"

A blinding light flashed in his peripheral vision, and the whole ship shuddered. Sammo gasped. "They just shot at us!"

The Ghruk's face returned looking seriously pissed. "For your insolence," he hissed. "Bring Sammo Yann to us or be destroyed."

"Hold, please."

Geddy suspended the conversation again, prompting a look of abject disbelief from Sammo. He threw his hands up. "That's it. We're dead."

"What arrangement?!"

Geddy continued to stare at Sammo until he let out a long sigh.

"The asteroid ... the one that came out of the Belt and almost hit Gundrun ... I sent it there."

— *Bingo!*

— That's my name-o.

He feigned shock. "How?"

"I'll tell you everything. Just get us the hell out of here!"

Geddy held his gaze for another couple of seconds,

letting the tension continue to build. The *Armstrong* was still safely in the *Fizmo's* hold, and they had their confession. No Zelnads necessary.

There was just one loose end.

"Why did Tatiana Semenov hire you."

"Later, man! Come on!"

But Geddy wasn't doing anything until Sammo told one more truth. He gave a brief shrug. "I've got all day."

Sammo gave a pained look, bringing his fist to his mouth as he considered his options. Lowering his hand, he said, "She hired me to broker a deal with them."

"With the Zelnads?" Sammo nodded, and Geddy's heart rate doubled. "A deal for what?"

"A baby mogorodon, okay?? Now get us the hell out of here!"

SILENCE HUNG between them for a tense few moments as Geddy processed Sammo's admission.

Tatiana, his ex, told both him and the Committee that a Myadani broker came to her about buying a breeding pair of mogorodons, ostensibly for commercial farming. Tati said she checked the guy out, discovered he wasn't legit, and walked away. How much of that was true?

When he visited her on Earth 3, she had a baby mogorodon in her aquarium. It seemed weird and dangerous, but he'd chalked it up as one of those rich-person whims — her way of showing dominion over Earth 3's native species. But what if she was just keeping it until it was old enough to transport? Maybe her money problems were bigger than anyone knew, and her Myadani broker was really a Zelnad.

"So, you helped her sell the Nads a mogorodon and took my ship as payment?" Geddy said. "My only way off the Deuce?"

"Obviously not the only way," Sammo noted.

His gaze kept shifting between Geddy and the screen, confused as to why anything could be more important than the Zelnads. Or, maybe just confused as to why they were still alive.

Finally, Geddy hit the simulation control button and killed the program. The Zelnad ships disappeared, and the screen revealed the truth — they'd never left the *Fiz*.

The color drained from Sammo's face. "What the ...?"

"Ta-da," Geddy said, getting out of the pilot's seat.

Sammo's mouth hung dumbly open as he stared out at the hold. Oz removed her headset as she strolled toward them. The rest of the crew gathered in front of the *Armstrong* looking quite pleased with themselves. Geddy wanted to be happier in the moment, but the revelation about Tati troubled him.

"You've gotta be kidding me." Sammo climbed out after Geddy. "That was just a sim?! It was so real. What the hell kind of ship is this? You tricked me!"

Every muscle fiber was tight as a guitar string as Geddy stomped down the ramp. At the bottom, he spun around to face Sammo. "I know how you did it."

"Did what?"

"The asteroid. You jumped it to just outside Gundrun. Then you set it on a collision course and flew off like the coward you are."

Sammo inhaled sharply, his bottom lip quivering. "They turned my sister. They said if I did what they wanted, they'd turn her back."

"And did they?" Geddy already knew the answer.

Sammo looked to the ground, his fists balled, holding his emotions in. When he looked up, pain darkened his eyes.

"Of course not. I begged them to turn me, too, but they wouldn't. They said I wasn't 'right,' whatever the hell that means."

— What *does* that mean?

— *I am not certain. Perhaps they are not as indiscriminate as we thought.*

Oz stepped forward and gave Geddy a look he knew well. *What the hell?* He turned back to Sammo, whose slick and cool façade had evaporated. After all he'd done, Geddy could only muster so much empathy for him.

The tablet in Jel's hand was still recording their conversation.

"What about Gundrun? You were just going to let all of those people die?"

He gave his head a sad shake. "No! It was supposed to be theater. They wanted to give Gundrun a scare so they'd join their stupid Coalition. I didn't know it was gonna break off a whole chunk of the damn moon!"

Sammo was a shyster of the highest order. His version of events couldn't be fully trusted, but Geddy believed the broad strokes. The Nads played him. They knew he'd do what they wanted before they even asked. Did they really turn his sister or did Sammo just choose to kiss the hand that fed him?

Still, there had to be a reckoning. Sammo was the key to

toppling the Zelnads' bullshit narrative. If tricking him did that, it would be worth it.

"What's really going on here, Starheart?" Sammo asked. "Tev, this ship, deceiving me ... who are you working for?"

Geddy looked up at him. "You'll find out soon enough."

CHAPTER TWENTY-SEVEN

NIRNAYA

THE PROTOCOL for contacting Verveik and the Committee was similar to the way Tev contacted Sammo. Geddy sent a challenge code via UDC to an unregistered satellite, then waited inside the *Armstrong* for the encrypted private channel to open. Sammo was back on the floor of the hold, again secured to the shelves behind the workbench area.

— *What do you think he will say?*

— Hopefully something along the lines of 'good job, Geddy.'

— *You think his confession will be enough?*

— It had better be.

The front screen flashed green, and he opened the channel. Commander Verveik appeared, wearing a stern expression.

"Hey, Chief. How's it hanging?"

He cocked his head. "It?"

"Sorry, human expression. I really need to work on my—"

"What is it, Captain?" he interrupted.

"I know what happened over Gundrun, I know who's responsible, and I've got a recorded confession."

The big man narrowed his eyes doubtfully. "Is that so?"

"An arms broker named Sammo Yann runs his operation out of a rock in the Elenian Belt. He outfitted it with engines, jumped it to Gundrun's solar system, and set it on a collision course. He's our guy."

The jubilant attaboy he'd hoped for didn't come right away. "Why would he confess to you?"

"Because I made him think he was going to die."

"What's his name?"

"Sammo Yann. The same asshole who stole my old ship."

Verveik paused. "Where are you now?"

Geddy could admit that his expectations for this contact were lofty. This was their first official mission, and they'd succeeded. But Tev died in the process. That had to mean something.

He blinked away his irritation at Verveik's lack of excitement. "Just outside the Belt. Commander, this is the proof we've been looking for. What you sent us to find."

"Bring him to Nirnaya Station," Verveik said. "Just you and him. I'll meet you there in two hours."

Long before the Alliance, there was the Intergalactic Justice Commission. Even though a true inter-world partnership wouldn't be in the cards for another two centuries, fifty-four member planets ratified a system of jurisprudence and built six identical stations to enforce it. Nirnaya was in the Core Quadrant, a relatively neutral location.

IJC judges were elected by the member planets and served aboard the station for compulsory one-year terms. It was a tremendous honor and a steppingstone for many with political ambitions.

Every trial was broadcast across the galaxy. Since the collapse of the Alliance some eighty years earlier, the IJC was the only meaningful interplanetary organization left. The only one with teeth, anyway. And it moved quickly.

Apparently, Verveik wanted this to move quickly, too. Geddy was heartened by his urgency but confused by his unemotional reaction to the news. No matter. Soon, everyone would know the truth.

"Nirnaya it is, boss."

Verveik gave a tight nod and blinked out.

Nirnaya Station looked like a double-ended lollipop set on its end. The larger sphere at the bottom was a prison called the Stocks where some ten thousand of the galaxy's hardest criminals were housed. The smaller end, the Scale, was home to the courts and judges.

Soon, everyone would know that Sammo was a Zelnad puppet who had set the Gundrun event in motion. The bigger conspiracy wouldn't be far behind. That would make people angry, and anger was the only force powerful enough to rebuild the Alliance in time to matter.

On seeing it, Sammo let out a long sigh. "I should've known."

Geddy ignored him and hailed them. "Nirnaya Station, this is the *Armstrong*. Requesting permission to dock." He could only assume Verveik was there and had him pre-cleared.

A stern-looking Dudiran woman's face appeared onscreen. She wore a dark maroon IJC uniform that looked tight enough around the neck to choke her. "Acknowledged, *Armstrong*. Proceed to dock 9B. A security detail will meet you there."

"Sounds good, Nirnaya. We'll see you in a few minutes." He disconnected.

"You might as well tell me," Sammo said.

"Tell you what?"

"What you know about the Zelnads." Geddy stared at him a moment, weighing the idea. "You really don't know?" Sammo shook his head. "They're immortal beings formed during the birth of the universe. They created civilization as we know it, and now they want to destroy it. All intelligent life, gone. History, culture, art ... everything."

He smirked as though Geddy was pulling his leg, but of course, it was the gospel truth. His lips formed a line, and he lowered his head.

"If that's what they want, then that's what's going to happen."

"Not in my galaxy."

Geddy lined up the *Armstrong* with dock 9B. The approach vector turned green, and he initiated the docking sequence.

Sammo's eyes seemed to dull, not focusing on anything. "Maybe they're right."

"Yeah, well, you'll have plenty of time to think about it in the Stocks.

"This isn't going to work, y'know."

Geddy shrugged. "Meh. I'm pretty used to shit not working."

"If I get convicted by the IJC, the Zelnads look even better."

The ship gently drifted into the airlock coupling, and the locks engaged. The display indicated a good seal.

Geddy unbuckled his restraint. "Why's that?"

"Because then they didn't just prevent a natural disaster. They stopped a terrorist attack."

— *I believe he is correct about that.*

— I know, and I hate it.

FOUR ARMED ESCORTS awaited them outside the airlock on 9B, all wearing the same maroon uniforms. The woman he'd spoken to strode forward to greet him while four Sarak guards quickly surrounded Sammo.

"Captain Starheart."

"Ma'am."

"Your weapon, please. Slowly."

He hesitated for a long few moments before unclipping his holster and handing her the big PDQ. She studied it briefly.

"Black tukrium," she said. "Gold skolthil inlays. Screvari-made, obviously."

"You know your weapons."

"I know the kind criminals prefer."

Geddy didn't take umbrage at this. Technically, he *was* a criminal when Tretiak gave it to him. She handed it to one of the Saraks, who departed with it. Geddy watched anxiously after him as she turned on her heels. "You can pick it up in the armory on your way out. This way, please."

The Sarak guards marched away first with Sammo fenced between them. Geddy and the woman fell in behind.

At the end of the brightly lit hallway, they turned right and stopped a couple doors down. One Sarak buzzed past a lock while another removed Sammo's wrist restraints. The door slid open, and they half-pushed him through it.

She gestured for Geddy to follow. He tentatively stepped through the threshold.

"Holy shit," Sammo muttered just in front of him, looking left. "It can't be."

Geddy came fully into the room, and the door slid shut behind him. Commander Verveik, his old boss Tretiak Bouche, and Zereth-Tinn, the shady Soturian he'd first met on Thegus, were seated on one side of a long table opposite the door. They were the de facto leaders of the Committee, the secret cabal of powerful people working to expose the Zelnad conspiracy and rebuild the Alliance.

The moment Geddy stepped fully inside, the door hissed closed, and the five of them were alone. Verveik's very presence was reassuring. For once, Geddy was squarely in the right, and he had delivered the man responsible for nearly destroying the commander's home world. Once his crimes were exposed, the rebuilding of the Alliance could finally begin in earnest.

Verveik rose, his head nearly scraping the ceiling, and gestured at the chair on the other side. "Hello, Captain. Have a seat."

Geddy did as requested, feeling a surge of pride to be part of this particular club.

"Otaro Verveik," Sammo said in a hushed tone, justifiably

awed at the sight of him. To most of the galaxy, he was a long-dead historical figure.

"Oh, Sammo," said Tretiak, feigning offense. "Aren't you going to say hi to me?"

"Or me," said Zereth-Tinn, coming fully out from behind the table. He marched right up to Sammo. "Not very brotherly of you."

Geddy must've gasped, because Zereth-Tinn turned to him and gave his usual *Please try to keep up* grin. "Oh, come on, Starheart. Don't tell me you couldn't see the resemblance."

— *Is it just me, or do they look nothing alike?*

— It's not just you, pal.

Zereth-Tinn was several centimeters taller, thinner, and carried himself differently. Sammo was schlubby by comparison. Their eyes and hair were similar, but the resemblance ended there.

"Can't say I do."

"He looks like his father. I look like mine."

Only then did Geddy realize that he wasn't just Sammo Yann. He was *Sammo-Yann*. Only Soturians from the upper crust used their full names like that. The firstborn child took the father's second name, and the second child, the mother's. Sammo-Yann and Zereth-Tinn were half-brothers.

Zereth-Tinn whapped Sammo's midsection with the back of his hand. "You're fat."

"And your breath smells like spignork dung," growled Sammo.

To Geddy's surprise, Zereth-Tinn started laughing, and the two men heartily embraced. While they did, Geddy noticed Sammo glance furtively at the blaster on Zereth-

Tinn's hip. Reflexively, his fingers twitched, but of course, his weapon had been taken.

— Aww, why did he get to keep *his* blaster?

— *You really think you'll need it?*

— No, but it makes me feel better.

Zereth-Tinn returned to the table. Geddy sat opposite Tretiak, but Sammo remained standing.

Verveik's withering gaze narrowed at Sammo. "Sammo-Yann, you stand accused of setting an asteroid on a collision course with Gundrun. What say you to this charge?"

Sammo's eyes briefly slid over to Geddy, then back to Verveik. He drew himself a bit taller. "They paid me a hundred million credits to outfit an asteroid with engines and jump it to a blind spot in Gundrun's defenses. I lit the engines and flew away."

A shot of adrenaline hit Geddy like a debutante's slap. They'd reeled in a Gundrun satellite they thought was scrap only to find out it wasn't. Shortly after that came the distress call from Gundrun. Did they cause the blind spot or was it already there? He might never know.

The men exchanged a grave look. Verveik tapped his fingers on the long table. "Did you know the Zelnads would intervene?"

"You think I just woke up one day and decided to kill four billion people?? Of course, I knew they'd intervene. But I didn't know it would shake out like it did."

"They could have failed," Zereth-Tinn said.

"They don't fail, brother. Trust me."

"You never said anything about money," Geddy said, drawing everyone's attention. "He told me they turned his sister."

Zereth-Tinn raised his eyebrows. "Sister?" He gave Sammo a disappointed shake of his head. "Oh, Mo ... was that really the best you could do?"

His reaction said it all. Sammo had no sister.

Sammo shot up out of his chair and backed away from the table as though there was somewhere he could go.

"I just told Starheart that so he wouldn't kill me, okay? Look, I'll tell you everything I know about the Zelnads. Whatever little club you have here, I'm an open book. I'm dead either way."

Zereth-Tinn looked at Verveik, then Tretiak. They only stared grimly back. He closed his eyes and sighed. "That much is true, brother."

The moment he opened his eyes, he shot back up out of his seat, drew his blaster in a flash, and shot Sammo dead.

CHAPTER TWENTY-EIGHT

FRONTIER JUSTICE

"WHAT THE *FUCK*?!" Geddy exclaimed, shoving his chair back as he shot to his feet.

Tendrils of smoke curled up out of the charred cavity in Sammo's chest. At least it was quick. Neither Tretiak, Verveik, nor Zereth-Tinn had any visible reaction.

Zereth-Tinn got up, holstered his blaster, and walked over to Sammo's corpse. He knelt and lovingly brushed his cheek. "Sorry, brother. Woe that these times are ours."

Geddy's eyes beseeched Verveik and Tretiak for some explanation.

"You were right to contact us," was all Verveik said.

"I brought him to face the music, not the end of a blaster!"

"There was no other choice." Zereth-Tinn returned to the table with a somber expression.

"I had evidence against him," Geddy protested. "And a confession!"

"A trial might've served justice, but not our cause. And as you know, Captain, there is no cause more just than ours."

Verveik growled. "A confession means nothing without concrete proof, and you don't have it."

Sammo had few positive qualities. He was a money-grubbing, unprincipled opportunist who ruined Geddy's life. He'd single-handedly given the black market its enthusiasm for Zelnad weapons. No one would mourn the guy except for warlords and mercs.

But in a way, he was also the reason Geddy was now captain of the *Fiz*. Why Oz and the rest of the crew were his family. That had to count for something, didn't it? It felt like he'd lured the man into a trap neither of them knew about. Verveik's logic held, but it didn't change the fact that two men were dead, and he had nothing to show for it.

"Am I wrong, Captain?" Verveik asked, irritated by Geddy's silence.

"No," Geddy said heavily.

The Sarak guards came in. With little more than a nod from Verveik, they carried Sammo's corpse away. Acrid smoke still hung in the air, stinging Geddy's nostrils. The door closed behind them as they departed. Zereth-Tinn ultimately broke the pregnant silence.

"As soon as they tracked that asteroid back to the Elenian Belt, I knew he was involved. I told Tretiak then and there that if he was proven guilty, I'd kill him myself."

"But you heard the Commander! We can't prove shit!"

"You proved it to me," Zereth-Tinn said with finality. "He would never confess to something unless he did it. But as far as a court goes, Verveik's right. If we didn't take him out, he'd walk."

"And make a new deal in which the Zelnads find out that Otaro Verveik is alive," Tretiak added.

"But he was your brother!" Geddy protested.

"*Half*-brother. And not the good half, believe me. Even so, it had to be done, and I could not allow anyone else do it."

Verveik said, "If I were you, Captain, I'd be less concerned about him and more about Myadan."

Geddy put his palms on the table and leaned forward, his outrage starting to ebb. "Myadan? What have you heard from Tatiana??"

Verveik activated a very thin holobar on the table, bringing up an image of the Earth-like planet. About two-thirds of it was green and blue. The rest was on its way, the galaxy's most ambitious terraforming project. Within the next century, it would fill in and become the largest animal sanctuary in history. Its only residents were descendants of the first terraformers to live on the surface, most of whom were Xellaran.

He zoomed in on a sprawling campus tucked between sharp-sloped mountains.

"The Myadan Xoo," he said grandly, pointing at the construction. "Already the largest collection of species in the galaxy. It's where we suspect the Zelnads are breeding your dangerous creatures. Miss Semenov has been angling to join their board of directors."

What Sammo told him about Tatiana was deeply upsetting. He didn't believe she knew what the Nads wanted with her pet mogorodon, but she had to know it wasn't good. Until he got to look her in the eye and learn the truth of it, he decided to keep that little tidbit to himself. After what he'd just seen, he couldn't be sure what the Committee would do to her.

Verveik cycled through photographs and video clips of

the Xoo. Geddy wasn't much for alien creatures, so he had never been there, but he'd heard it was practically a city unto itself.

"We believe the Zelnads are operating between these mountains where the old atmospheric processors used to be. It's completely hidden from the Xoo and the spaceport, and there may be spaces underground."

"Underground?" Geddy asked.

"Permanent terraforming facilities," Verveik said. "Myadan started as a desolate, class six exoplanet with no atmosphere, so people would work there for years. Decades, even. They built a whole facility underground for the workers to live. It was filled in so they could build the Xoo on top of it. We're betting it was connected to the processors, and that that area of the facility wasn't filled in."

"All right, so what's the plan?"

Verveik flicked off the display and folded his giant hands. "The Xoo board is a who's who of powerful people. Once Miss Semenov joins their ranks, she'll use her influence to find out what's going on."

Geddy thought he knew what was going on, but after Durandia, he wasn't so sure. These guys didn't know what happened there, and they didn't need to. He'd talked to Smegmo about helping Minister Napthar get the city back on its feet, and a small fleet of supply ships were already on their way. Geddy asked him to keep it on the down low until he had more information.

— *This is how it all works, isn't it? Powerful men, alone in a room, deciding which strings to pull when.*

— I suppose so. I've never been in that room before.

— *I don't like it.*

— Me, neither. But it's what we've got.

"You're putting all your eggs in Tatiana Semenov's basket?" Geddy asked, laughing. "A woman who had her nipples augmented for a destination wedding just so she'd look hotter in white than the bride? Who kept a mogorodon as a pet? You mean that Tatiana Semenov?"

"This is our best lead," Verveik said, bristling at Geddy's growing irritation. "We need to tread lightly. I'd suggest you do the same, Captain."

"What about the fleet?" Geddy asked. "Don't you need pilots? Crews? Training them will take months, right?"

"Public opinion won't turn against the Zelnads overnight," Zereth-Tinn said. "We should have plenty of time."

That seemed like magical thinking to Geddy. Stopping the Zelnads relied on two things remaining secret — the existence of a vast New Alliance fleet and their possession of the jump tech. If either one came to light, the Nads would be forced to act swiftly. And then neither of those things would matter. They weren't ready, and they wouldn't *be* ready unless they started taking some risks.

Everything needed to move faster. If they failed, the Zelnads would destroy Sagacea and eliminate the possibility of civilization ever forming again. For all anyone knew, they'd already done it.

"What are your orders?" Geddy asked, biting his tongue.

"Rest and regroup somewhere. Take this Dr. Krezek home. When we know more about Myadan, we'll be in touch."

Geddy frowned. "You want to sideline us *now*? We're just finding our groove!"

"This is a strategic game," Verveik answered. "We win by moving the right pieces at the right time."

"What about finding their fleet?"

"Parmhar Tardigan has nearly finished his deep-space scanner," Verveik assured him. "We'll find them soon enough."

"What if they find us first?"

The big man drew himself up, head and shoulders taller than even Tretiak, who had several centimeters on Geddy. Even though he seemed weary, his presence was imposing.

"Sometimes, Captain, you just have to hope."

— *That is a tall order for you.*

— Yeah, but I'm working on it.

He stood and glanced at the spot where Sammo's body had just been. There was no blood, no nothing. Like he was never there.

"I need to talk to Tatiana," Geddy said to Verveik.

"That's out of the question."

"Why?"

"We believe the Zelnads have infiltrated the Xoo's leadership. She's already in grave danger. All the more reason to give her a wide berth."

"But–"

Verveik's expression hardened. "Stay away from Myadan, Captain. Are we clear?"

The words he wanted to say formed in his throat, but he swallowed them. "Then what am I supposed to do?"

"Go back to your crew and lie low until I contact you," he said gruffly.

Geddy bit the inside of his lip hard enough to draw blood. But he gave a tight nod and got up. "Sir, yes sir."

— The only thing I don't like about the military is being ordered around.

— *What about your problem with authority?*

— That, too.

On his way out, he passed the spot where Sammo had died. A deep pang of guilt churned in his guts. Maybe he'd deserved what he got, and maybe it was the only way, but that didn't make it justice. Bile rose in his throat, but he swallowed it down with everything else.

The door opened as he approached, and he didn't look back.

CHAPTER TWENTY-NINE

TANTU'KAH

GEDDY ENTERED the bridge of the *Fizmo* expecting to find it empty. The same sun that had shone on old Elenia for billions of years still burned brightly behind them, casting the broken planet's features into sharp relief. Studying its pock-marked landscape, you could easily discern the remains of a vast ocean basin. An egg-shaped continent dense with mountains. An island chain resembling a curved sword.

Guilt clung to his soul like tar. It was just as foul, just as stubborn. He settled into Denk's seat and put his feet up on the console. Sleep was out of the question.

— *It has a certain stark beauty.*

— Lately, that's the only kind of beauty there is.

— *You know that is not true.*

— Then why does it sound right?

— *Because you are in distress.*

That much was certain. Five days had passed since Sammo and Tev's deaths — two men he neither liked nor respected. So why did it bother him so much?

"The longer you look at it, the more intriguing it becomes."

Geddy whirled at the unexpected sound of Doc's voice. He stood at the back of the bridge, the light rebounding off Elenia just brightly enough to cast shadows across his face. Geddy smiled at his friend.

"Kinda like a hemorrhoid." Geddy patted the seat beside him. "Join the insomnia club. We're small but growing."

Tardigan settled into the ordinarily empty seat beside him.

"I've been keeping odd hours. Ehrmut loves to talk science but suffice it to say I am ... unaccustomed to so much intellectual conversation."

Geddy chuckled to himself. "You don't say."

"Currently, we are collaborating on a device capable of detecting his sex pheromone and a chemical blocker should we encounter it."

The whole pheromone thing seemed like a stretch until he'd seen firsthand how powerful it could be. "It's that strong?"

"Let's just say he is deeply concerned."

For a couple minutes, neither of them spoke. The ruin of Elenia filled the entire screen. It was as though a beautiful building was bombed that no one bothered to raze.

"It's very curious, you know," Doc mused.

"What's that?"

Tardigan lifted his chin at the broken planet. "The so-called cataclysm. No natural forces at the core of a planet could shatter it like that."

Geddy quartered toward him, frowning. "Then why is that the story?"

The tale of Elenia was a favorite of young kids, boys especially, because it was about a beautiful, ancient planet mysteriously blowing up. When you were eight, that was cool as shit. Now, it just made him sad.

"History is composed of stories. The ones that stand the test of time are those that most people prefer to believe. Or prefer to tell."

"So ... that's not the story?"

"The truth is that nobody knows. All science knows for certain is that the core didn't explode like a bomb. It had to be something else."

Geddy gave a sidelong grin. "Something tells me you have a theory."

Doc pointed his finger at a concave section that still clung stubbornly to the largest chunk of planet. "Do you see that piece that looks like an eggshell? The one that is thinner than the rest?"

"That part that looks like it should've broken off?"

"Yes. Now follow the jagged edge down to where it meets the main part of the sphere."

He spotted what Doc was referring to immediately. A perfectly straight line, perpendicular to the core. It had to be hundreds, if not thousands of kilometers long.

"Why haven't I seen that before?" Geddy asked.

"It is usually in shadow. This is the only time of day you can see it. I have studied it since we first arrived."

"Almost looks like it was drilled," Geddy noted.

"An astute observation, Captain. And yet, ancient Elenia did not possess any such technology."

He let that hang in the air for a few seconds, giving

Geddy an opportunity to connect the same dots. It didn't take long.

"You don't think the Zelnads ...?"

Doc replied, "I've estimated both the volume of material in the Belt and what is clearly missing from the planetary sphere. Even accounting for asteroids knocked out of orbit over the ages, a vast amount of material is missing."

"Tukrium?"

Doc could only shrug because they would never know for sure. "It is merely a theory. If true, it would mean the planet did not explode, but rather, broke apart."

He thought about this a moment and nodded. "You're right. The other story's better."

"To what do you attribute your insomnia, Captain?"

Geddy picked at one fingernail while his eyes drifted down to the console. "Tev and Sammo."

"Ah," he said knowingly. "Guilt is an unwelcome bedfellow."

"It didn't work out like I thought."

"Very little has," Doc pointed out, "yet here we are. Ornean mystics call it *tantu'kah*." Geddy gave doc a quizzical look. "It roughly translates to 'elastic thread.' It is the notion that our path in life flexes. The further we stretch it, the more it resists. But it never breaks."

He didn't believe in fate or destiny or that things happened for a reason. But the universe did seem to have a funny way of returning to the mean.

"Existential entropy," Geddy said. "I could get behind that. What happens when your *tantu'kah* stretches too far?"

"Then it returns you to where you should be, sometimes forcefully."

Geddy tapped his fingers together. "Seems like it would hurt."

"It's supposed to."

CHAPTER THIRTY

NINETY DAYS?

Oz's HEAD nestled in the crook of Geddy's shoulder, her bright red locks gently pulsing in time with her heart as they lay together in the dark. Under any other circumstance, he would've been happy to stay here forever. But two weeks had passed with no word from Verveik, and he was getting antsy. That, plus his lingering guilt, had him in a sour mood. Oz was the only thing buoyant enough to lift him out of it for a while.

"You're thinking about Tev and Sammo," Oz whispered in the dark. She always said she couldn't read his mind, but sometimes he got the feeling she was. Maybe he wasn't as cagey as he thought.

He nodded and pulled her closer. She ran her long nails lightly up and down the divot running down the center of his chest, circled his navel a couple of times, and slowly returned. Man, he loved that.

"Want to talk about it?"

Oz lived in a world of emotions. Like a watchmaker, she knew exactly how their mechanisms worked and how to fix them. Geddy, meanwhile, had about as much facility with emotions as Voprot had with intransitive verbs.

It wasn't the talking that fixed it — it was how she made it all seem okay, whatever it was.

"I know you didn't like Tev," he said. "Hell, *nobody* liked Tev. But he didn't deserve to die."

"And Sammo?"

"I'm not sure what he deserved."

"If he deserved it, would that take away your guilt?"

The truth was, he wasn't sad Sammo was dead, and frankly, he wasn't exactly torn up about Tev, either. Maybe it wasn't his fault they died, but it wasn't *not* his fault, either. That's what he couldn't square.

As always, she was exactly right. Who deserved what wasn't up to him, and it wouldn't have mattered anyway.

"No."

"Then you need to let it go. Whether war is coming or something else, people are going to die. We're one tiny part of one little galaxy, Geddy. One of millions, probably. The Zelnads have been at this for eons."

Geddy's breathing became shallow. "Are we arrogant to think we can stop them?"

Her fingers paused mid-stroke, and she lifted her head off his shoulder to look him in the eyes. In the dim light of his quarters, her big yellow irises resembled binary stars.

"Don't you dare think that, Geddy Starheart."

He looked away, unwilling to bear the intensity of her gaze.

"It's a legit question. I mean, what if we're fighting an unwinnable war instead of enjoying the time we have left?"

She let out a long sigh and returned her head to its spot

where it fit so well. "Let's make a deal. We won't make love again until we've stopped them."

Geddy snapped his head back, reading her face for a sign she was kidding. Nope. "What purpose would that serve, exactly?"

"To remind us what's at stake."

"What if we're still fighting these assholes in ten years?" he asked.

"Fine. We'll make it a rolling ninety-day thing, then."

"Ninety days?"

She gave an exasperated sigh. "Think of it as incentive."

Oz was the only thing keeping him afloat. He didn't like this idea at all, yet something about it intrigued him. Didn't top athletes abstain for a while before the big game?

"I think of it as torture. And not the fun kind."

Her eyes rolled. "Oh, please. You'll live."

"I'd be more worried about you," Geddy teased.

"Me?"

"I mean, you're pretty insatiable."

A mischievous grin formed on her beautiful face. "Is that because I can't be sated, or I can't be sated by *you*?"

— *She has a way of turning things around on you, doesn't she?*

— Yes, damnit.

He gave a rueful laugh. "No further questions."

After a long pause, she asked, "Have you ever been to the Myadan Xoo?"

"No. Why?"

"What if we checked it out?" She quickly clarified, "Just as tourists."

He gave his head a decisive shake, rejecting the idea out of hand. "Not an option. Verveik said to steer clear."

"Yeah, but he meant in our *official* capacity, right? Why would he care if we just saw some animals and ate balefna fluff?"

Geddy wasn't much for touristy stuff, and the thought of being around a bunch of weird creatures made his eye twitch. But then again, they'd been through quite a lot, and sitting around the *Fiz* waiting for orders from Verveik wasn't as relaxing as it sounded.

— *You* could *use the distraction.*

— Wait — you'd be on board with this?

— *Your head has not been a very hospitable place lately.*

Maybe a little side trip would do everyone some good. If he didn't like it, they probably had an overpriced cafeteria with terrible food where he could wait.

"What does Eli say?" she asked.

"As usual, he agrees with you. Y'know, the two of you are supposed to keep me *out* of trouble."

She raised her eyebrows expectantly. "So ...?"

Geddy heaved a sigh. "Fine, let's go to the damn Xoo."

"Ha! I knew you'd crack."

"One question — did this no-sex thing start the moment you said it or ...?"

She batted her swooping eyelashes and rolled on top of him. "Well, I mean, it's a new rule, so it's not quite firm yet."

"Ah. Well, speaking of firm ..."

CHAPTER THIRTY-ONE

R&R

A private landing pad at the Myadan Xoo's spaceport was eye-wateringly expensive, but unfortunately, it was the only way to ensure no one got too curious about the *Armstrong*. The transponder was modded to show Zihnian registry, though it didn't look Zihnian in the slightest. Considering the rest of the spaceport was filled with small, chartered transports and family-size starships, a tukrium warship dripping with weaponry belonged in a private landing pad.

Geddy unbuckled and stretched, glad as always that fresh air was just around the corner. Myadan's engineered atmosphere was said to have a touch more oxygen than most habitable worlds. After the Durandian Underground, that fact alone seemed worth the trip.

"Captain, may I have a word with you and the crew?" Doc said as Krezek joined them on the bridge.

"What's up, Doc?" Geddy asked, allowing himself a private chuckle.

Krezek handed Doc a small rectangular device on a chain. One side was plain, the other had a small display. Doc held it up for everyone to see. "Dr. Krezek and I made a device capable of detecting his sex pheromone in the air. If the Zelnads are operating on Myadan as we suspect, it may show us the way. Or warn us if levels become dangerous."

Krezek picked up from there. "I cannot stress enough how powerful this substance is."

"Captain, would you do us the honor?" Doc held it out for Geddy. It was about half the length of his finger with a metal housing. "It will alert you with a vibration if the measurement exceeds one hundred parts per million."

"Is it anything like the stuff we used on the crypsids?" Denk asked.

"This is far more concentrated," Krezek replied. "Being exposed for more than a few seconds will result in ... an irresistible and animalistic compulsion to procreate."

The crew exchanged uncomfortable looks.

"How irresistible, exactly?" Jel asked.

"A biological imperative on par with the will to live," Krezek replied.

"Perfect."

"However," Krezek excitedly unrolled a bundle of small auto-injectors for them to see, "since I created the molecule, I was able to create a protein that blocks the pheromone from olfactory receptors."

"Like an antidote?" asked Denk.

"Not exactly. This is strictly a preventative measure," Krezek corrected. "If the sensor buzzes, you should all inject yourselves immediately."

He handed them out. The one for Voprot was twice the size of the others.

"How long do they work?" Oz asked.

"An hour, give or take."

Geddy tucked the small metal cylinder into his pocket and patted it, briefly meeting Oz's concerned expression. "Thanks, Ehrmut. You've given us all a lot to worry about."

The private pad included a dedicated attendant, who appeared very confused when the crew descended the ramp. He was a young Vyeph a few centimeters shorter than Geddy, with six skinny arms and scaly yellow skin that flashed iridescent when the light caught it just so. His face was wide and flat, with tiny red eyes and a concave nose.

"Welcome to the Myadan Xoo, friends. I'm Deepa, your personal attendant. Quite the ship you've got there."

"Thanks! It's a rental," Geddy said.

The kid gave a nervous chuckle, like he wasn't quite sure if Geddy was kidding. "Heh, well, our standard package includes a full interior cleaning, so just leave the ramp down, and I'll–"

Geddy tapped his device to close the ramp. As it raised, he slipped the kid a hundred-credit square. "How about we trade the cleaning for your discretion?"

He grinned greedily and tucked the square in his pants pocket. "I am at your service." He folded himself into a low bow. "Enjoy your time at the Xoo."

"Why's it spelled with an X?" Geddy asked.

"The X is for xenomorph," the kid explained. "Most of our creatures will be alien to you."

"Perfect. We're all big, big fans of alien creatures."

The kid practically tripped over himself to open the door, and they passed into the main hangar. In stark contrast to Durandia, it buzzed with activity. As they'd noticed coming in, it was mostly families and couples, many of whom walked hand-in-hand as they followed the yellow lines toward the arched exit.

The wide plaza that separated the spaceport from the Xoo's main entrance was lined with heavily landscaped mounds exploding with trees and flowers. Chirping birds flitted between them as though on cue. Each square stone tile underfoot was engraved with the name of a Xoo benefactor, along with an image of their favorite animal. Geddy recognized a couple of names as former clients of the Double A auction.

A twenty-five-meter-high wall encircled the vast property. Thick vines encrusted most of it, but they did little to mask its imposing nature. Was it keeping things in or out?

"Whoa ..." said a little Napnap kid walking beside Voprot, his voice full of wonderment. He craned his neck to meet the big lizard's eyes. "Do you live here?"

Voprot frowned and shook his head. "Voprot not part of Xoo."

"Yet," Geddy muttered, earning an elbow in the ribs from Oz.

The Visitor Center's roof came to parabolic peaks that seemed to mirror the actual mountains in the near distance, which was where Verveik suspected the breeding facility was.

Enormous glass doors parted as the throngs streamed inside. A looping holographic presentation had already begun to play overhead in the cavernous atrium. Everyone's head craned back to take it all in as loudspeakers blared the voice of Oleptau Duvon, a famous Zorran actor whose basso profundo tone lent gravity to the canned production. Geddy and the crew lined up along a metal railing to watch.

The hologram depicted Myadan as a lifeless brown rock rotating alone in space.

"Just seven hundred years ago, Myadan was a class six exoplanet incapable of sustaining life. Its razor-thin atmosphere was a toxic mix of methane, ammonia, and carbon dioxide."

A lone starship faded into view, and the camera followed it to the surface.

"One day, a Xellaran explorer named Quadle Yun landed on Myadan, not far from where you're currently standing. His environmental readings suggested the planet was a perfect candidate for terraforming. The government of Xellara conducted its own study and agreed to fund the atmospheric processing that would eventually turn this dead planet into the cradle of life it has since become."

The camera zoomed in close on the planet, depicting a colossal array of atmospheric processors tucked into the mountains. Their flared shape reminded Geddy of trumpet bells. An animated diagram showed the methane, ammonia, and CO_2 coming in while oxygen, nitrogen, and hydrogen were belched back out.

"For four hundred and fifty years, the processors churned, powered by Myadan's only sun. Then, one day, a sensor array recorded the first evidence of water vapor. From there, Myadan was off to the races. Less than a century later, the planet's atmosphere and temperature became capable of sustaining life."

On the near side of the mountains, giant earth movers were shown excavating a deep, long arc. A simulated time lapse ensued as Oleptau's dramatic narration continued.

"Terraformers first came to Myadan nearly two hundred

and fifty years ago. A vast underground complex was constructed to house them and their equipment until the atmosphere became breathable. They planted trees and flowers and introduced helpful bacteria and single-celled organisms into the soil."

— *That must be the one Verveik mentioned.*

— Why did I never learn about that?

— *You never visited the Xoo.*

The camera, which had flown through a bit of the terraforming facility, zoomed out to reveal animation of a planet transformed. What had been brown and rocky had become a verdant patch that spread outward. A puffy blanket of low clouds parted to reveal a pale blue sky and an orange-red sun. A small group of Xellaran workers emerged from their underground home and cautiously removed their helmets, taking a deep, nourishing breath for the first time.

"After Myadan City was established, smaller communities popped up along the so-called Floral Frontier. Some terraformers departed while others remained to settle the land and look after the animals. Xenobiologists helped introduce new species from around the galaxy. Species that could live in harmony."

The terraforming equipment and atmospheric processors faded away, and animals took their place. Something like a slimy, six-legged giraffe nibbled on leaves. Shimmering blue beetles constructed multi-room houses with pebbles.

Duvon continued. "Soon, word spread about Myadan's remarkable biological diversity. Xenomorph safaris became all the rage, and a thriving tourism industry sprang forth. Investors realized that a little refinement was all they needed to make Myadan one of the galaxy's top attractions. And so, the Xoo was born. Forty years later, it's still going strong."

"What happened to the terraforming facility?" Denk wondered aloud.

"They filled it in and built the Xoo on top of it," Geddy said smugly, turning to Doc and Krezek. "Isn't that right?"

Doc replied, "That is my understanding, Captain."

"On behalf of the entire Myadan Xoo family, thank you for visiting," intoned Duvon, a medium closeup of his handsome face floating overhead. The camera widened to reveal him surrounded by goofy animals that Geddy doubted were real. "My friends look forward to meeting you. Please proceed to the ticket kiosk and be sure to ask about our new X-Pass, which gives smart Xoogoers unprecedented access behind the scenes at our beautiful park."

He gave a phony laugh as a bird resembling a hairy pigeon landed on his shoulder and pecked him playfully, then the holograms faded out and the lights came back up.

Denk, unsurprisingly, wore an ecstatic grin. "I'm *totally* getting the X-Pass!"

"Voprot want X-Pass, too."

"Samesies," Oz echoed, batting her eyelashes at Geddy. "How about you, *Captain*? What pass will you get?"

"Whichever one gets me into the bar. I could really use a—"

"Geddy, look!" Voprot said, pointing at a sign over the ticket window. "It say no alcohol."

Panic seized him. He jerked his head in the direction of Voprot's clawed finger. The digital sign read, *In the interest of our animals' safety and security, we have suspended the sale of*

alcoholic beverages indefinitely. We apologize for any incon-
venience.

His heart bottomed out. On one hand, he was weirdly proud that Voprot could read, but on the other ... Being in the vacuum of space for more than a couple days made a man thirsty.

"Maybe I should wait in the ship."

Oz grabbed his hand and started dragging him toward the ticket window. "Not a chance, fuddy-duddy. We're gonna have so much fun!"

"Fun." Geddy rolled his eyes. "I can hardly wait."

CHAPTER THIRTY-TWO

NEW XOO REVUE

AFTER PAYING for everyone's X-Passes, Geddy passed through the doors and onto a raised semicircular terrace that overlooked the park's central feature — a vast round lagoon ringed with trees and a crowded walking path. An underwater dome structure protruded just above the surface, from which spat orchestrated jets of water.

A sprawling map of the Xoo's exhibits was carved into the stone beneath their feet. The lagoon was represented by a scaled version of the fountain in front of them. It tumbled over a dome that reminded Geddy of the Bubbles on Earth 3.

"That's WetWorld," said a beaming young Xellaran that approached from behind him. He wore a bright yellow vest with the Xoo's logo.

Geddy regarded him, then the fountain, as Oz looked on. "WetWorld, you say? Tell us more."

It was hard to tell whether he was caught off-guard or didn't get it. Given his obvious youth, it could've gone either way. He struck Geddy as a bit delicate, but in an exuberant, charmingly naïve way.

"Sure thing! WetWorld is our ocean habitat here at the Myadan Xoo. It's the most biologically diverse body of water in the entire galaxy, with more than two thousand aquatic species!"

"Cool, cool," Geddy said, winking suggestively at Oz. "And how long should a man like me devote to WetWorld?"

"You should plan on at least an hour."

"An hour? That's a long time to be down in WetWorld."

Oz shrugged. "Depends who you ask."

"*Anyway* ..." The kid's demeanor freshened. "We recommend you start this way," he pointed toward the right side of the lagoon, "so you can finish with the mogorodon."

Geddy sucked in a breath. "Mogorodon?"

"It's our newest exhibit. Don't worry, though, it's completely separate from the lagoon. Otherwise, we'd go from two thousand species to just one real fast. Heh, heh."

"Thanks for the info." He grabbed Oz's arm and pulled her toward Jel and the others, who were all leaning their elbows on the railing between. "Come on. We're starting over here."

"Don't you want to check out WetWorld?" Denk asked hopefully.

"Later," Geddy said over his shoulder. "Ninety days later."

"Aw, man ..." Denk muttered, kicking at the ground.

"He's kidding, Denk," Oz assured him. "Today, we're *all* going to WetWorld."

A ramp descending from the left side of the terrace joined the broad walkway that branched toward the lagoon. It was crowded with visitors, most of whom were moving in the opposite direction. Where the path split, a sign pointed left to the West Lagoon Trail and the Mogorodon Exhibit. Geddy followed the sign, leading them down another ramp that curled downward toward a darkened, arched tunnel. A feeder line of xoogoers stretched outside and halfway down the length of the Visitor Center.

Geddy despaired until he noticed another sign that read, *X-Pass Holders.* An arrow pointed to an adjacent entrance.

"That's what I'm talkin' about!" Denk raced toward it with Voprot close at his heels.

The rest of them followed, continuing down the tunnel via a section of the ramp that had been blocked off to everyone else. The side-eye from the ordinary ticketholders in line ranged from jealousy to contempt, which gave Geddy a pleasing shot of smugness. A sensor over the tunnel read their passes and flashed green as they passed through a force field door.

Underwater sounds met their ears, piped in over speakers hidden in the simulated rock. They continued down past more holograms depicting the life cycle, favorite foods, unique morphology, and mating habits of the mogorodon.

"Huh," Jeledine remarked, studying the glowing text beside an animation that highlighted the creature's mind-blowing scale. "I didn't know it was the largest conventional animal in the galaxy."

"Oh, yes," Doc Tardigan said. "It is so large that it requires five brains."

"Voprot only have one brain," said the lizard.

"And that's if he rounds up," Geddy whispered to Oz, who couldn't help but laugh.

After descending through the gauntlet of facts, the tunnel leveled out, and the already crowded space swelled with people. A strip of thick windows down one side revealed an immense water tank that ran at least partly under the Visitor Center. People were lined up six or seven deep to catch a glimpse.

The tank was roughly the size of a typical terrestrial hangar, big enough to house a moderately sized transport. In the lower left corner was a cage that ran the full width of the tank. The entire bottom was sandy, with ribbons of bright green kelp that gently swayed with the current. A simulated reef had been built up, replete with a phony shipwreck.

Geddy scanned the tank for a sign of the creature but didn't see anything.

"Where the hell is it?" he asked no one in particular. "Isn't it the size of a damn ..." The throng sucked in a collective gasp, and the pale-yellow belly of the mogorodon slid into view, lazily gliding past as though showing off. "... house?"

Little kids pressed their faces to the glass, eyes wide, while about half the adults took an unconscious step back. The creature turned away before its full length was revealed. As it swam away, Geddy judged it to be at least forty meters long. Its presence filled him with dread.

No way this was the same one from Tati's aquarium. No way. The last time he saw it, it would've fit in a bathtub. This thing was basically a dinosaur with a long, flat snout overflowing with teeth and a sinuous, paddle-like tail covered in long vertical spines. The rest of its body was encrusted with thick scales that appeared jet-black in the slightly cloudy water.

"Hey Doc, how fast do these things grow?"

Tardigan was clearly delighted by the question. "They

reach full size in approximately three years. I'd estimate this one is between one and two years old. Remarkable, isn't it?"

"That's one word for it."

— So it cannot be Tatiana's. Was Sammo lying?

— I'm more interested in this tank.

— Why?

— Because I'm betting it was part of the terraforming facility.

— Which would mean it wasn't really buried.

Oz cleared her throat, yanking him from his internal conversation with Eli. "What's he saying?" she whispered.

"Sammo told me he brokered the sale of Tatiana's pet mogorodon to the Nads."

Her face registered surprise. He hadn't mentioned that part of the conversation. "Pet mogorodon? You don't think ...?"

"No, no. It was just a juvenile. It wouldn't be this big already."

"Doesn't mean she didn't do it."

He shook his head. "Nor does it mean it isn't here somewhere."

"A breeding pair, maybe?" she flared her eyebrows.

By merely sticking close to Voprot, Denk easily wound up at the front with the little kids. They all pressed their palms and noses to the glass and clearly were having the time of their lives. It brought a smile to Geddy's face. Maybe he'd judged the Xoo too soon.

Jel came up on his other side. "I knew they were big, but damn."

"C'mon," Geddy said. "Let's get this over with." He

tapped Denk and Voprot and motioned that they were moving on. "You guys coming?"

"We'll catch up with ya, Cap," Denk said, his and Voprot's eyes never leaving the mogorodon as it made lazy figure eights around the tank. "Feeding time's in five minutes." He pointed at a timer over the tank.

"What do they feed it? A truck?"

He was about to turn away from the thing when it slowed and came to a stop right in front of the window, much to the delight of the children. Its basketball-sized eyes stared straight ahead.

At him.

His neck hair stood on end. Back in Tati's lavish digs on Earth 3, he and the baby mogorodon had a moment he'd never forget. Its bright yellow eyes seemed to pierce his very soul, and he remembered feeling a certain cold intelligence behind its murderous stare.

"Dr. Krezek??" came a female voice behind them.

Krezek turned at the sound of his name. "My goodness! Iondra?"

Geddy and Oz watched as he warmly embraced a uniformed Xoo employee. It wouldn't have been that remarkable save for one very notable detail.

She was Kigantean.

CHAPTER THIRTY-THREE

IONDRA

THE KIGANTEAN WOMAN was markedly shorter than Voprot, with pale green skin and less severe angles in her face. She wore the same yellow vest as the kid outside.

"What are you doing here?" she asked. "Are you on sabbatical?"

Iondra's diction was perfect. There was a slight hiss to her voice, like air was escaping between her sharp rows of teeth, which were a bit further apart than Voprot's. Otherwise, she was clearly intelligent and quite articulate.

"A story for another time," Krezek explained. "I'd like you to meet my new friends."

He introduced all of them except for Denk and Voprot, who were still plastered to the glass. The carcass of some hooved creature Geddy didn't recognize hit the surface with a splash and slowly sank, leaving a trail of cloudy water behind it. The mogorodon swung its giant head away from the window, jetted across in a blink, and consumed it in two clean bites, earning a volley of gasps and cheers.

The commotion prompted Iondra to glance in that direction, and she did a double take. Voprot turned around wearing a big, silly grin that fell the moment he locked eyes with her.

The rest of the crowd moved on through the other end of the viewing area, seemingly oblivious to the laser-like connection between the two Kiganteans.

— *Now this is a pleasant surprise.*

— I'm a little uncomfortable.

Denk's eyes darted back and forth between the two of them. Neither had spoken. "Whoa, Lady Voprot! Do you guys know each other?"

Voprot had frozen in place, his clawed fingers splayed and his mouth half open.

Iondra took a couple steps forward and nervously extended her hand. "Why, hello there. I'm Iondra. What's your name?"

Rather than take her hand, Voprot puffed out the sacs in his neck, formed his hands into claws, and made his arms into L shapes over his head. His pupils narrowed to slits as his eyes rolled back, and he splayed his legs wide. Iondra's head gave a quizzical tilt, and she withdrew her hand, taking a step back.

"Oh, okay ..."

Voprot began tottering back and forth from one leg to the other, maintaining the distance between his legs like a caricature of a court jester. All the while, he huffed out staccato, guttural grunts in a repeating rhythm, turning himself in a slow circle as mothers hurried their children toward the exit.

— What the hell is happening?

— *He appears to be in some kind of trance.*

Thinking back to the Champion's Party on Thegus,

Voprot had entered a similar state while doing his version of a dance. This seemed different. Instinctive.

Iondra took another step back. Raising a hand to her chest, she gave an embarrassed laugh as passers-by cleared out, their faces registering alarm. "It's okay, everyone ... I think."

"Cap, what's he doing?" Denk asked.

"The tarantella, maybe?"

Doc sidled excitedly up to Geddy and whispered, "We may well be the first people in more than a century to witness a Kigantean mating dance."

"Mating? They only just met."

"Sometimes, the heart just knows." Doc's eyes sparked with wonder.

Since no one else was willing to break this weird spell, and Iondra was officially mortified, Geddy jumped in and grabbed Voprot's arm. "Hey!"

Voprot stopped, his pupils returning to normal size. He regarded the quizzical stares around him before his eyes focused on Geddy.

"What happened?" Voprot asked.

"You, uh ... kinda ... went away." He had no idea what to say.

Iondra came to the rescue, her expression brightening. "You had a moment of reverie."

"You are ... Kigantean." Voprot stated the obvious.

"I was adopted and raised on Afolos. I've never set foot on Kigantu. Is it beautiful?"

Geddy coughed to cover his convulsive laughter.

"It beautiful like you," Voprot said. Iondra gave an embarrassed smile and looked away.

She took Voprot's arm and guided him away from the viewing window so the next batch of people could move in. "Let's get you some fresh air."

"How do you guys know each other?" Oz asked her.

"I was one of Dr. Krezek's lab assistants." She turned to Krezek and asked, "How long has it been? Seven years?"

"At least," Krezek said. "Oh, I'm just delighted to see you, my dear. I thought you were still at the wildlife sanctuary on Dudira."

"I was, but the Xoo lured me away."

"A better opportunity?" Krezek asked.

"Assistant director of donor relations." Her tone carried a note of embarrassment, and she shrugged. "It gets my foot in the door."

"Well, good for you, my dear. Good for you, indeed."

Meanwhile, Voprot still seemed dazed. Geddy had seen this look before on Xellara when he was seduced by a Nurithean. It was easy to forget it was still a teenager.

"Well, listen, I've got some time," Iondra said. "Could I interest you all in a private tour?"

"We'd love that," Oz said.

"Great! Follow me." She turned to leave but hesitated, concerned about Voprot's state. "Is he okay?"

"Depends who you ask," Geddy said, throwing a wink at Oz. They continued out of the viewing area through a tunnel that ran beneath the terrace. "So, how long have you worked here?"

"Almost two years," she said.

"Do you happen to know if the mogorodon tank was part of the old terraforming facility?"

She cocked her head quizzically. "You know, I'm not actually sure. It took a long time to construct, that's for sure."

The tunnel curved left and climbed, and they emerged on the opposite side of the terrace. Wayfinding signs pointed to various areas of the park, which had fanciful, alliterative names like Bird Boulevard and Reptile Row.

"How do you all know Dr. Krezek?" Iondra asked.

"He ... consulted on a recent mission in Durandia. I guess he enjoys our company."

She heaved a sigh. "Must be nice, traveling the galaxy with your friends."

It was such a simple way to put it, yet so resonant. Geddy smiled back. "Y'know, it really is. Hey, sorry about Voprot back there. He hasn't seen another of his kind in a long time."

"It was charming in a way," she said demurely. She clapped her hands together and addressed the group. "Who's ready for a trip down Herbivore Highway?"

CHAPTER THIRTY-FOUR

WETWORLD

Iondra's tour of the Xoo was far more enjoyable than Geddy expected. He wasn't keen on alien creatures, especially the ones that wanted to kill, bite, or lay eggs in him, but the stout enclosures put him largely at ease. Her encyclopedic knowledge of, and enthusiasm for her work impressed even Doc.

Some particularly biodiverse worlds, like Temeruria and Ecke, had their own sections. Otherwise, it was roughly organized by ecosystem — rivers, mountains, arboreal forests, plains, and so forth. Some animals had shrunk into hidden corners of their enclosures as though terrified of being seen while others seemed to enjoy the attention.

Given the Xoo's obvious popularity, it was difficult to imagine why a secret Zelnad breeding facility would be anywhere nearby. The mountains that interested Verveik were plainly visible from most areas of the park. It just didn't strike him as a likely location for anything nefarious. The terraforming facility, on the other hand, kept popping into his mind.

Denk and Voprot stopped at every little food stand along the wide path and bought at least one of whatever they were selling. Nurdo rings. Balefna fluff cones. They boasted that nothing was made from animals or animal products, which seemed considerate.

It took almost six hours just to make it around the lagoon and back to where they started in front of the Visitor Center. Iondra said they should save the best for last, meaning WetWorld. Everyone besides Denk and Voprot was feeling peckish by then, so they stopped at the cafeteria for some lunch before heading back out.

The lagoon path gently descended as it curled toward the water. As soon as they passed the concrete retaining wall, it became a clear tunnel that afforded a 360-degree view of the water as it wound down like a hollow glass snake.

The lagoon teemed with aquatic life so dense in places that it filled Geddy's entire field of vision. All manner of fish, eels, and jellies swam or drifted by while crustaceans and bottom-feeding critters crawled through a technicolor coral forest. Along the way, animated placards described the seem-ingly infinite variety of species. Sunlight danced on the silvery surface well above them, beams piercing the water like an otherworldly mirror ball.

Earth 2 had an artificial lagoon as well. A couple of oper-ators ran submarine tours out of Laguna Luxe mall back in the day, but that wasn't something Geddy would've done in a million years. He'd seen nature documentaries here and there, but otherwise, his entire existence was on land or in space. Oceans and lakes were just blue geographic features, and he rarely gave a single thought to the life they supported.

But being underwater with them filled him with unexpected awe.

"You're looking at the largest curated collection of aquatic life in the galaxy," Iondra said. "It's also the largest artificial lake by volume, with five point eight *billion* liters of water. A state-of-the-art filtration system keeps it clean, and sensors throughout the lagoon maintain the appropriate salinity."

Iondra had an engaging style that drew people to her. Before long, taggers-along had joined the crew to listen to her erudition. All the while, however, Voprot had remained at the back of their group, barely making eye contact with anyone.

— *You should talk to him.*

— About what?

— *You know about what.*

— Ugh. Do I have to?

— *He is still a teenager.*

— At best.

— *Were you not awkward as a teenager?*

— Guess I was too busy picking tourists' pockets to notice.

As they wound their way deeper, Geddy dropped back to walk beside Voprot.

"You okay there, pal?"

"Voprot fine. How are you?"

"Iondra really knows her stuff, huh?"

"Yes," he said stiffly, staring at the floor.

"You like her, don't you?"

"Yes."

"Sorry your mating dance didn't work."

He hesitated before answering. "Voprot not understand what happen. Voprot not really expect to mate with her."

"Okay, then what's the problem?" Geddy asked.

"She smart. Voprot not."

Rather than argue that point, Geddy chose a different tack. "So, you complement each other. That's a good thing. You should talk to her."

"Voprot not know what to say."

"Know any poetry?" His eyes widened with panic. "Just kidding. You managed to charm that Nurithean babe back on Xellara. The one you were in love with?"

"That not need talking."

"Fair enough. But a girl like Iondra isn't gonna fall for some mating dance or ... y'know ... eat your molted skin."

"She not?"

He shook his head. "Not without getting to know you first. A girl like her responds to character. Authenticity. Just be yourself. If it's meant to be, it's meant to be."

The big lizard grinned. "Geddy always have Voprot's back."

Geddy managed a weak smile through his guilt. He hadn't been very nice to Voprot, but the big guy remained stalwart.

— *You give good advice. Why do you make such bad decisions?*

— Personal branding.

As the see-through tunnel continued downward, the outline of the underwater dome appeared through the faintly cloudy water. It stood perhaps twenty meters tall and twice as wide, and Xoo patrons could be discerned through its clear wall. It reminded Geddy very much of the Bubbles back on Earth 3, though it wasn't nearly so large.

Iondra turned and smiled as she walked backwards, delivering her shpiel with practiced ease. "You're looking at the WetWorld Exploration Center. Not only does it afford guests an unbeatable view of our underwater habitat, but it's also frequently rented out for parties. In fact, the annual Patron Appreciation Gala is being held there tonight."

Eventually, the tunnel reached the bottom of the lagoon and widened as they entered the dome. It was even larger than it first appeared. If the dome had seams anywhere, they were invisible. A circular gift shop section stood at the center, and interactive displays were sprinkled around the perimeter. A group of workers were erecting a small stage along the far edge.

Its cost had to be staggering. No wonder they had so many patrons.

Iondra gestured grandly about her. "Welcome to the WWEC."

A placard affixed to the wall near the entrance highlighted the dome's major donors. Perched at the top, in bigger letters than the rest, was THE SEMENOV FAMILY FOUNDATION.

Oz and Geddy exchanged a look. No wonder Verveik tapped Tatiana to look into Myadan. Ivan bankrolled a big chunk of the Xoo's main attraction through the foundation, which she now ran. That would give her access and influence. What had she learned already?

The rest of the crew wandered off in awe to investigate the displays. Geddy and Oz remained near Iondra. He surreptitiously checked the pheromone detector around his neck. Nothing.

"So, about this gala tonight," Geddy said, tucking the device back under his shirt. "Any chance Tatiana Semenov is on the guest list?"

Iondra seemed caught off-guard by the question. "You know Ms. Semenov?"

"Intimately," Oz answered for him.

"As it happens, she's being named to the Xoo board tonight."

Again, Oz's eyes met his. Tati's way of looking into Myadan was to worm her way inside the Xoo's upper echelon. Verveik said to leave her alone, but while she was politicking, the Zelnads were racing toward their endgame. He needed to talk to her.

"I don't suppose there's a chance we could get on that list?" he asked.

Iondra laughed at the notion. "Sorry, but it's exclusively for our biggest patrons and the board. Unless ..."

His ears perked up. "Unless?"

"Unless you happen to have a tuxedo and know how to tend bar."

A broad grin met his lips. "Iondra, this is your lucky day."

CHAPTER THIRTY-FIVE

PATRON-IZING

THE CREW'S day at the Xoo served its purpose, helping to release much of the tension that had formed since Nirnaya. Bypassing the most crowded parts of popular sections like Amphibian Alley helped them whiz through the exhibits. Voprot and Denk opted to stay until they closed at six. Everyone else headed back to the spaceport around four.

After showering in the private landing pad's awesome facilities, they ate a hearty dinner at the hangar bar and gathered around the table in the *Armstrong's* galley for some hard-earned Kailorian gin.

Geddy related his conversation with Iondra in the WWEC and that he'd arranged to tend bar to get in front of Tatiana without blowing her cover.

"Are you sure that's a good idea?" Doc asked. "If Zelnads have infiltrated the Xoo board, she's in a dangerous position."

"All the more reason for her to know about Krezek's pheromone, Durandia, and everything else. Maybe she's got an idea what's really going on here."

Verveik had ordered him to stay away from Myadan.

He'd left that small detail out when Oz cajoled him to come to the Xoo. Now that they were there, he had to try to speak with Tatiana. The more actionable intel they had, the better. Waiting was a luxury they couldn't afford.

"The pheromone detector ..." said Krezek. "Did it alert you at all today?"

Geddy removed the device from inside his shirt and held it up. It hadn't vibrated, and the little readout still said zero. "No, nothing."

"And Eli?" Doc asked. "Did he detect any Zelnads?"

Geddy sipped from his glass. "Nope. Of course, I didn't expect they'd be walking around the Xoo."

"Perhaps they aren't here after all," Krezek said.

It was possible, but Geddy felt in his bones that they were. Tati had to have information.

"This terraforming facility they talked about in the video ..." Geddy began. "It was pretty well-built, yeah?"

"Yes, almost like an army barracks. Home to engineers, equipment, supplies. A small city unto itself," Doc said. "I believe the original schematics were entered in the intergalactic archives for their historical merit. Why do you ask?"

"If it wasn't buried or demolished, would it still be usable?"

Doc nodded. "It would've been made of reinforced concrete and completely sealed off. I don't see why not."

"They're here. I fucking know it."

Oz checked her watch, stood, and gave Geddy's shoulder a mocking pat. "Time to suit up for your shift."

Geddy still had his very expensive tux from the IASS gala back on Xellara. The memory of strolling toward the convention center with Oz on his arm, both dressed to the nines, hit hard. What a weird and terrifyingly wonderful night that was.

He got up and finished his drink in one big swallow. "Listen, I don't know what to expect in there. Stay awake at least until you hear from me."

Oz yawned and stretched her arms, making a show of how tired she was. "Yeah, okay. We'll be right here on standby."

GEDDY TOOK a quick inventory of his banquet bar. It was a typical setup for this kind of event, with lots of premium liquor and a good wine selection.

This was how he and Tati first met. He took a side gig bartending for the express purpose of meeting rich, hot women. The company he worked for got tapped to cater an event in the Semenov's penthouse at the Laguna Luxe tower. Tati came up and ordered a martini, which he'd made well enough to keep her coming back for more.

It led to a very memorable night and a passionate, if highly dysfunctional relationship that only ended because she thought he was dead.

Iondra approached wearing something like a dress. Her long tail snaked out underneath the swishy orange material. She awkwardly smoothed the fabric as she walked.

"Wow, Iondra, you look incredible."

She rolled her eyes. "Ugh. I hate dressing up, but thank you. You don't look so bad yourself. I must admit, I was surprised you had a tuxedo."

"I was surprised it still fit," he joked.

"You got everything you need? Our regular bartender should be here within the hour."

"I'll manage, thanks."

She leaned in close. "Listen, if anyone knew I told you Miss Semenov was on the guest list ..."

"Don't worry," he assured her. "I won't get you in trouble."

Ten minutes later, the lights dimmed, and patrons began to arrive through the tube. The first several were single men who ordered drinks before wandering aimlessly around the crystal-clear walls. Several species were bioluminescent, giving the appearance of organic vessels moving through space. Not unlike the Zelnad research vessel they'd dropped in the Kigantean desert.

Tati came in about thirty minutes later wearing a surprisingly tasteful gold dress that nearly matched her hair. It clung to her sinuous physique, as all her dresses did, but it went past her knees, which was almost unheard of.

She exchanged pleasantries with some of the other patrons as she came in. By then, pretty much everyone had a drink in their hand, and the string ensemble on stage was humming away.

Geddy gave her his most shit-eating grin. "Hiya Tots. Extra dry martini?"

Tati's icy blue eyes popped wide, her face reddening with rage. "What the *fuck?!*"

He sighed and motioned her to calm down. "Take it down a notch! I'll explain. Lemme make you a drink."

She forced a bright smile as some Dudiran fat cat walked by, his eyes roaming up and down her body. Some part of her relished being gawked at, but it had to get old after a while.

"Every time I bat my eyelashes at these dopes, my soul dies a little," she said when he was out of earshot. "Now, what the hell are you doing here??"

He scooped ice into a martini glass and filled it with club soda. That made the glass colder. "Listen, something big's going down here. What have you found out?"

"That anyone with a family legacy, good looks, and a fifteen million credit gift can break the glass ceiling."

"Whoa, fifteen?" He dumped the ice mixture and poured in a bit of vermouth, swirling it around to coat the inside. One, two, three swirls. Dump.

"What do you *think* is going on?" she asked.

"We think the Zelnads are using the terraforming facility below the Xoo to breed deadly creatures," Geddy said, scooping more ice into a shaker before pouring in the gin. "I'm not leaving until I know what's down th–"

"Well, if it isn't the lady of the evening," said a tall Temerurian behind her, his tone cool and even.

— Interesting choice of words.

— *Zelnad alert!*

— I had a hunch.

Geddy gave the tin a light shake and listened as Tati's demeanor shifted back into schmooze mode.

"Mr. Chairman," she cooed. "Aren't you looking dapper?"

He half expected the guy to put his arm around her or remark on her figure, but he kept a respectful distance and only looked her in the eye. Definitely a Zelnad.

"Not nearly so much as you, Ms. Semenov."

Tati's thin smile only lasted a second. The pheromone sensor around Geddy's neck pulsed rhythmically. As the two of them made small talk, he turned sideways long enough to sneak a look at the tiny readout. Fifty-six parts per million. It hadn't registered anything all day.

He tucked it back inside his shirt and turned to face them, then poured Tati's martini into the chilled glass.

"Have you seen the tank we built for your pet? I understand he's quite the hit," he said.

Tatiana swallowed and looked away. "I'll be sure to stop by."

— *That can't be her mogorodon, can it?*

On seeing the creature, Geddy had dismissed the idea it might be the one from her aquarium. Then again, it had seemed to recognize him. Donating it must have been part of her deal to get on the board.

Geddy slid her drink across the bar. "Your martini, Miss. Extra dry." He pointed at the Temerurian. "Anything for you, Sir?"

"No, thank you." He barely glanced in Geddy's direction, then did a double take. His eyes lingered for an uncomfortably long moment.

— *Uh-oh. Is the bracelet not working?*

— No, I trust Jel. He recognizes me.

— *From where?*

— No idea.

The gentleman merely smiled and shook his head. "I ... just came to let Miss Semenov know I will see her at dinner."

"You're not staying?" she asked, taking her drink by the stem. Her nails had just been done.

"I've been called away," he said through a phony smile. "But please, enjoy the party."

"I always do," she said, flashing her brilliant white teeth.

He met Geddy's eyes and gave a tiny nod, then strode purposefully toward the tube that led up through the lagoon.

Tati dropped her smile and took a gulp of her martini. "Ugh. He gives me the creeps."

"Who was that?"

"Duke Marcourt. Chair of the Xoo board."

"Duke? As in ..."

"Temerurian royalty. He holds the lease to the tukrium mines."

If he was a royal, then he was part of Oz's extended family. Temeruria had become the Zelnads' go-to source of tukrium, which made the royals stupid rich. Now, it seemed the Zelnads had effectively joined their family.

"He's also a Zelnad," Geddy whispered.

"What?! For real?" Her eyes shot over to him as he receded. "How do you know?"

"Eli can sense it. Where's he going?"

"Hell if I know. Now look, I don't know what your deal is, but if you screw this up for me, I will ..."

Iondra had posted up near the entrance. Marcourt stopped to whisper something to her before continuing up the tube, alone.

"Are you listening to me??" Tatiana demanded, drawing his eyes back to her.

"Sorry, I've gotta go."

Her face pinched in confusion as he stepped out from behind the bar. "Oh. Well ... good."

"I'll stay out of your way," he said over his shoulder. "Congrats."

Iondra stepped away from the wall, frowning as Geddy approached. "Where do you think you're going?"

"I just need some fresh air." Marcourt disappeared as Geddy anxiously skirted around Iondra and started up the tube. "Cover for me."

"What are you talking about? You've still got fifteen minutes in your shift!"

But he was already racing up the tunnel. After a few seconds, he caught up to where he could just see a sliver of Marcourt's lower leg around the inside of the curve. The air grew cooler and fresher as he climbed, and when reached the edge of the lagoon, his head jerked from side to side looking for the duke. A flash of movement from between the palm trees caught his attention. Marcourt was heading back toward the Visitor Center.

Geddy stole down the empty walking path after him, passing two more late arrivals on their way to the WWEC. Instead of turning left toward the main entrance, Marcourt veered right toward the outer ring of exhibits. Just before the entrance to Bird Boulevard, he squeezed between a pair of shrubs and vanished once again.

As Geddy neared the spot, the soft chirping of birds was the only sound. He slipped through the shrubs and found a set of steps leading down to a concrete box, well hidden by vines, with a single door. It slid shut just as he spotted it. A closer look revealed a discreet security panel to the side.

— *Where do you think it goes?*

— It's gotta be the terraforming facility.

— *If so, Verveik is focused on the wrong area.*

— Yeah, but he's got enough on his plate. We're right here.

— *Geddy* ...

He lifted his arm and opened a channel back to the *Armstrong*.

"Oz, you copy?"

A few seconds passed. "Hey Ged, it's Jel. Everyone's asleep. How's it going?"

"Wake them up and meet me at the Xoo entrance. I think I just found our breeding facility."

CHAPTER THIRTY-SIX

WHAT EXHIBIT IS THIS?

GEDDY STEPPED out from between the shrubs when he came face to face with Iondra, her big arms crossed defiantly.

Shit.

"What do you think you're doing?" she asked.

She didn't know anything about anything, but if he was going to get the crew inside the park after hours, he'd need her help.

"Iondra, there's a lot you don't know."

She looked past him and squinted. "What's back there?"

"A door."

"What? What door?" She brushed past him and pushed between the shrubs, stopping abruptly on the other side. "Oh, my! *That* door."

He came up beside her. "I think it goes into the terraforming facility."

"What makes you think that?"

"Duke Marcourt's a Zelnad, and I have reason to believe the Zelnads are using the facility as a base of operations. I followed him here. He just went through that door."

Iondra's eyelashes fluttered, and she shook her head. "Duke Marcourt is a Temerurian royal. He's been board president for–"

"Yeah, yeah, I know. But he's gone. A Zelnad has taken over his consciousness."

"A Zelnad ... what?"

"Look, you shouldn't be involved with this. I just need to get my friends inside, then you can go back to your party."

Her expression hardened. "Who are you, really? Where's Dr. Krezek?" She searched around as though he might suddenly appear, but they were very much alone.

"Iondra, we believe the Zelnads are using the terraforming facility to breed deadly creatures. Right under our feet, right now."

She reflexively glanced down. "Deadly creatures? What're you talking about? The Zelnads are, like, heroes."

Geddy lips pressed together, and he shook his head. "In fact, they're an ancient race bent on destroying civilization. We're trying to stop them, and we need your help."

She paused. "You do know how crazy that sounds, right?"

Geddy nodded. "My crew is on their way from the spaceport. We need to get through that door."

Something seemed to click into place. "Well ... I have heard strange noises late at night recently. Only on the lower levels, and only faintly, but ..."

"What kind of noises?"

"Sometimes like a motor. Other times more like an animal."

"All the more reason to check it out."

An inner conflict played across her face. "But the patrons ..."

"Once my crew's inside, you can head straight back. The patrons won't know a thing."

Her eyes drifted down to the steps. "Y'know, I never should've taken this stupid job. I'm a damn biochemist, not some glorified party planner. I just wanted 'Myadan Xoo' on my resume." She swung her giant head up to the stars, her eyes glassy. "What kind of scientist sells herself out to get ahead?"

Geddy gave an encouraging smile. "You took the wrong job for the wrong reasons. It happens." Turning more serious, he said, "But if we don't stop the Zelnads, there won't be jobs anymore. There won't be any ... anything. Please."

As many other poor souls had done, she searched his eyes for any sign he might be pulling her leg. Finding nothing, she said, "Screw it. I'm coming with you."

"What??"

— Well, that was unexpected.

— *Your pitch is getting tighter.*

— Do you really think so?

— *I would quit my job, too.*

She turned on her heels and marched away. "There's a service entrance on the west side of the building," she called over her shoulder. "Tell your crew to be there in half an hour."

She went back through the shrubs. Geddy called after her, "Wait — where are you going?"

"To lose this ridiculous outfit."

THE SERVICE ENTRANCE was only manned during daylight hours and wasn't visible from the main entrance due to the landscaping. Iondra said she received deliveries all the time and had the credentials required to open it. Geddy had just heard from Oz that they were waiting outside.

She activated the motor, and a section of the high wall around the Xoo slid aside to reveal Denk, Voprot, Jeledine with Hughey, and Oz with Morpho on her shoulder. As soon as they were close, Morpho hopped over to Geddy's left shoulder, his favorite spot.

"Dr. Krezek?" Iondra asked hopefully.

"He and Doc Tardigan are running ops from the ship. They tracked down the original schematics for the terraforming facility."

"What's that?" she asked Geddy, staring at the black blob on his shoulder.

"Morpho, meet Iondra. Iondra, Morpho. He's a synthetic organism whose hobbies include saving my life."

Morpho gave his customary salute.

"Nice to meet you, Morpho," Iondra said, then noticed Hughey floating just off the ground beside Jel. "And who might this be?"

Jel said, "That's Hughey Twoey, my shifter bot. I see what he sees." She pointed at her left eye, which bore the faint glow of the special contact lens.

"Thanks for helping us, Iondra," added Denk. "This probably seems kinda weird, but you can trust us."

Iondra pressed the button to close the entrance behind them. Once the door locked into place, she studied them a moment, her eyes lingering on their weapons.

"You're ... armed."

"We frequently resort to violence," Geddy said. "If it makes you uncomfortable, you should—"

"Should I have one?"

"No," Oz said firmly. "We'll take it from here."

"Actually ..." Geddy began, "... Iondra will be joining us."

Oz blinked. "She what?"

"I won't get in the way, I promise," Iondra said. "I might even be useful."

The look on Oz's face indicated her discomfort.

"I told her what's going on," Geddy explained. "She's heard noises."

"Voprot keep her safe," the big lizard said, stepping forward. Iondra met his eyes and smiled.

"See? Nothing to worry about," Geddy said to Oz, though it was clear she still didn't like the idea.

"Before we get too carried away ..." Jel removed a small hard case from her cargo pocket and cracked it open to reveal her signature long-range earpieces. "Clearest comms in the galaxy, right here. Insane range, and they mold to your ears."

Everyone reached in and took an earpiece out of the case.

"You want to be heard over the network, just hold your hand close to your ear, like this." She demonstrated, cupping her right hand over her ear. "Testing one, two ..."

"I've gotcha loud and clear!" Denk said. The others nodded.

Oz adjusted her scabbard harness and handed Geddy his PDQ still in the holster, which she'd brought from the ship. "For the record, I think this is a bad idea."

"I have a lot of those," Geddy said.

Geddy fastened the holster around his waist, appreciating the contrast between the tux and the weapon.

"You're seriously wearing that?" She regarded his outfit doubtfully.

He shrugged. "We're just poking our heads in, right? I already took off the bowtie."

Oz rolled her eyes and shook her head. Geddy led them through the heavily treed landscaping around the Visitor Center. They were about to step onto the path near the secret door when Iondra stopped them.

"Wait — the patrons are moving into the banquet room."

She pointed down the path back toward the lagoon. Sure enough, people were leaving the tunnel and meandering toward the Visitor Center for dinner. But it was pretty far away, and none were looking in their direction.

"It's fine," Geddy said. "Let's go."

He s led the others through the shrubs and down the steps to the concrete housing that framed the door.

"This is where Marcourt went." He gestured at the security panel beside it and turned to Jel. "Think you can bypass it?"

Jel brushed past him to inspect the panel, running her fingers over its smooth black surface. "Uf ... I've never seen one like this before. Looks like Zelnad tech."

— *Put your hand on it.*

— Huh? Why?

— *Just try.*

"Hang on ... Eli wants me to try something," Geddy said, reaching past Jel. He pressed his hand to the panel. It turned green, and the door slid aside, revealing a dark stairwell leading down. "Whoa."

"How did you do that?" Jel demanded.

He was about to say he had no idea when a memory hit him.

Back on Verdithea, where Verveik was hiding, they met a Kailorian scientist named Dennimore. He'd developed a device to detect the so-called Zelnad harmonic, a unique electromagnetic signature that could identify friend from foe. But Zelnads and Sagaceans like Eli had the same harmonic, so when Dennimore scanned him, he set the thing off. Convincing Verveik he wasn't a Zelnad took some careful explanation.

"The harmonic," Oz said behind him, having realized the same thing.

"Who's Eli?" Iondra repeated.

"He's a microscopic alien who lives in Cap's head," Denk explained matter-of-factly.

"I might've omitted a few details," Geddy said to Iondra. "The point is, Eli's not a Zelnad. He's a Sagacean. Sagaceans good. Zelnads bad."

"Um ... okay ..."

"It's not too late to change your mind," Oz reminded her, but Iondra's expression only displayed determination.

"All right, Hughey, recon time," Jel said, and Hughey floated silently into the darkness. A minute later, Jel said, "Looks like we've got a long hallway ... and another security door."

"That's it?" Geddy asked. "Can Hughey get past the door?"

"Hughey, see if you can get around it." A minute passed, and Jel shook her head. "No dice. It's sealed tight."

"No opening's too tight for me," Geddy announced, and winked at Oz before descending the steps.

Behind him, Jel heaved a sigh. "Walked right into that one."

"See what I have to deal with?" Oz asked.

CHAPTER THIRTY-SEVEN

SO IT BEGINS

GEDDY STOOD in front of the vault-like door at the end of the nondescript hallway but hesitated to press his hand to the panel. The tactical situation sucked. They were basically stacked single-file in a confined space with no idea what might be on the other side of the door. For all they knew, a Zelnad security team would be waiting to grease them the moment it opened.

— *Could there be another way in?*

— Maybe, but this is the way we're going.

— *What does the pheromone detector say?*

Geddy consulted the device around his neck. It read just twelve parts per million.

"I'm still detecting a bit of the pheromone," he said, leaving it hanging outside his shirt this time. "Probably residual from Marcourt passing through."

"Marcourt?" Oz asked warily. "As in, Duke Reni Marcourt?"

"You know him?" inquired Iondra.

"He's my cousin. And, apparently, a Zelnad? Ugh... as if I needed another reason to hate my family."

Iondra gasped. "Your cousin? Wouldn't that make you—"

"A royal, yes." Oz let out an exasperated sigh, refusing to entertain any further questions regarding her royal lineage. "Geddy, are you gonna open the door or just knock?"

Geddy took a deep breath and unholstered the PDQ. "All right. Be ready for anything. You, especially, Morph."

Morpho could absorb and dissipate the energy from blaster bolts and had shielded Geddy in the past. Hopefully it wouldn't be necessary here.

— Anything detected on the other side?

— *No, nothing. But these walls look thick.*

He put his hand to the panel, and the door slid open. As it did, Iondra gasped. Her hand clasped Voprot's wrist. He leaned forward, assuming a fighting stance as he bared his jagged teeth, his lips curling into a tittering snarl. Every muscle in the Kigantean's body tensed like cables, standing out beneath his scaly skin.

"What?" Geddy asked. "What's wrong?"

The lizard's prodigious tongue flicked in the air. "Voprot ... er ... *I* smell ranses."

"Ranses?" Iondra asked. "I don't understand. It was like a jolt of electricity through my whole body."

"Ranses enemies of Kiganteans," Voprot affirmed.

"But I've never even seen one in real life."

"Instincts powerful."

Kiganteans had dealt with ranses for millennia before Aquebba was settled. They were the only ones who knew how to survive in the unforgiving desert and its fearsome, nearly indestructible predators.

They'd entered near the ceiling of a colossal warehouse that opened below where they stood, still deeper underground. It had been turned into a desert habitat. Pale sand covered the entire floor, dotted with columns of black volcanic rock, scrub brush, and cacti.

It bore a disturbing resemblance to Kigantu.

"Looks abandoned," Oz observed.

Geddy turned the pheromone detector over in his fingers and checked the reading. It had risen to almost eighty parts per million. The pheromone was down here somewhere, and they were getting closer to its source.

Doc's voice spoke in his ear like he was standing there with them. "Hello, Captain. Do you read me? I have your position. What are you seeing?"

He cupped his hand over his ear. "Yeah, I read you. We came in through a long hallway, and now we're in some giant warehouse. Looks like they've converted it into a ranse habitat."

"Ah, yes, okay. According to the schematic, that room was once used to store labrozite, a high explosive used for excavations. That explains why it is set apart from the rest of the facility."

Labrozite had been used to excavate the geothermal tunnels back on Earth 2. It was also what Geddy had used to find enough shinium to build his ship — and to release the flood of methane that eventually forced the planet's evacuation.

"What's on the other side?"

"Another hallway to the right."

Krezek's voice interrupted. "What about the pheromone?"

"Eighty PPM," Geddy said. "The doors on these rooms are sealed tight, but I think we're on the right track."

"Please watch your levels and be prepared to inject your blockers. The pheromone is quite fast acting."

Geddy turned to check with the others, who all nodded. All except Iondra.

"Pheromone blocker?" she asked.

"Oh, right, I almost forgot." Jel dug into her jacket pocket and produced one of the larger autoinjectors and held it out for Iondra. "Krezek made you one, too. Just in case."

"Why?" she asked hesitantly.

Krezek helpfully replied. "The Zelnads forced me to make an ultra-powerful pheromone to compel fast reproduction. It's imperative that you protect yourself from its effects."

She hesitantly took the tube and tucked it into her vest pocket. "Sex pheromone ... Is this going to keep getting weirder?"

"Most likely," Geddy said.

An elevated walkway with waist-high rails spanned its width, ending in another door ten or twelve meters up. A small structure was set off to the side of the walkway that Geddy judged to be a lab or observation room. It merely confirmed what he already suspected. The Nads wanted ranses for the same reason they wanted crypsids and mogorodons — to sweep across planets and eliminate the dominant species, whatever it was. So why was no one there?

"Why don't any of you seem very surprised?" Iondra asked.

"A while back, we found a derelict Xellaran ship bound for Myadan," Geddy explained. "It was transporting ranses. Didn't work out so hot for them."

"Or Captain Bykite," Denk correctly noted, referring to his former captain.

"Looks like an abandoned testing facility," Geddy said, venturing inside. "Let's check it out. Jel, make sure we get all this documented."

"Yep, on it," she replied. Hughey, who had re-formed beside Jel, took off to explore the space.

"Check it out??" Iondra regarded him like he was insane. "Shouldn't we get ... I don't know ... backup or something?"

"Where's the fun in that?" Geddy asked.

The sand below remained inert as they crossed the walkway. A large, rust-colored shape stained the sand below like an inkblot. Geddy recognized it immediately, and he could see Voprot did, too.

"W-what's that?" Denk said, pointing at it.

"The equivalent of a ranse dirty plate," Geddy said.

Denk's mouth dropped open, and he stuttered, "What do they eat?"

Geddy and Voprot replied in unison. "Everything."

RANSES DIDN'T ANNOUNCE THEMSELVES, which made them especially terrifying. On his first day in Aquebba, an old space pirate described how they hunted. They'd lie still in the sand two or three meters below the surface, sensing tiny vibrations or changes in density that indicated someone was walking or standing above them. They'd attack from directly underneath, launching straight up out of the sand with such force that they could "cleave a man in half."

"Where is everybody?" Jel whispered.

"Maybe they went union," Geddy quipped.

The group crossed the walkway to the small observation room. Geddy entered and looked around. Two vacant terminals with dormant holoscreens were dark, their corresponding chairs pushed under the built-in desk. Apart from that, there was a small refrigerator and a pair of empty hooks mounted on the wall. Voprot and Iondra remained outside, both still visibly on edge.

Oz came in behind him. "Not much for decorating."

"Jel, I don't suppose you can get into their systems," Geddy said.

"I can try. No promises."

Jel pulled out a chair, sat down at a terminal, and touched the holoscreen. As soon as she did, another Zelnad-detecting security pad opened in the desk. She turned around and looked expectantly up at him.

Geddy pressed his hand to it. It sank back into the desk and the screen lit up with an interface.

"Bingo," Jel said, her fingers tapping and moving panels around on the screen. "Let's see ... we've got like a million readings here. Temperature, humidity, density ..."

"Can you tell what this place is?"

She swiped past a couple screens and landed on one detailing ranse biology. There were diagrams of ranses from different angles, measurements, and blood chemistry. Jel scrolled up, the panels of data seemingly endless.

"Studying ranses, I guess. I don't really know what I'm looking at."

"Maybe I can help." Iondra came in through the door at a low crouch. Oz stepped back to make room for her.

"I thought you didn't know much about ranses," Geddy said.

"No, but maybe I can make sense of the data." Her eyes narrowed as she studied the screen. "May I?" Jel pushed her chair aside while Iondra's dulled, painted claws swiped through the data. She stopped at a long table. "Interesting ..."

"What is it?"

She pointed at the table. "These are destruction dates. There are twenty-five, maybe thirty subjects. And look ... these physical measurements increase with each record. Length. Girth. Bite strength. Scale thickness."

"What's that mean?" Jel asked.

Iondra pulled away from the screen to meet their eyes. "I can't be sure, but I think someone's been trying to build a bigger and better ranse."

An invisible hand squeezed Geddy's heart. An ordinary ranse could turn a caravan into a constellation of bloodstains in minutes. He didn't want to find out what an engineered super-ranse could do.

— *Did they perfect the ultimate killing machine?*

— Or did they move on to something even deadlier?

Geddy gulped. "Let's keep moving."

Jel flicked off the holoscreen. "Hughey, we're heading out."

Geddy, Jel, and Iondra joined Oz, Denk, and Voprot on the walkway and headed toward the door on the opposite side about thirty meters away. Halfway there, red lights along the walkway and over the door began to flash.

"W-what's happening? What do these lights mean?" Panic filled Denk's saucer-sized eyes.

Before anyone could reply, a chunky, motorized sound came from below them along the far wall.

"What was that?" Oz asked.

At ground level, a door slid open, and a mechanism shoved a plump ruminant creature inside the habitat. The motor re-engaged, and the door closed behind it. The poor animal gave a loud, mournful bray that echoed through the cavernous room.

"Feeding time." Geddy took off toward the door. "Run."

The terrified beast shuffled through the sand, sniffing warily as brayed in fear. It wandered directly under the walkway.

Ten meters short of the door, Oz whapped Geddy on the back. "Stop."

He turned back to find Voprot and Iondra facing the opposite direction. Voprot's lips curled back, his razor-sharp teeth bared. He chuffed as he stared down. Iondra pressed close to him, a similar expression on her face.

Geddy's finger tensed on the PDQ's trigger a moment before the sand under them exploded.

An average ranse was about as long as a man was tall, with dense bones and scales that rivaled metal. They bore a passing resemblance to centipedes. Every feature, especially its rock-hard, bullet-shaped head, was made to slice through the sand like a knife. Its speed through the sand was unmatched.

The one that took the creature was at least six or seven meters long. The blistering ferocity of the attack propelled it right through the hapless creature like a blood bag and into the underside of the metal walkway. It wrenched violently to the left, and Geddy's feet left the ground as his fingers fruitlessly sought the railing. Morpho, caught entirely off-guard, couldn't stop them from falling.

The mega-ranse, a glistening red instrument of death, screeched and recoiled from the impact before plunging back into the sand as quickly as it had come.

Geddy landed flat on his back, the sand providing little cushioning as the impact forced the air from his lungs. Gasping, his eyes focused on the twisted walkway above. It had been wrenched nearly ninety degrees by the impact and dumped every last one of them onto the sand.

"Do not move!" ordered Voprot.

— *Geddy, are you okay?*

— Meh. I hardly ever use my lungs anyway.

He pushed himself to a sitting position, still gasping for air.

— *Then get up!*

Geddy's head lolled to the side. Voprot and Iondra were already on their feet. Jel was curled into a ball on her side, spitting out sand and coughing violently. Oz was on one knee, blades drawn. The remains of the butchered animal were just a couple meters away. It looked like it had swallowed a bomb.

"Everyone okay?" Oz did a quick visual check of the crew. "Ged?"

"I'm good. Hey, Morph ..." Geddy croaked. "Find us a way out of here." Morpho jumped from his shoulder, skittered across the sand until he could stick a tendril to the wall, and inspected the door through which the animal had emerged.

"Ohmystars, ohmystars ..." muttered Iondra, sounding as though she might hyperventilate.

Geddy shakily stood at the same time as Jel their blasters pointed at the ground.

Voprot's nostrils flared as he sniffed the air. "Voprot ... er, *I* draw ranses away. Run to rock when I say."

A relatively flat piece of black volcanic rock jutted out of the sand about fifteen meters away. Under the circumstances, it might as well have been on another planet.

Geddy opened his mouth to protest, but this was Voprot's realm. "You heard the lizard. Everyone, get ready to run when he says."

"Trust Voprot," the big lizard said. He splayed his claws, fell to all fours, and took off across the sand in the opposite direction.

CHAPTER THIRTY-EIGHT

RANSE WITH THE DEVIL

Voprot darted so lightly across the sand he barely left prints, not unlike Morpho back in the myre on Durandia. He stopped about twenty meters away, and with a flick of his wrist, his electric whip unfurled, settling into an S shape behind him. He widened his stance and raised his right leg high into the air, then brought it down like a pile driver.

Geddy felt the impact through his feet.

"Go now!" Voprot hissed.

Everyone bolted for the rock. Iondra and Oz reached it first, easily bounding up to the top. Oz immediately spun to help Jel and Denk up.

As Geddy planted his left foot to jump, the ground beneath him seemed to thrust upward and collapse at the same time. Several sets of hands grabbed his jacket and yanked him up as the gigantic ranse's toothy maw snapped at the air where he'd just been. Oz and the others hoisted him the rest of the way onto the rock, and he whirled in time to see it plunge back into the sand in a puff of dust.

He clambered to his feet, his heart thudding in his chest. "Phew, that was close."

"You okay Cap?" Denk asked.

Voprot stomped on the sand again, harder this time. He fell into a low crouch, his legs splayed, his claws lightly brushing the sand. A moment later, he flipped backwards and barely avoiding a geyser of sand that erupted where he'd been standing. The glowing blue whip flashed through the sand cloud and wrapped around the middle of the outstretched ranse before it could clear the sand.

Voprot gave the whip a mighty yank. A twinge of disappointment settled on Geddy as nothing happened. But then the two halves of the ranse fell heavily into the sand on either side of him, and his prodigious tongue tasted the air.

Undaunted, the head half hissed and slithered at him. Geddy took careful aim from where he stood and turned it to ash, then dispatched the tail section for good measure.

As Voprot prepared his whip again, a second one burst through the sand directly behind him and lunged at his back. But Voprot was directly between Geddy and the ranse, making a shot impossible.

"Behind you, V!" Denk cried to his best friend.

Voprot spun too late. The ranse opened its huge mandibles wide enough to swallow him. Tumbling backwards, Voprot held its mouth open just inches from his face, its full weight on top of him as he grunted with effort.

Geddy and Oz leapt from the rock. Oz bolted across the sand, her glowing blades slicing through the air as her arms pumped. Voprot growled as he struggled to hold the ranse's head back. Oz gave a fierce battle cry as she ran up the ranse's back and buried her blades in its neck. It wrenched violently, ripping the blades from her hands.

Before it could make another move, Geddy unleashed a bolt into its thrashing face. It fell to the sand as cinders.

"Hughey, help Morpho with the door!" Jel shouted from the rock.

Geddy whirled. The door through which the cow-like animal had come stood partly open. Morpho had wrapped himself around the edge, but strained to hold it open against the motor. Hughey descended from overhead like a tiny metallic flock of starlings and flowed through the gap between the door and the wall to disable it.

Voprot had initially drawn the ranses away, but now all three of them were out in the open on the far side of the twisted walkway. Jel, Denk, and Iondra were still on the rock. They both had a good twenty meters to cover to reach the door.

Voprot kipped to his feet and snaked the whip back behind him while Oz retrieve her blades. They'd been blasted five meters apart by Geddy's kill shot. An eerie silence descended over them.

"How many more??" Geddy asked.

"Voprot think two!" Voprot replied.

A burning smell accompanied an electric sizzle from the direction of the door. A puff of white smoke indicated that Hughey had successfully fried the motor. Morpho's elastic body snapped back like a rubber band, and the door slid fully open.

"Everyone get ready to run to the door!" Geddy said. "I'm gonna draw them—"

Before he could finish the sentence, Iondra leapt from the rock and ran in the opposite direction.

— What the hell's she doing?!

— *Same as Voprot did!*

"Iondra, no!" Voprot bellowed.

She hadn't taken three steps before the sand boiled under her feet. Though the ranse's jaws missed her leg, the upward force sent her tumbling ass over teakettle. She landed half on one shoulder and half on her neck, which bent grotesquely to the side. Geddy gasped as she lay unmoving.

But the attack seemed to awaken something deep within her. Something primal.

She rolled sideways and popped to her feet, legs spread wide like Voprot, her claws flashing in the air. She hissed and slammed her foot down like a piledriver.

This was their shot. "Go! Go! Go!" Geddy yelled, motioning toward the door.

Jel and Denk leapt from the rock and bolted for the door, sand kicking up behind their heels. Oz covered the distance in a flash, just beating them there.

But a jolt of adrenaline sent Geddy racing toward Iondra instead. His feet struggled for purchase in the sand like he was running underwater. He leveled the PDQ at the ground near her feet, hoping he'd have a shot when the ranse struck. Instead, it burst up right behind her and reared back like a cobra about to strike.

He didn't have a shot.

"Iondra, watch out!" Denk cried from the door.

She whirled. The ranse's insectoid jaws snapped at her back. Just before impact, a blaster shot rang out, and its head jerked back, smoking.

Denk stood fast just outside the door, his blaster leveled. But it wasn't half as powerful as the PDQ, and he'd only managed to piss it off. Iondra scampered away as Denk kept firing. Every shot sent the thing reeling back, but it didn't die.

"Go, Iondra!"

She bolted for the door, opening a few meters in between her and the wounded ranse. Geddy took dead aim at its head and turned it to dust as Voprot skidded to a stop beside him.

"Come on!"

Geddy didn't take orders from Voprot, but his tone left no room for discussion. He followed Iondra as best he could with Voprot close at his heels.

———

GEDDY ONLY HAD five meters to go before joining everyone on the other side of the door when Voprot grabbed his jacket and yanked him back so hard he dropped the PDQ.

"Hey! What—"

A curtain of sand shot up right in front of him, spraying sand into his face. He stumbled backwards into Voprot as the last super-ranse launched skyward, its momentum taking the PDQ with it.

The giant creature reached its apex and descended upon them with its mandibles open wide. Voprot shoved Geddy out of the way and unfurled his whip, but the ranse was simply too close.

Geddy could see what was about to happen as though in slow motion. He and Voprot were about to become a ranse buffet, and nothing could be done about it.

As though in a dream, Iondra pressed her feet against

the wall and launched herself at the ranse, slamming into its side with such force that the infernal creature jolted several meters sideways before it toppled to the sand, dazed by the blow. She bounced off and landed on all fours, her prodigious tail coiled around her like she'd done it a thousand times. Even she seemed surprised by what she'd done.

Before it could retreat, Geddy lurched forward and grabbed the PDQ from where it had fallen. He aimed a full charge at the writhing, disoriented predator before it could right itself. Even though it burst into ash with one shot, Geddy kept firing, again and again, until the sand beneath was a puddle of molten glass.

— *I think you got it.*

— Yeah, maybe.

"Iondra!" said Voprot as he hurried over to her. "Are you okay?"

"I ... I think so," she said, brushing herself off. "I don't know what came over me."

"You're sure that's the last one?" Geddy asked Voprot.

"Yes, Vop– er, *I* am sure."

"Cap!" Denk called. "We found a way through!"

Geddy holstered the PDQ and heaved a sigh.

— What do I call myself now? Geddy Deady? Ranse Macabre?

— *How about 'lucky?'*

They were all very lucky at that moment. He holstered the PDQ and walked over to Voprot. "Thanks for saving me back there, buddy. And Iondra, wow. You're an animal!" Oz turned to him, wide-eyed in horror. "Oh, *shit.* No, no. I mean ..."

She laughed it off. "No, you're right. I *was* an animal for once. And it felt *good*. My shoulder notwithstanding."

A cut on her shoulder seeped blood from where she struck the ranse, but it wasn't serious. She used her long, snakelike tongue to lick it.

"Are you okay?" Voprot asked her.

"It's nothing."

"You ... are good ranse fighter," he stammered.

She gave a sheepish grin and replied, "You're not so bad yourself."

CHAPTER THIRTY-NINE

WHAT HAVE WE HERE?

THE DOOR that Morpho and Hughey had forced open led to a much smaller, industrial-looking rectangular room covered in tile. Clusters of pipes and conduit crowded the ceiling. Bare spots on the floor and the walls suggested the recent removal of old fixtures. A mechanism like a conveyor belt ran from the door straight back to an elongated pen along the back wall, where two more of the docile ruminant creatures lay awaiting their gruesome fate. Two metal troughs ran up and down its length, one with water and one with a pulpy mash of food.

"What is this place?" Oz asked, her blades still at the ready.

"A vending machine," Geddy said.

"Looks fully automated," Jel noted. She approached the doomed creatures and leaned over the metal railing around their pen. "What are these things, anyway?"

"Tayras," Iondra said. "Farm animals introduced to Myadan from Nichu."

Jel grimaced and shook her head. "It's so cruel. We should disable the whole damn system."

— *I think you were right. Whatever experiment this was, it has been abandoned.*

— Yeah, but in favor of what?

In a very short timeframe, the Zelnads had created super-ranses that conventional weapons could barely scratch. But apparently, that wasn't good enough. What if they'd done the same with mogorodons, or the dreaded skysnakes? The thought gave him a shudder.

A closed door in the back corner was the only way out, though it didn't appear to have any kind of security and wasn't sealed as tight as the perimeter doors.

"Let's see what's behind door A," Geddy said to Jel.

She directed Hughey to investigate. A portion of his nanobots split off and slipped easily through the gap around the door. Everyone looked expectantly at Jel.

"It's clear. Just a curved hallway to the right."

Geddy's eyes met each of theirs in turn, seeking tacit agreement that they were good to proceed. But of course, they were in this to the end. His main concern was Iondra, but if anything, she seemed galvanized by what just happened. Not to mention pretty cagey.

He threw the door open and lunged into the lit hallway PDQ-first, but as Hughey had shown them, it sat empty and disappeared to the left.

Geddy pressed his finger to his ear. "Doc, can you still read me?"

"Yes, captain, but the signal is spotty."

Jel gave her head a grim shake, as though she expected this. "I was worried about that. There's gotta be half a click's worth of reinforced concrete between us and the *Armstrong*. I could use Hughey as a sort of antenna, but then he wouldn't be our eyes anymore."

Doc's calm intellect was reassuring, and Krezek's expertise on the pheromone might still come in handy. But he and Jel both had the same schematics on their devices, and he wasn't about to give up Hughey's recon capabilities.

"All right. Looks like we'll lose you soon. Anything up ahead we should know about?"

"I believe that corridor will take you to the gymnasium."

"Gymnasium?'"

As he was talking, Oz caught his eye with a sudden movement. She stuck her hand out to steady herself against the wall. Her other hand trailed lightly over her chest.

— *Is she okay?*

— I dunno. She doesn't look distressed, exactly ...

"This facility was home to several hundred terraformers on twenty, even thirty-year stretches. Regular exercise was critical for their health."

He barely heard what Doc said. Oz's situation, whatever it was, had his full attention. "Hey, are you–" The pheromone detector buzzed against his chest like a trapped bee. He fished it out and consulted the display. Three hundred thirty-seven parts per million and rising quickly.

"Oh, shit. Everyone, I think we'd better–"

Before he could finish, Oz shoved him against the wall and stuck her tongue down his throat as her hand gripped his crotch.

— *The pheromone's hitting her.*

— Maybe we ought to bottle this stuff ...

— *Give her your blocker!*

It took every ounce of willpower he had, but he managed to push Oz away long enough to yank the autoinjector from his pocket, press it into her neck, and pop the end with his thumb.

"Ow!" she pulled back, rubbing her neck.

"Ninety days, remember? A deal's a deal." Geddy asked. "Everyone, inject your blockers! Sorry about that. On multiple levels. Are you okay?"

"That was ... phew." She gave her head a cleansing shake. "It's weird. I can feel my body fighting the effects."

The same effects began to hit him. For a brief, shining moment it was like being fifteen again. "My turn, I guess."

She rubbed her neck, still looking a bit dazed, and handed him the little cylinder she'd brought for herself. He winced as he administered the blocker on himself. "The pheromone level just spiked. We're getting close to some-thing. Anyone else feeling frisky?"

"A little," Jel said. "For a second, I thought I might kiss Denk."

Denk rubbed his neck where he'd injected himself and forced a chuckle. "Heh, yeah. Good thing that didn't happen."

Geddy cupped his ear again. "Hey, Krezek, you read?"

"Yes, I'm here," he said through a crackle of interference.

"The meter's almost at four hundred. We all took the blocker."

He sighed with relief. "Good. You should be safe for the next hour or so, but it all depends on your biochemistry."

"Roger that. Hey, we're gonna lose you any second. I'll ping you when we're back in range." He lowered his hand and scanned the group. "Everyone feeling okay?" When he was met with nods, he said, "Let's see what's around the bend. Jel?"

"On it," she said, looking a bit dazed. "Hughey, check it out."

Hughey's tiny, scale-like bots formed a sphere, and he floated off down the corridor. Jel's eyes got their usual distant look as she focused on watching the feed.

"Okay, a short way up, we've got a branch to the left."

"Take it," Geddy said.

"Go left, Hughey," she directed. A few moments passed, and she sucked in a quick breath. "We've got voices."

"Can you make it out?"

"Not really. It's echoey and there's a lot of background noise. Hughey, see if you can get closer to the speakers. Not too close, though."

Several nerve-wracking seconds passed. They didn't know whether there were ten Nads down here or a thousand. Again, not a great situation. Verveik would be furious if he knew what they were doing, but he'd take the heat if anything went south. Something big was happening here. He could feel it in his bones.

Jel's face, which had been pinched in concentration, went slack. The color spilled from her cheeks.

"What is it?" Geddy took an anxious step toward her.

She closed her eyes and gave her head a little shake as though to clear it. "The gym. It's way bigger than I expected. And full of ... pods."

"Pods? Seed pods? Pulsating fleshy pods? Dolphins? What?" Geddy asked.

She shook her head. "No, nothing like that. I think

they're cloning pods. Hughey, get closer to one of the pods. I wanna see what's inside."

"Ranses?" Denk asked hesitantly. He, too, assumed the worst.

"No, not ranses." Jel turned to Geddy with her mouth hanging open. "I think they're humans."

GEDDY TOOK off down the corridor, partly to give him a few seconds' head start to think and partly because he couldn't believe what Jel said until he saw it with his own eyes.

— *I do not understand. Why would they be cloning humans?*

— Your guess is as good as mine.

— *Perhaps it is for their army.*

— The old super-soldier plan? I dunno. Doesn't sound like their M.O.

As soon as he took the left branch, he could feel the air change. It was warmer, and a faint chemical smell that reminded him of formaldehyde hung in the humid air. The closer he got to the gym, the easier it was to understand Jel's awe.

The others caught up a moment later. They'd come in on an elevated track that encircled a cavernous, sunken room more like an underground fieldhouse than a gym. Lines for its running lanes were still plainly visible. A metal railing ran along the inside.

Eight floor-to-ceiling towers were crowded into the space, four on one side and four on the other, with a wide central aisle. Each tower was packed with rows of large cylindrical pods about two meters apart. Humanoids floated in cloudy pink liquid, each tower representing a different stage of growth.

Thick cables led from the base of each tower to a square control center on the near the end of the main aisle. Two technicians monitored a bank of holoscreens. A large cylindrical tank of faintly yellow liquid bubbled behind them, a cluster of eight tubes leading away from its base.

"That must be the pheromone," Geddy said, pointing at the cylinder.

Just outside the flat black banks of computers that formed the control center's perimeter was an adult-sized pod suspended from a beefy, C-shaped armature bolted to the floor. Its clear lid faced away so they couldn't see what was inside.

The beings inside the tower pods, however, were plain to see as they drew near. The nearest one was a male child, maybe seven or eight, and naked, with a mop of light brown hair that floated and shimmered in the column of fluid. A mask covered his entire face, an air tube snaking up and through the top. Bubbles escaped rhythmically from ports in the side. Oval devices covered his eyes. A faint glow came from underneath them, suggesting they were tiny displays.

Every pod in the tower was identical, suggesting they were cloned at the same time. The ones in the next tower heading across the gym were several years older.

Dim bluish lights overhead gave the scene an otherworldly cast. The crew lined up along the railing, agape at the scale of the operation, whatever it was.

"Holy hell," muttered Oz. "How is this possible?"

"The Xoo closed for three months last year for maintenance," Iondra said. "Marcourt gave the whole staff a paid sabbatical."

"Wow, you must have great benefits!" Denk noted.

"Meanwhile, the Nads moved in," Geddy said. "And built whatever the hell this is." He cupped his ear. "Doc, do you read?" No reply. "Doc?"

Geddy had hoped for Doc's guidance. What would the Nads want with human clones when they could easily take over any species they wished?

"What we do now?" asked Voprot, a little too loudly.

As though in reply, the faint echo of voices came bubbling up from the floor, and they reflexively took a step back from the railing. The ventilation system running overhead muffled their conversation but also gave them additional cover.

"There's four of them," Jel said. "Looks like two Orneans, a Screvari, and some Temerurian guy in a tux?"

"That's Marcourt," Geddy whispered, and turned to Oz. "Would he remember you?"

She shrugged. "Maybe? I only met him once or twice as a kid."

He turned back to Jel. "Any audio yet?"

"It's still rough. I'll try to clean it up. In the meantime ..." She removed her small tablet from an inner pocket and swiped through a couple of screens. "Patching Hughey's feed through ..."

As she'd done in Temeruria, Jel's device now mirrored her contact lens so they all could see. Hughey was a few meters above and behind the four Zelnads. Marcourt strolled slowly between the rows with his arms folded behind his back. The male Screvari walked astride him, and the Orneans followed.

"... ahead of schedule," finished the Screvari. "Gestation time is down to three months."

"Good. And the programming?" Marcourt asked.

"We start at preadolescence when the brain is at its most plastic. Combining images of the female with the slow drip of pheromone has a cumulative effect. By the time they reach maturity, they can think of nothing else."

Marcourt nodded, seemingly pleased with this. "And speaking of the female ..."

"The beta is fully functional. We can begin production immediately."

"Show me."

The Screvari gestured at the single hanging pod on the floor. "We've already modified the male programming to match her final physical profile."

They stopped just outside the control center, studying the suspended pod with clinical interest. Hughey shifted his elevated position to get a clearer view. This particular pod did not contain liquid, suggesting the growing process was complete. Soft lights inside the pod competed with the reflection of those overhead, o details. The female was blond with curves in all the right places. She, too, was naked, her eyes closed.

— At least they have good taste.

Eli was silent. Hughey pushed in a bit, and her body was revealed in its full glory Geddy squinted to get a better look, and his heart stopped.

The female clone looked exactly like Tatiana.

CHAPTER FORTY

TATI-DOUBLE

"HOLY SHIT," said Oz. "Is that ... ? That can't be ..."

Geddy averted his eyes and rubbed his temples in a vain effort to find an explanation for what he'd just seen. The male clones were somehow being programmed to desire this particular female.

— Eli, help me out.

—*It appears this is a cloning* and *a breeding program. The breeding presumably occurs later.*

— Yeah, but to what end?

"You guys know her?" Denk asked.

"She's my ex," Geddy said.

"Uf," Denk said, raising his eyebrows at Oz. "Awkward!"

Meanwhile, the Zelnads continued their conversation.

"It's vital we keep her separated from the males," said one of the Orneans. "They are rather ... aggressive. The combination of programming and pheromone works almost too well."

"And once they are deployed?"

"Mating will begin immediately."

"Ew," Jel said.

"This doesn't make sense. They want to *end* civilization, not ..." Geddy trailed off.

It took shape before he could finish the sentence. He saw it in Oz's face, too. The others hadn't quite caught up.

"What?" Denk asked.

"The Zelnads went looking for the most dangerous creatures in our galaxy," Geddy said. "And they found us."

Human history was fraught to say the least, but he never imagined his species was more dangerous than ranses or mogorodons. And why did the female clone look like Tatiana?

"Look!" Jel said, pointing to the far side of the gym.

Another pair of Zelnads wheeled a second pod armature down the central aisle toward Marcourt and the others. An adult male was inside, the first they'd seen.

"What's this?" asked Marcourt, turning away from the Tati-double.

"We thought you would like to see a brief demonstration of their ... affinity," said one of the Orneans. "The pheromone has greatly augmented the effects of their neuro-visual programming."

The two Nads wheeling the male in were Zihnian. Marcourt took a couple steps back to make room, and they positioned the pod opposite the Tati-double so the two clones faced each other.

The moment the male saw the Tati-double, he threw himself against the inside of the pod, scratching at it with animalistic desperation. Spittle flew from its mouth, and a low, guttural wail escaped his lips. At the same time, the female awoke and pounded her fists against the inside of her pod and cried as though being tortured.

But that wasn't the most interesting part.

Hughey changed position so they had a clear view of the pathetic, sex-starved male pounding on the side of the cage. The extent of his excitement was on full display and pressed against the glass.

Geddy's stomach dropped through his feet, followed by a wave of nausea.

The clone looked exactly like him.

Judging by their slack-jawed expressions, the rest of the crew realized it, too. He was the same height, had the same color hair, and roughly the same build. Both he and the Tati-double were at least ten years younger, though he never had abs like that.

"Um ..." Oz said. Given the situation, it was the perfect sentiment.

"Hey, Geddy ..." began Voprot.

"I know, pal. It looks like me."

"Only younger and way buffer," Oz noted.

"Impressive," said a clearly pleased Marcourt. "I've seen enough."

The Orneans turned the male back around and wheeled him away from where they'd come. He wailed in despair. The Tati-double pounded her open hands against the inside of the pod and bawled.

His and Tati's DNA wouldn't have been hard to find. His would've been all over the *Penetrator*, which the Nads had for a time. They could've gotten hers from just about anywhere. But why them?

"What's the plan here, boss?" asked Jel.

Geddy's first inclination was to charge the PDQ and start

laying waste to the whole abominable scene. But a better idea began to form.

"Keep getting footage of the facility. We need to find the other adult males and get them out of here."

The crew exchanged confused looks.

"What? Why?" Oz asked.

He squared up to her and the others. "The New Alliance needs pilots, right?"

Verveik had a vast fleet of ships hidden in the Karrea Ion Storm, but nobody to fly them. If his talent for flying was hereditary, maybe they'd have it, too.

Oz looked sideways at him. "You can't be serious."

"There's only a handful of Nads here. We capture them, free the males and the Tati-double, and bring them to Verveik. This is the smoking gun," Geddy urged.

"Okay, first off, we don't know how many Nads there really are. Second, what are we supposed to do with hundreds of horny, brainwashed clones? And third, 'Tati-double?' Is that supposed to be cute?"

"You have a better idea?" He regarded the young clones nearby and felt a powerful empathy for them. "They didn't ask for this."

Oz's big eyes drifted over to Marcourt and the others, then back to Geddy, shaking her head. "No. We're soldiers now. Let's tell Verveik what we found and wait for orders. In case you hadn't noticed, taking matters into our own hands hasn't gone so well."

He understood her reticence. Their prisoners on Durandia wound up dead. But he was just as reluctant to let Verveik and Tretiak decide. After all, he'd hand-delivered Sammo *and* a confession about the Gundrun event, and it cost both Sammo and Tev their lives. What if Verveik decided to keep this under wraps, too?

"We're not even supposed to be here, remember? Verveik would say to stand down and let Tatiana's long game play out. But I don't think we have that kind of time, and Eli agrees."

An inner debate played out on her face. Coming to the Xoo was her idea, after all, and everything about this operation violated intergalactic laws around cloning. Why wait for Tatiana to work sensitive back channels when they could blow this whole thing open, right here and now?

After several seconds, she closed her eyes and sighed, then searched the faces of the crew. Finally, she shrugged. "All right. Then let's expose these assholes once and for all."

CHAPTER FORTY-ONE

THE GAGGLE

GEDDY and the crew descended the steps to the gym floor and crept along the space between the left towers and the wall. It was weird to notice the remnants of an old athletic facility amid the cloning operation. Faded banners on the wall bore vaguely inspirational messages aimed at terraformers like *PUSH THROUGH THE PAIN* and *CHANGING WORLDS TOGETHER*. Tracks for old divider curtains still hung from the ceiling, though the curtains themselves had been removed.

The clones in the second tower appeared to be around thirteen — the same age he was when he lost his parents and stowed away on a ship bound for Kigantu.

Those in the third tower were around seventeen. By the time he reached that ripe old age, he was among the best pilots in Aquebba. Tretiak let him make his first solo run to Doxx-Mora to collect an artifact for the auction. He made five thousand credits in a game of uguinok and felt like a total badass until a pirate accused him of cheating and beat him within an inch of his life.

As expected, the last tower held adult clones. They were not in pods but some kind of haptic suits, suspended in an anti-gravity field. Helmets covered their heads, with a flickering light underneath similar to what they'd seen in the first tower. Occasionally, they would reach out as though interacting with whatever simulation was playing out on their retinas.

He turned to Oz and smiled. "As far as your gangbang fantasy goes, I could roll with it in this case."

She shot him an acid look. "I don't have a gangbang fantasy."

"You mean you *didn't*."

She eyed the clones and their impressive physiques before returning her gaze to Geddy. "If I did have a gangbang fantasy, I'm not sure you'd make the cut with these guys around."

Geddy silently cursed his clones and their two-point-seven percent body fat as he thought about his response. "Yeah, well, that's where experience comes into play. Besides, I think these guys only have eyes for ..." He trailed off when he realized she'd moved out of earshot.

Each level had ten rows of ten clones on each side, with eight levels in each of the eight towers. Even he could do that math. There were more than six thousand copies of him in here.

"Jel, take Denk and Iondra, and see if there's a way to cut the clones' feed. Oz, Voprot, and I will deal with Marcourt and the others. Morph stays with me."

"Then what?" Jel asked.

"Then we free the clones and lead them out of here like the pied piper. Easy-peasy."

Jel looked at him through the tops of her eyes. "Mmm... famous last words."

"Voprot– er, *I* want to stay with Iondra," lamented the lizard.

"It's okay, pal. Jel and Denk will keep her safe."

Iondra placed a gentle hand on Voprot's arm and looked him in the eyes. "I'll be okay." They held eye contact until Voprot gave a small nod.

"You can count on us, Cap!" Denk said. "C'mon, guys. Let's unplug these knuckleheads."

Geddy headed back down the outer aisle with Oz and Voprot following. Between the second and third tower, he took a quick peek around the corner. Finding it still clear, he stole between the thirteen- and seventeen-year-olds with his PDQ still at the ready and stopped at the corner. Oz drew her blades and Voprot readied his whip.

Peering around the corner, he found Marcourt and the two Orneans still talking in the control area. The Screvari had returned.

Cupping a hand around his ear, he whispered, "Jel, is the coast still clear?"

"Hold, please." A few moments later, she said, "Still just the four guys and two technicians."

"Roger that." He turned to Voprot and Oz. "You two flank them. Once you're in position, we'll move in together. Oz, take their weapons. Voprot, make sure they don't escape."

"All right," said Oz, biting her lip. "Come on, V."

— *She does that when she doesn't like your ideas.*

— I know it well.

Oz and Voprot disappeared around the outer corner of the tower, leaving Geddy surrounded by his clones.

— *I don't like this.*

— What's not to like?

— *It seems too easy.*

— Yeah, well, let's not look a gift horse in the mouth.

He waited with his back pressed to the corner support, staring at one of the adolescent clones in the third tower. The kid's face was largely obscured, but the rest of him was like looking into a mirror from twenty-five years ago. The reddish-brown hair. The big feet. The well-defined ribcage.

— *You were cute once. And look so innocent.*

— Yeah, and I wound up doing a lot of shit I didn't intend. Just like this poor kid's gonna do.

While he waited for Oz and Voprot to get into position, he ventured another peek around the corner. The edge of Voprot's head poked out from behind the first tower on his side. Several seconds later, Oz's lily-white face appeared from the first tower on the other side.

Showtime.

Geddy huffed a couple of deep breaths, then emerged fully into the central corridor between the rows with the PDQ leveled.

One of the Orneans spotted him and gave a little gasp, followed by the other scientist and the Screvari. Marcourt, whose back was to him, slowly turned to face him.

"You're late for dinner," Geddy said, drawing closer.

Oz and Voprot stepped out from where they were hiding and moved in behind them.

Marcourt's eyes narrowed, but he didn't appear overly concerned. Or surprised. Hopefully, that was just Zelnad stoicism.

"You," he said.

"Surprise, Duke Marcourt," Geddy said.

"I am no more Duke Marcourt than you are Edgar Kepler, Mr. Starheart." Oz sheathed her blades while she patted them down. He took one look at her and squinted. "Wait, I know you ..." He closed his eyes to access Marcourt's memory. "Aunt Nandra's long-lost daughter, isn't it?"

She glared at him. "We're not related anymore." After finishing her pat-down of the others, she took a couple of steps back. "They're clean."

"And what ..." he began, his eyes narrowed at Morpho, "... might you be?"

"Never mind him."

Marcourt gestured calmly at the coffin-like pod holding the whimpering Tati-double. Geddy had been careful to avoid being seen by her. "Would you care to meet our female beta? Something tells me she'd be most eager to make your acquaintance."

"Been there, done her," Geddy said, throwing Oz an apologetic look. "How'd you get my DNA?"

Marcourt smirked. "It wasn't exactly hard to find, Mr. Starheart. It was all over your ship, your residence ... a mall kiosk on Earth 2 ..."

Oz closed her eyes and gave her head a slow shake.

"Yeah, okay. But why her and why me, specifically?"

"Because in every model we ran on every world, your particular combination of traits eventually led to complete environmental, moral, intellectual, educational, and societal collapse, ending in self-destruction."

Geddy had never entertained, seriously or in jest, the idea of having kids with Tatiana. Apparently, he'd made the right call.

"Mom always said I'd eventually herald the apocalypse."

"Of all the galaxies we've cleansed, no intelligent species has shown less interest in its own long-term survival than humankind. Not even ranses would destroy their own habitat," he noted. "You've successfully destroyed two planets and are making quick work of a third."

"Yeah, but we invented rock and roll. And I think maybe fire?"

The Zelnad smirked, looking him up and down like he was a turd. "Perhaps you should have invented forethought."

"Third time's a charm," Geddy said, echoing the sign over the entrance to the Bubbles on Earth 3. "We invented that saying, too, asshole."

"A fine example of your contributions to the universe."

Geddy's hand tightened around the PDQ.

- *He's baiting you. Do not fall for it.*

Marcourt continued, "With accelerated breeding and gestation, this germ line will establish dominion quickly. After that, its self-destruction is a mathematical certainty."

"You're pretty forthcoming about your evil plans," Oz noted.

Marcourt gave Oz a brief glance before returning to Geddy. "Thousands of galaxies have already been cleansed, and thousands more will follow. Nothing you do or do not do will change that."

Geddy considered this. "Then why hide behind bullshit stories and underground lairs?"

"Expedience."

"I thought time had no meaning for you."

"The longer we observe civilization, the more eager we've become to author its end."

— *He is stalling. And he would not be truthful in any case.*

— *Stalling for what?*

"Voprot tired of talk." The lizard cracked his whip from behind them.

"I was just thinking the same thing." Geddy activated his earpiece. "Jel, how we coming?" When there was no reply, he shot Oz a worried look. "Jel?"

A shuffling sound came from behind him. He spun around. Jel, Denk, and Iondra approached with their hands in the air. At least a dozen Nads were behind them brandishing short rifles.

Shit.

"Sorry, Cap," Denk said. "They got the drop on us."

In his peripheral vision, more Nads appeared from between the towers. Geddy spun back to find more coming in behind Voprot. There were hundreds now, nearly all Screvari.

— Guess we know why he was stalling.

— *What are you going to do?*

Marcourt's lips twisted into a grin. "Your hubris is always your undoing. Now, if you'll excuse me, I have a banquet to attend."

The Screvari beside him said, "What should we do with them?"

He gave an indifferent shrug. "It does not matter."

As he turned to leave, the vat of bubbling, piss-yellow pheromone next to the control center rose suddenly from its base, popping the bolts. It hovered three meters in the air, stretching taut the tubes connected to it.

Taking a couple steps back, Marcourt's eyes widened in fear. "Wha ...? Who is doing that?"

Geddy spotted Doc and Krezek first. They were up on the track. Doc held the gravity gun, keeping the vat aloft. Krezek stood beside him.

Marcourt followed Geddy's gaze, and the Nads swung their weapons in that direction.

"Drop your weapons," Doc ordered. "Or I drop this."

Marcourt grinned, his gaze shifting back and forth between Doc and Geddy. "Antigravity technology. I wonder where you got it."

At that moment, Doc and Krezek simultaneously lifted off the ground. A pair of Zelnad-Screvari appeared from behind them holding similar gravity guns. Doc twisted in midair, straining to maintain control of the vat. The oily liquid swished back and forth as Doc's arms shook.

Sighing, Marcourt turned to Geddy. A handful of Zelnads came marching up behind him and leveled their rifles at Oz and Voprot.

— *We need to do something!*

— I've been noodling on a terrible idea.

— *I expect nothing less.*

One of the Screvari lieutenants strolled up to Geddy and

admired the PDQ, which was still leveled at Marcourt. "Impressive weapon."

"I get that a lot."

He held out his hand and looked expectantly at him.

Geddy smiled back. The PDQ was fully charged and he had an itchy trigger finger. "Let the games begin."

In one smooth motion, Geddy raised his arm at the hovering vat and fired.

CHAPTER FORTY-TWO

RISQUE BUSINESS

THE ALARM SOUNDED IMMEDIATELY, an electronic *whing whing* that would've seemed anemic in a less echoey space. The cloud of vaporized pheromone was strong enough to sting Geddy's eyes as it washed over him. He fell to one knee and rubbed his eyes, breathing shallowly while he waited for his vision to clear. Sweat poured from his forehead, underarms, and crotch as his body reacted. Even with the blocker, his head swam.

Though his eyes were pinched shut, he could sense the chaos unfolding around him. The thin *tink, tink* of weapons and buckles hitting the floor. Staggered footsteps. Moaning.

Moaning?

Oh, right.

He forced one eye open and instantly wished he hadn't. He was facing right and looking down the gap between the second and third tower.

At least two dozen Zelnad-Screvari, a mix of males and females, were acting like it was closing time. Rifles were cast aside. Tongues were thrust enthusiastically into mouths.

— *Wow, that stuff really works.*

— Krezek's sitting on a gold mine.

"Geddy, holy shit, are you okay?" asked Jel from his right, her hands slipping under his arm.

He got slowly to his feet, steadying himself against her. "What's happening?"

"The adults are coming out of their trance, and fast."

He leaned sideways to get a good look at the tower with the adults. A handful had already taken off their helmets and were stumbling around, sniffing the air in search of the Tati-double.

"Oz?! Where are you?"

He whirled back to the control center. The two Ornean scientists had their eyes closed, presumably trying to stave off the pheromone's effects through concentrated effort. Marcourt and the Screvari were both gone. He spotted Oz across the control center. She had fallen to her knees as well. Geddy and Jel reached her as shakily got to her feet.

"You okay?" Geddy asked.

"I think so. A warning would've been nice."

"Sorry, I didn't know what else to do. C'mon ..." He pivoted back to the left and took a couple quick steps toward the Tati-double's pod. "Help me get this open."

"What?" Oz asked warily. "Why?"

He jerked his head toward the clones. "To get them out."

Oz gave her head a clearing shake. "Hold up. You want to use a clone of your *ex* to lure clones of *you* away so they can become Alliance pilots?"

"It's not as insane as it sounds. Even Eli thinks it's a good idea."

— *I do?*

"Captain!" called Tardigan from up above. When Geddy blew the tank, the soldier holding Doc and Krezek in the gravity field dropped his gun, and with it, Doc and Krezek. Other than Doc having a small bloody gash on his forehead, they looked okay, but he'd want to get them fully checked out once they were back on the ship. "This way! Quickly!"

Geddy nodded and whirled back in time to see the pod open. The Tati-double locked her eyes on him and tried to leap right out of the pod. Oz pinned her left arm to her back and held her fast.

"Sorry, sweetie. That one's mine."

"Voprot, pick her up!" Geddy said. "We've gotta go!"

Voprot ran over and wrapped up the Tati-double in his thick arms. He tossed her over his right shoulder like a sack of potatoes. "Where I take shiny hairless woman?"

"Follow Doc!"

The Tati-double stretched toward Geddy, and cried, "I need him!"

— It's kind of an ego trip.

— ... *which you totally needed.*

Iondra and Denk raced up the steps, shoving amorous Zelnads out of their way. Iondra glanced nervously over her shoulder as the adult male clones spotted the Tati-double in Voprot's arms.

"They see her," Geddy said. "Time to go!"

Voprot took off up the steps with Jel and Oz in tow. Geddy stayed back, firing quick blasts at the clones' feet to keep them at a safe distance as they jockeyed for position like sperm on the hunt for a lone egg.

"This way! Follow Ehrmut!" shouted Doc, pointing down the same hallway where they'd entered the gym.

Krezek ran ahead, motioning for everyone to follow. Doc brandished the gravity gun as he waited for Geddy to reach him.

"What're you doing here?" Geddy asked.

"After we lost contact, I had a feeling you might be in trouble."

"That's usually a good instinct." The clones reached the top of the steps and scrambled toward them. Geddy scorched the concrete at their feet, and they jumped back. "Trust me, you don't wanna get caught between them and the female."

They took off after Denk and the others. Doc said, "I look forward to learning what is going on."

The moment they burst into the main corridor, a barrage of blaster fire from the right forced them in the other direction. A wall of Zelnad-Screvari in protective masks advanced in squadrons, using arched concrete supports as cover. Bolts sizzled past, tearing chunks of concrete off the wall. Geddy charged up the PDQ and unleashed a shot at the ceiling, sending a pile of debris raining down in front of them. Thick dust plumed in the air. Geddy pulled his tux jacket over his mouth and nose. Even still, his body was racked with coughs.

Doc grabbed his arm and tugged him away. The gaggle of horned-out clones came skidding into the corridor, likely only tracking the Tati-double through smell at this point and continued their frenzied pursuit. They clearly hadn't done much, if any, actual running because they tripped over each other constantly and were panting like dogs.

— At least you are in better shape than someone.

— Wow, really? An alien spore with no metabolism is commenting on my fitness level? During a gunfight?

— If you die, I die. It wouldn't kill you to do more cardio.

A fresh volley of blaster fire rang out, and several the clones went down. Geddy felt an instant pang of regret, as though he'd watched himself die.

"I hope you know another way out!" Geddy called out as he followed behind Doc.

"According to the schematics, there is another exit."

Fifty meters up, the corridor came to a T. "This way, everyone!" Krezek's voice echoed down the right corridor, and they gave chase.

"I don't suppose you saw where Marcourt went?" Geddy asked.

"The Temerurian? No, I'm sorry."

Maybe he was immune to the pheromone, or maybe he just managed to get out before the cloud filled the room. At any rate, he was in the wind.

Geddy didn't love that his clones were effectively human shields now, but as they rounded the corner, wild-eyed and desperate, it seemed at least several hundred were still alive. Perhaps the Nads were reticent about killing their new creations. Or, more likely, they still intended to grow the rest to adulthood and these were an acceptable loss.

The corridor ended in a narrow set of steps leading up. Geddy ran up backwards, giving cover for Doc while making sure the clones were still chasing them.

When they reached the top of the steps, they found Krezek and the others. The short hallway ended at a concrete wall.

"They seriously built a stairwell to a dead end!" Oz paced back and forth in the small space. "Now what??"

Geddy spun back just as the clones began up the steps

after them. If he didn't shoot them himself, they'd tear through all of them to reach the Tati-double.

— *How are you going to control them?*

Geddy's hand tightened around the PDQ.

— Drugs? Violence, maybe?

"What is the pheromone reading?" Doc asked.

He glanced at the readout. "Six thousand, four hundred thirty-two parts per million."

"Cap, I'm feeling kinda ... funny ..." Denk steadied himself against the wall.

"Shit, I think the blocker's wearing off." Geddy looked up at the ceiling. "What's above us?"

Doc whipped out his comm device and pulled up the schematic. "My best guess is the east side of the Visitor Center."

"Everyone stand back!" He raised the PDQ at the ceiling and took one final glance over his shoulder. The clones were already halfway up the steps.

"Are you out of your mind?!" Oz asked, backing up.

"It's either this or we fight Zelnads while simultaneously ripping each other's clothes off."

"Aw, hell," she said, and turned her back to him. She, Denk, Voprot with the Tati-double, Iondra, and Krezek pressed tight to the far wall. Doc put his fingers in his ears and winced in anticipation.

Geddy covered his face with his left arm and gave the pistol a long squeeze to charge it. When he let go, the resulting blast sent stinging bits of exploding concrete ricocheting painfully off his arms and head. The rumble traveled up through his feet as a couple metric tons of concrete fell, and dust again filled his lungs. A metallic sound, like lunch trays falling out of a racing vehicle, met his ears.

Moving air tousled his hair, tickling his forehead. The smell of roasted meat hit his nostrils, making him salivate. He licked his lips, which were coated in dust, choked on the dryness, and spit out as much as he could. Somewhere below, invisible through the dust cloud, he could hear the clones coughing. At least they weren't dead.

He turned toward the hole in the ceiling and squinted through the bright light.

Dust and concentrated pheromone vapor billowed through the hole in the ceiling as though under pressure, which it sort of was. The ventilation system in the gym circulated huge volumes of air. It had nowhere to go.

"Everyone okay?" he asked.

"Vop– er, I am okay, Geddy!" said Voprot. "Slippery woman okay, too. Dust make less slippery!"

"That's great, buddy."

"We're all right," Oz said. "Except my mouth is cement mixer." A fit of spitting and coughing drove the point home.

Doc stepped up next to Geddy, and Geddy gave his back a pat. "You good?"

"I smell food, Captain. It may indicate a head injury. Am I bleeding?"

Geddy gave him a quick once over but saw no blood except for scratches from the exploding concrete. "I don't think so."

Light streamed in from the giant hole he'd created. Among the rubble were several large chafing dishes. Meat, pasta, and a colorful medley of seasonal root vegetables covered half the crew, making it look like they'd just had an epic food fight.

"Where the hell did we come out?" Geddy asked, shoving the metal parts aside. When his hand came up full of dark red sauce, he grimaced. "Ugh, disgusting. You gotta wonder about any meat that needs so much sauce. Especially at a zoo."

Denk's entire left side was spattered with the stuff, so much that Geddy needed a double take to ensure he wasn't covered in blood. When Denk brought his own sauce-covered hand up in front of his face, he gave it a tentative lick.

"Oh, it's good, though, Cap. Puttanesca, I think."

"How do we get out of here?" Oz asked.

Geddy managed to scramble onto a large block that had fallen from the ceiling. Grabbing jagged pieces of rebar for leverage, he hoisted himself up through the rough hole.

"I'm gonna check it out. Hopefully it's a kitchen and not ..." Once he felt steady, he raised his eyes. "... the dining hall."

A room full of nattily dressed Xoo patrons stared back. Marcourt was among them.

So was Tatiana.

CHAPTER FORTY-THREE

NOW IT'S A PARTY

THE HOLE GEDDY blasted through the concrete ceiling of the dead end had turned the high-end buffet of the patron dinner into a war zone. Two hundred stunned and terrified faces stared back at him.

"Oh, *shit*." The realization of what they'd done slowly made its way through his brain.

Marcourt took off running toward the back of the room. Geddy aimed at him but didn't fire. The door opened, and he vanished into the night.

The pheromone vapor was already flooding the banquet hall and entering the upturned noses of the Xoo's wealthiest patrons. The same stuff that had just turned a few hundred exhausted clones into mindless sex fiends. This could only go one way.

He called back into the hole, "We've gotta go!" Then he faced the crowd again, giving a nervous laugh as he tried to extract himself from the tangle of metal, concrete, and food. "Um ... nothing to see here, folks. We'll be out of your hair in a few minutes."

Geddy clambered to his feet, stumbling over an upturned and partly shattered table as he fell toward a predictably apoplectic Tatiana.

Wild-eyed and beside herself with rage, she planted herself in front of him and caught him by his upper arms, likely keeping him from falling. "*What have you done now?!*"

"Tots, I know you're mad, but I need to get you out of here." He grabbed her right forearm and half-dragged her toward the back of the banquet hall, checking anxiously over his shoulder. "*Especially* you."

Several patrons were already groping each other. The sound of descending zippers came from every direction. Voprot leapt out of the hole with the Tati-double still in his sinewy arms, both of them covered head to toe in gray dust. Iondra climbed out next and turned to hoist Krezek up.

Tatiana's face twisted into a mask of incredulity. "Who are they? And who's the naked woman?" At once, her face softened, and she placed a palm on his chest. "Damn, Eddie, have you been working out?"

— *Oh no, it's happening!*

— Fresh air. We need fresh air!

The detector around his neck continued to buzz insistently. Two thousand fifty parts per million and rising faster than the digits could keep up. He grabbed Tati's hand and ran toward the doors on the far side. Looking over his shoulder, he called, "Outside! We need to get outside! Are the clones still behind you?"

"Ooh," Tati cooed. "Are we going somewhere private?"

"Sure, Tots," he said, anxiously checking over his shoulder. The others were all out now and starting to follow. The first clone arm shot through and braced itself against the floor.

"Yeah, and they're coming fast! Go! Go!" Oz said, drawing her blades and backing away.

Tatiana continued to paw at him as he hauled her toward the door. For a brief moment, Geddy actually thought he and Tati *should* go somewhere private. That it was a good idea. He managed to shove the thought away for the moment.

— Now my blocker's wearing off, too.

— *Stay strong! You're almost outside!*

The door was less than five meters away. Tati's other hand had stretched down his abdomen. His hand wrapped around her thin wrist like a vise. "Shit, you *have* been working out. I mean, look at your pecs. I'll let you feel mine if I can feel yours."

Geddy burst through the door into the main lobby of the Visitor Center, which was empty and dark save for green and blue lights up in the atrium. If most of the pheromone stayed inside that room, they might get out of this mess.

Voprot burst through the door next, followed by the others, and finally the clones. He couldn't know how long it would stay in their systems, but until it wore off, he needed to give them a very wide berth. He dashed across the lobby toward the Xoo entrance. They needed fresh air immediately.

Geddy barreled through the door onto the semicircular terrace and took deep lungfuls of fresh air while Tati continued her efforts to remove his clothes. He stiff-armed her and trotted away, which wasn't that hard since she was still in heels.

The others came through the row of doors nearly in unison, still trailing dust as they stumbled onto the terrace. Through the glass, Geddy spotted the first of the clones running at full speed toward the door. Like a trapped bird only seeing a tree outside, all the clone saw was the Tati-double in Voprot's arms.

He hit the glass so hard that it spiderwebbed out, then the weight of those behind him did the rest, streaming through the broken door.

— *Not very smart, are they?*

— We'll work on it.

"Iondra, we need someplace safe, right now!" he called to her.

A broad grin crossed her lizard lips. "I know just the place. Follow me!"

"Tots, I need you to run as fast as you can."

"Why?"

"Because ... you wanted somewhere private, right?"

He dropped her arm and took off running after Iondra. Thankfully, his ruse worked. Tati kicked off her heels and gave chase, clearly anxious to get her reward.

Iondra sprinted down the right side, where she'd begun her tour earlier. A short way down the path, she angled right toward a locked enclosure that resembled many of the other exhibits. A pair of thiscus trees formed a tangled canopy over a little pool of water, with rocks and stumps in between. It clearly wasn't part of the regular Xoo. Beyond it, well-hidden by trees and shrubs, was a one-level structure that followed the contour of the outer wall.

"This is the herbivore clinic," Iondra said over her shoulder. "The recovery area is empty at the moment. We'll be safe there."

She ran ahead of Voprot and waved her credentials in front of the habitat's outer door. It slid open, and she hurried them inside, locking it just as the first naked clones appeared on the path, looking dazed and spent.

— *They are like zombies only somehow more pathetic.*

— We call it adolescence.

Tati caught up, but the fresh air pumping through her had begun to clear her pheromone fog. She raised her fingers to her temple. "Ugh, my head. What's wrong with me?"

"Duke Marcourt's a Zelnad. I followed him to a secret entrance to the old terraforming facility under the Xoo. They're growing clones based on engineered versions of me and you because, apparently, we are the worst people in the galaxy."

She blinked rapidly, shaking her head. "Marcourt's a Zelnad?"

"That's the most shocking detail??"

"But the patrons ..."

"You all inhaled a super-powerful sex pheromone. The fresh air is flushing it from your system. We freed some of the Geddy clones so we can train them to be Alliance pilots." He turned to Oz. "Did I miss anything?" She shook her head no.

Tati gave a droll look over the tops of her eyes. "Okay, first off, I'd never have kids with you. And second of all, what the *fuck* are you talking about?"

Oz said, "Verveik sent us to find proof of what the Zelnads were up to, and we did. Technically."

"Verveik *sent you here*?" she said, thin-lipped.

"Well, not exactly," Geddy admitted. "In fact, he specifically said not to come here."

She rolled her eyes. "But, being you, you came anyway."

"*We* came," Oz corrected. "Together."

"We got X-Passes," Denk noted. "All in all, it was a really good day."

Tati scowled and shook her head, ignoring Denk. "Why don't I remember anything?"

"It's a side effect of the pheromone," Krezek explained. "The subject's sexual psychosis is so powerful that external stimuli don't register. The result is a form of amnesia."

Geddy gasped with delight. "Which means the patrons won't remember anything?" Krezek nodded. "Tots, did you hear that? Your cover's not blown. You can still get on the Xoo board."

"What good's that gonna do now?"

"It's a who's who of the galaxy's most powerful," Iondra said. "Whatever you people are trying to do, you'll need their help."

"How do we know they're not all Zelnads?" Tati asked.

"Eli would've detected them."

She stared at him for a moment. "Ah yes, the alien in your head." He nodded.

The profoundly exhausted and naked clones finally reached the high-impact shell of the enclosure and pressed against it, the sight of *two* Tatianas bringing fresh energy to their dopey exertions. There was nothing they could do besides paw ineffectually at the glass.

"I dunno," Tati lamented as she looked the clones up and down. "You were never that ripped."

Geddy frowned at her assessment.

"I think you look good for your age, Cap," Denk offered.

Tatiana walked over to an aerial photo of the Xoo and stared at the area labeled WetWorld.

"My father made the lead gift to build that stupid dome,"

Tati said. "It didn't make sense because he didn't give two shits about animals." Shaking her head, she turned back to Geddy. "He said it was to win the salvage contract for the old terraforming facility, which he did. An exclusive deal worth eight figures."

"But ... the facility is still intact."

"Interesting, isn't it?"

HOURS PASSED in the empty herbivore habitat while the clones very slowly came out of their pheromone-addled fever dream. Nobody wanted to venture outside until they were completely settled down. By now, the patrons had likely gotten their wits about them and wandered into the night spent, profoundly confused, and hungry.

Iondra had found a comically large pair of Xoo coveralls for the Tati-clone to wear. She'd sat beside the little manmade pond for hours, fixated on the male clones outside until most had passed out in the neatly trimmed grass. The desire that burned in the Tati-double's eyes showed that her programming was just as strong.

"You should go talk to her," Geddy said to Tatiana.

"Why?"

"She didn't ask for this. She must be scared to death."

"Since when do you care about anyone's state of mind?"

He flared his eyebrows. "That's fair."

"I didn't want to sell them Mogues. I only did it to get on the board." After a pause, she ruefully added, "Dad would be so proud."

Her pet mogorodon had quickly gone from being the size

of a small alligator to the size of a starship. Even so, she still considered it her pet. "Mogues?"

"Not too original, I guess."

"Look, I know we threw a wrench into your operation. But I've got a feeling the Nads are a lot further along than we thought. We're running out of time."

"Guess you would know," she admitted.

"You wanted to find out what they were up to here. Now we know. But Iondra was right — we're gonna need those people in there, and soon."

"The people currently fucking in the banquet room?"

"Actually, they should be winding down by now. But everything's still in play. The whole galaxy needs to know what they were doing here."

Tati eyed the younger version of her and chewed thoughtfully on her lip. "All right, I'll talk to her. But you're coming with me."

He gave her a warm smile. "Yeah, okay."

Oz gave him an anxious look as he and Tati walked over to the Tati-double. Geddy winked that it was under control. When she noticed them approach, the Tati-double rose and tugged awkwardly at the coveralls.

"Hi," Tati said, offering her hand. "I'm Tatiana Semenov."

The female clone's face was still smeared with concrete dust. She regarded Tati's hand curiously but didn't take it. "I'm ... I don't know who I am."

"I like your hair. It's ... untamed."

The Tati-double gave a nervous laugh and sheepishly said, "I like your dress."

— *Aww. What a lovely gesture.*

The real Tatiana pursed her lips and gave a pained smile.

In one smooth motion, she yanked Geddy's blaster from his holster, leveled it at the Tati-double's head, and pulled the trigger. It took a long moment for her headless body to topple over, the stump of her neck still smoking from the blast as it rolled into the little pond.

While everyone stood stupefied, Tati sighed and handed the weapon back to Geddy.

"There can be only one."

CHAPTER FORTY-FOUR

THE MUSIC

COMMANDER VERVEIK STOOD in front of the window for a long time with his back to Geddy, staring out at the stars. They'd just finished watching Denk's footage from the myre, Jeledine's footage from the Xoo, and a lengthy recorded brief from Tatiana. Between that and what they already knew about the late Sammo-Yann, it painted a compelling picture.

As Dr. Krezek promised, the Xoo patrons remembered nothing from their giant interspecies orgy. All they knew was that they attended a buffet dinner and somehow wound up naked, sweaty, and physically spent. After killing her clone with Geddy's blaster, Tatiana returned to the banquet hall to discover they still weren't done. She waited outside until the moaning stopped then slipped inside. Afterward, she simply claimed to be a victim of the same disturbing amnesia.

The jagged hole in the concrete beneath the ruined buffet raised its share of questions as well. The Zelnad formerly known as Duke Marcourt, chair of the Xoo board, wasn't available to explain why the centuries-old terraforming facility was not, in fact, buried. A team of IJC investigators entered the facility the next morning and discovered the hastily abandoned cloning facility, the immature Geddy clones still intact. They ordered the Xoo closed until further notice and brought in a task force to care for the clones while the courts determined their status.

The so-called "Myadan incident" was only five days old, but the news had spread through the galaxy. Geddy had made the deeply uncomfortable call to Verveik a few hours after it happened. Ever since, the galactic rumor mill was buzzing, and the Committee was fanning the flames about Zelnad involvement. Everything Marcourt said had been recorded. It still wasn't an airtight case legally, but the court of public opinion mattered more.

Geddy rented a small transport to take the clones up to the *Fizmo* in the wee hours of the morning. Iondra helped slip them out through the service entrance before the Xoo opened. Once they were settled in the hold, Verveik's orders were to jump back to Nirnaya Station for a full debrief. The crew remained in the *Fiz* with the clones while Geddy met privately with the commander.

"Do you know how I survived sixty-six years alone in the Kigantean desert, Captain?" the big Gundrun asked calmly.

"Pizza and porn?"

If he could almost hear Eli shaking his head.

— *Something tells me he's not in the mood for your comic stylings.*

— Is it the smoke coming out of his ears?

Stone-faced, Verveik huffed and slowly turned around. "I raised a garden."

Geddy gave him a doubtful look, for this was impossible

to conceive. Anyone who found so much as a shrub on Kigantu took a selfie with it. "A garden, sir? On Kigantu?"

"Much like Durandia, it was once covered in water. The sand is too salty to grow anything, so I took what precious water I could spare from my portable condenser and rinsed it, a handful at a time, until it was clean. Then I began mixing in organic material — animal bones, bugs, even some of my own blood. You can probably imagine what I used for fertilizer."

"Did you look into hydroponics?" Verveik's acid look made him put up his hands in surrender. "Sorry, I'm done."

"My ship's emergency kit contained a single packet of esnip seeds. No more than fifty or sixty. But I cultivated them, and they grew. After my supplies ran out, I only had a cup of water and an esnip. Day in, day out, until I was ready to leave."

Geddy gulped. He had a pretty good notion where this was headed. He'd been standing at attention for a solid ten minutes, and his lower back was screaming.

"That's an astonishing story, sir."

"Do you understand why I told it?"

— To prove that real men garden?

— *I think he's talking about being meticulous and patient.*

— Oh, that makes more sense.

"That you survived because you were meticulous and patient?"

Verveik's eyebrows arched. "Did Eli tell you that?"

"No! Well, yes. But I would've gotten there on my own."

— *Liar.*

"Had I simply stuck those seeds in the dirt and hoped for the best, I'd be dead."

"All right, look ... I know I messed up, and I'm sorry. But

now we've got footage, the Myadan rumors, a bunch of sore Xoo patrons, and two hundred seventy-eight conscripts for the New Alliance. That's not nothing."

"So once the galaxy knows the truth, then what? You think they'll suddenly change their minds about the Zelnads and run to us?"

"Umm ... kinda?"

"I ordered you in no uncertain terms to stay away from Myadan and await further orders. Did I not?"

Guilt and a generous sprinkle of shame fell over him. He was the first commissioned officer of the New Alliance, but addition to ignoring one of his first orders, he'd thrown a big wrench into the Committee's plans. Two men wound up dead in the process.

"It could've been worse."

Verveik rubbed his forehead as though it suddenly hurt. "'It could've been worse.' Something tells me this won't be the last time I hear that."

"I'd expect not, sir."

The hulking Gundrun shook his head and let out a long sigh. "Tell me, Captain — what would you do if you were me?"

— *Tell him what you told me yesterday.*

— *Really? It's pretty half-baked.*

— *But it is sound reasoning. That may never happen again.*

— *Cute.*

He cleared his throat. "Permission to share a theory, sir?"

Verveik rolled his eyes. "Skip the military protocols. You don't know them, anyway. What's your theory?"

"That maybe we've been following the wrong thread."

"How so?"

Geddy hesitated to say it, but he and Eli had talked a lot about it since Myadan. Something about the events of the past several weeks didn't sit right.

"This all started because of shinium. They need it to destroy Sagacea. That's their endgame. You heard Marcourt. Getting rid of us is almost an afterthought."

The big man raised his eyebrows. "So the cloning operation was what? A distraction?"

"I think it's just one operation of many. Almost like terrorist cells. I know how this sounds, but I don't think their hearts were in it."

"Explain."

"Back on Durandia, our prisoners stopped running from the crypsids the moment they saw daylight. At the time, it seemed like they were trying to trap us in the tunnel, but I think they realized we weren't going to kill them."

"You believe they ... wanted to die?"

"Eli said it's really hard to take full control of someone's consciousness. That it would only be possible if the host is unable or unwilling to resist," Geddy said. "What if not all Zelnads have complete control? It would result in a kind of psychological stalemate."

He could tell that Ververik wanted to dismiss the theory, but he couldn't. "That would explain how you lot got the best of them."

— *Was that a dig at us?*

— I believe it was.

— *Pretty fair, really.*

— Succeeding in spite of ourselves. That's the *Fizmo* motto.

"There's more," Geddy said. "An associate of mine claims to know a guy who *used to be* a Zelnad. A Basoan named Lestiko."

"Used to be?"

"He told her he 'broke through,' whatever that means," Geddy said.

"And you trust this 'associate' of yours?"

"Oddly enough, I do. Look, the Nads are a threat to all of us. Not just the good guys and not just governments," Geddy said. "You said it yourself — the Alliance needs allies. We need to cast a wider net."

Verveik's eyes drifted around the room as he pondered this, nodding. "You mean … unsavories?"

"It's a world I know well. As does Tretiak. Allegiance can be bought. Armies, too."

The big man crossed his arms like this was all a bit too much and stared Geddy down over the tops of his eyes. "From what I understand, your old friend Eilgars has given you pretty much unlimited funds. How you spend it isn't my concern."

His meaning was clear. Geddy had permission to get his hands dirty.

He smiled broadly and took a few steps forward. "Then if it's all the same to you, I'm gonna chase down this lead. If there's a way the hosts can take back control, we need to find it."

"I agree," Verveik said.

Geddy's eyes popped wide. "You do??"

"Your evidence should help dissolve the Coalition, but we can't build an army until we prove there's an imminent threat. That means following the tukrium."

"Did Parmhar Tardigan finish his deep-space scanner?"

Doc's brother had developed technology that could identify tukrium deposits from incredible distances. He'd hoped to sell it to the mining industry, but now he was developing it so the Committee could track down the Zelnad fleet they knew was out there.

"He should have a working prototype in a couple weeks," Verveik confirmed.

"Your orders, then, sir?" he asked.

"See if there's anything to this 'former Zelnad' business. In the meantime, I'll get things sorted with the IJC and use your evidence to dismantle the Coalition."

"And the clones?"

"Start training them up. Mr. Zirhof's company is nearly done retrofitting the Alliance fleet with the Zelnads' bubble jump tech. We need to be ready."

Geddy beamed and gave him a tight nod. "Very good, sir."

After a long pause, Verveik replied, "Captain, you're the most insubordinate, impetuous, and shortsighted soldier I've ever encountered."

Geddy cocked his head and waited several seconds, but Verveik didn't say anything else. "Is there a 'but' coming, sir?"

"No."

GEDDY STOOD outside the airlock quietly studying the listless clones in the hold. There was only room because the *Armstrong* was docked separately at the station. They'd been given standard-issue prison jumpsuits and bedrolls from the

Stocks on Nirnaya Station. All but a few were curled up dreaming whatever clones dreamed about. At this point, that was still probably Tatiana. However, Krezek's pheromone had largely worn off, and with it, their slobbering sexual aggression. They'd been programmed to survive at all costs, multiply, and dominate all life, but now they just looked scared.

The court was still debating what to do with them. The law stated that illegal clones had no status and must be humanely destroyed, however there was no precedent for this many, and the IJC had taken over responsibility for all the immature clones still on Myadan.

Eli was quite certain that none of the clones were Zelnads themselves, which had been a chief concern.

"They look confused." Oz came up behind him holding a cup of tea and joined him at the window, running her fingers lightly down his back.

"They get that from me."

She chuckled and locked eyes with him. "You're really gonna make us ask?"

"Us?" He spun around to find the whole crew and Dr. Krezek had filed into the back of the bridge to hear how it went with Verveik. Geddy scratched the back of his head. "He was pissed. The Committee has a lot of moving parts, and we gummed up the works pretty good."

He paused a long time on purpose.

Oz rolled her hands over one another. "Is there a but?"

"*But* he agreed we should find Lestiko. In the meantime, he'll use our evidence to dissolve the Coalition and convince them war is coming."

"Sounds easy enough," Jel said sarcastically.

"Parmhar's scanning tech will be key," Doc said.

"Speaking of which, his prototype's almost done. And Zirhof's outfitting the fleet with the bubble drive. We can start training the clones as soon as the IJC clears them."

Zirhof of Zorr was one of Geddy's oldest friends. He was a collector and business magnate who occasionally bought Old Earth arcana from the Double A. He had decoded the quantum cubes from their Old Earth salvage op and found the same jump tech used by the Zelnads. That would help level the playing field, at least.

"Where is this operation of your brother's?" Krezek asked Tardigan.

Doc gave a pained smile. "Afolos, as it happens."

The look between them said it all. Dr. Krezek had been indispensable, but he wasn't part of the crew. He didn't have to return to Afolos, but he had to go *somewhere*. They had shit to do.

He gave a deferential smile and lowered his head. "Which is where I will leave you."

"You're sure?" Geddy asked. "We can drop you off anywhere."

Krezek waved it off. "Thank you, but it's time I went home. Ever since Durandia, I've been bursting with new research ideas. Besides ..." he turned sheepishly to Doc. "Something tells me this won't be our last encounter."

"I hope you're right," Doc said, grinning like Geddy had never seen.

— *They are very cute.*

— That's not a word I just throw around, but yeah. They kinda are.

— *If everyone realized how little time they have, they would never stop loving.*

— That's good. You should put it on a bumper sticker.

— *A what?*

— Never mind.

CHAPTER FORTY-FIVE

TRAINING DAY

THE *STALWART* WAS one of sixty-eight heavy destroyers in the New Alliance fleet, but among them, it was unique. The hangar, which normally would've been a parking lot for forty close-support fighters and two troop transports had been converted into a pilot training center. In place of ships, rows of simulators lined the hangar.

Pilots' performance on the sims was used to create new custom mission scenarios. Geddy had been across the galaxy but had never heard of a training facility of this caliber. His old man would've been impressed.

It took a judge on Nirnaya Station less than an hour to reach a decision about the clones. Galactic law not only forbade the cloning of intelligent species but also dictated that illegal clones be humanely destroyed. However, Tretiak and Everett Hau had helped spread the Myadan story far and wide. IJC member planets overwhelmingly favored granting the clones legal status, and the court had little choice but to agree.

The video evidence they'd collected played on multiple

IJC broadcasts. Anti-Zelnad stories had begun to spread, and the other members of the Coalition were facing tough questions. Pritchard, who had led the Zelnads' coming-out party at the IASS show, was a ghost. The entire galaxy now knew that the Nads were up to no good.

In presenting his evidence to the court, Verveik also proved to billions of people that he was alive and well. And that he stood for justice. That would be key.

Geddy stopped by one of his clone pilots-in-training, Geddy 114, as he studied a looping replay of an atmospheric dogfight. "Stumped?"

"What do you call that move again?"

"A barrel roll," Geddy replied.

"What's a barrel?"

"Something that holds beer."

"What's beer?" asked 114.

Geddy drew the picture with his hands as he spoke. "Imagine a supreme being of infinite kindness and love. A beautiful woman with big, plump titties. Beer is what would come out of those titties. Understand?"

"I ... think so?"

"Atta boy." He left 114 to figure that out and continued strolling through the rows.

Twenty-six days earlier, the rest of the crew had been *officially* welcomed to the Alliance by Commander Verveik. Geddy had never seen Denk so puffed up as when Verveik shook his hand and said, "Welcome to the Alliance, young man."

It felt weird to be in the position of flight instructor and weirder still to be strolling between his doppelgängers as his voice echoed through the hangar. The acoustics weren't ideal, but there was ample space for a class of nearly three hundred, and they spent most of their days in the simulators now.

"Have I ever told you guys about the Ponley Point race?"

The clone next to him groaned and muttered, "Only about a thousand times this week."

— *Apparently, sarcasm is genetic.*

— Is that really what I sound like?

— *Yes.*

Geddy ignored him, continuing his stroll down the middle of the hangar.

"So, I'm trying to get us some much-needed scratch for the *Fizmo* by winning at Ponley, but all I have is this Ring War-era Kailorian fighter that's slower than me reaching for the check at dinner ..."

A handful of the Geddys still asked after Tatiana. Geddy would gently and patiently remind them that she was gone, and they would be crestfallen all over again.

Denk didn't think he had it in him to teach, but he was content to program most of the combat scenarios. Geddy would outline the mission parameters, suggest a couple twists, and Denk was off to the races.

In fact, Geddy had taken to spending the last hour of his day in the simulator just to keep his edge. All they knew about Zelnad ships was that they could vanish in one instant and show up behind you in the next. Adapting to that was going to be tough.

"Anyway," he continued, "I'm neck and neck with this guy in the Suicide Plunge, and we are really pushing those engines, right? I mean, we are screaming. I've gotta kill my speed immediately, so what do I do?"

"You invert and give 'er hell," several clones said in unison. "*We know.*"

Geddy was teaching them to fly, but Oz was teaching them to be soldiers. Everything from physical training to diet and discipline was her responsibility, and she'd taken to it with relish. Maybe it reminded her of her days with the Xellaran resistance. In any event, she wanted to whip these guys into shape. If they became good enough, they could train others, who could train still more. New clones would be maturing soon.

Rather than jump Dr. Krezek straight to Afolos, he and Doc had charted a private transport to turn the journey into a vacation. The timing was ideal since Parmhar's prototype wouldn't be ready for another few weeks. Besides, there wasn't much for Doc to do just yet.

In the space of a very long day on Myadan, Iondra had become Voprot's reason for living. Whether it was the astronomical circumstances of their meeting or the subtle influences of the pheromone, those two had formed a real connection. Voprot was determined to become as smart and articulate as she, which was easy to admire but difficult to imagine. She'd stayed on Myadan to oversee the cloning operation and agreed to pass information back to the Committee as the IJC's investigation unfolded.

"Officer on deck!" shouted one of the clones near the front, and they all leapt to their feet like they'd sat on a nail.

Oz marched down the stairs beside the elevated computer cluster with a stern look on her face. She often worked out side-by-side with the clones, and man, the extra effort was starting to show.

— Remind me to stay on her good side.

— I do. Quite frequently, in fact.

"As you were, gentlemen."

They returned to their seats and returned to their quiet study. Oz allowed a thin smile as she strolled up to Geddy.

"Captain Starheart."

"First Officer Nargonis. First among officers and first in my ooey-gooey heart."

She skipped the classic Oz eye roll and leaned in close.

"They're here."

CHAPTER FORTY-SIX

UNSAVORIES

THE *STALWART'S* upper hangar was much smaller than the lower. It was designed to hold small transports, such as for crew changes or guests of officers. Four additional close-support fighters were lined up along one side to protect an escape if it ever came to that.

They were in orbit over the remote gas giant Sulrinda, not far from the Karrea Ion Storm where the Alliance fleet was hidden. As soon as their meeting was over, they would jump back. Verveik wasn't crazy about the idea, but seeing the ship in all its glory was a necessary bit of theater.

Jel's ship, *Bogart*, appeared first through the hangar doors and settled onto the landing pad beside the fighters. A second, much larger ship came in right behind her. It was a pure custom job made from good used parts. The kind you had to scour the galaxy to find but couldn't actually obtain unless you were exceptionally rich, clever, or scary. It looked almost as mean as the *Armstrong* and barely fit in the main bay.

"You okay?" he asked Oz, unsure whether she'd actually *seen* the ship that had abducted her back on Verdithea.

"I'm fine," she tersely replied, biting her lower lip. Below them, the bay doors closed, and the hangar began to re-pressurize. "She won't believe you."

"Stay positive." He patted her on the shoulder. "C'mon, let's say hi."

The pressure warning light turned green, and it hissed open. The big ship's ramp lowered, and three figures descended through the shadow. Queen Tymeri emerged first, flanked by her brutish Screvari lieutenant, Horschus, and the Nichuan twins, one of whom now sported a robotic hand.

Jeledine exited the belly of her ship and gave a long stretch before heading over to join them. They all converged at the edge of the landing pad where Jel joined Geddy and Oz. There would be no handshakes.

"Thanks for taking time away," Geddy said. "I know pirating is a full-time job."

"I heard Sulrinda's nice this time of year."

"When it's not raining ammonia, it's quite lovely."

Tymeri allowed a smirk as her eyes roamed around the hold. "Nice ship. Are you and your girlfriend renting it for the weekend?"

"It's an Alliance destroyer."

She gave a smile like she knew she was being had. "Sure, it is. And I suppose those are real uniforms, too."

Oz shook her head and muttered, "Told you."

Tymeri's eyes swung back and forth between the three of them, searching for signs of deception. "How about you tell me why I'm here, and I'll think about suspending my disbelief."

"I have a one-time offer to make."

"I'm listening."

"I want to retain your services," Geddy said.

She guffawed. "What do I look like, a lawyer? Besides, we work alone."

"For ten million credits, I'm hoping you'll make an exception."

She exchanged a skeptical look with her crew, then wetly chuckled. "Bullshit."

Geddy gave a patronizing smile. "Come on. I want to show you something."

He led them across the hangar to where the close support fighters were parked, a nimble and well-armored platform called Chimera because of its flexibility. He was still getting the hang of flying it.

The front shield had a squared-off teardrop shape that widened as it raked back, giving the impression of a scowl. Clusters of armaments hung from its thick, curved wings, which could be lengthened for greater control in atmospheric flight. Coolest of all, the whole cockpit rested on a gimbal that could keep it leveled at the enemy as the ship itself reconfigured or instantly rotated to face any direction.

He ran his fingers along the wingtip. "This is an Alliance Chimera. Toward the end of the Ring War, they built almost eleven hundred of these puppies. They've never been flown."

Tymeri barked a laugh but quickly saw he wasn't kidding. "You're serious?"

"We're still learning her capabilities. What we don't know are the capabilities of our enemy. Or where to find them."

She looked at him askance. "The Zelnads? They're not *my* enemy."

"You've seen the evidence. They're everyone's enemy. Now, someday soon, Tymeri, I'm going to call on you. When I do, you come running. That's the deal. No questions, no bullshit. Do that, and you'll have your ten mil."

She raised a ridged chitinous face part resembling an eyebrow and exchanged a look with Horschus. "Come running? Like a good little dog? Fat chance."

"In good faith, I've been authorized to advance you a million. In exchange for your word, of course. And your discretion."

Her face remained implacable. You never wanted to play cards against a Ceonian.

"The Alliance died decades ago."

"We're resurrecting it," Geddy said.

"Why?"

"Because war is coming."

"You mean all that shit you told us in the cave ..."

"... was true," Geddy confirmed.

"I don't suppose I can get this deal in writing?"

He gave her a crooked grin. "It doesn't work that way. But you have my word."

She equivocated for a few seconds, measured the hopeful looks of her men, and extended the device on her exoskeletal wrist.

"Then prove you're sincere."

Geddy used the device on his wrist to deposit the million in Tymeri's account. She showed her men the balance, and their eyebrows flared approvingly.

"I'll be damned. All right, Starheart. Looks like you bought yourself a pirate crew."

"Excellent."

"Is there anything else?" she asked.

"Actually, yes. Tell me where I can find Lestiko."

Tymeri nodded. "Basoa. Outside Guntto."

"Could you be a little more specific?" Oz asked, irritated.

"He moves around a lot. But just ask around. You'll find him," Tymeri said.

"Okay, then," Geddy said.

"You'd better hold up your end, or I'll kill you myself," Oz reminded her.

She gave a bemused grin. "C'mon, boys. Drinks are on me."

They turned around and went back to their ship. Oz sneered and huffed. "I sure hope you're right about this."

"Me, too."

Jel pursed her lips and swished them back and forth. "She's in deep to some bad people. Oz's ransom was supposed to get her out from under it."

"What if she flakes?" Oz asked.

A sly grin spread across her face. "Then we'll track her with the device Hughey just placed on her ship."

Sure enough, Hughey's nanobot cloud reformed right next to her.

"I should've known," Geddy said.

"I like to hedge my bets." She clapped her hands. "Well, I guess I'll leave you guys to it. I've got a Basoan kid to track down."

They both hugged her goodbye, and she trotted off toward the *Bogart*.

As she powered up, Oz and Geddy returned through the airlock. The hangar doors opened once again, and they watched Tymeri's ship leave, followed by Jel's.

"Well, I hope no one took our parking spot," Geddy said.

They got back on the elevator and returned to the bridge. Geddy sat at the controls and hailed Verveik. A few seconds later, his giant head appeared on the front display.

Geddy reflexively sat taller in his chair. "Hey, Commander, how's it hanging?"

"Captain. First Officer Nargonis. I presume our guest agreed to the deal?"

"Reluctantly, but yeah."

"Good. How are my pilots doing?"

"Chips off the ol' block. Oz enjoys disciplining them." She punched his shoulder. "Ow! See?"

"Keep at it. The next batch will be there soon along some new recruits from the former Coalition. You need to look like you know what you're doing."

"That's kinda my thing."

The corner of Verveik's mouth twitched, which was the closest he ever got to a smile. "We'll see you back in the cloud. And no joyrides. That's an order."

Geddy saluted. "Aye aye, sir."

Verveik blinked out, leaving Geddy and Oz alone on the bridge.

"Thanks for not killing Tymeri," he said. "I know that was hard."

"Anything for the cause."

He wrapped his arms around her waist as they both watched the ship's progress back toward the rest of the fleet. "So, about this ninety-day rule ..."

"The one where we don't have sex?"

"That's the one." He started kissing her neck. "Has that been, you know, ratified yet?"

Her breathing deepened and she relaxed deeper into his embrace, reaching back with her fingers to stroke his hair.

"It's still under review. You know bureaucrats ..."

"So technically we're free to–"

Geddy's fingers had just begun to fumble with her pants when Verveik popped back on screen. They jumped apart.

"Ho! Hey, hello again, sir." He unconsciously smoothed his hair. "Was there something else?"

Verveik squinted imperiously. "I forgot to say, take as much time as you need getting back. I figure you could both use a little R and R."

"R and R. Yes, sir, that's exactly what we need. Thank you."

"As you were."

He blinked out again, and they broke up laughing.

Geddy laced his arms around her again. "You heard the Commander. As we were."

"You think I like doling out discipline, huh?" she asked.

"I was just joking."

She attempted a stern scowl. "I'm not. Drop and give me twenty."

His lips upturned and his eyebrows flared. "Twenty what?"

"Pushups, dummy."

He gave a frown and backed her up against the wall. "In a *row?*"

Oz's hands roamed all over him, her breath hot in his ear. "Why am I so hot for you all of a sudden?"

He kissed her elegant neck up and down. "My charm? My boyish good looks?"

"No, that's not it."

— *You didn't wash all your clothes from Myadan, did you?*

— What? Of course, I did. Everything but my socks.

— *... which still have sex pheromone stuck to them.*

— Oh, do they? Shoot.

— *Uh huh. I'm gonna go now.*

— Sounds good. Pick me up some cigarettes while you're out.

Again, Eli was gone. Disconnected. He always gave Geddy the courtesy when he and Oz were about to get busy, but the first few seconds were jarring.

"Is Eli giving us the room?"

He shrugged. "Yeah, but I think he secretly likes to watch."

THE END

THANK you for reading *Xeno Xoo*. Geddy and the crew will return.

Please, please give *Xeno Xoo* a rating on Amazon, if not a short written review, but only if you liked it. If you didn't, please email me at cp@cpjames.com and tell me why or I'll just keep writing books you hate.

If you haven't already, head over to reassembly. cpjames.com and nab a complimentary copy of *Geddy's Gambit*, a prequel novella from Geddy's henchman days.

The Cytocorp Saga: A Dystopian Adventure

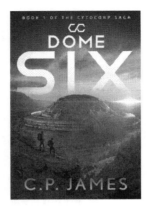

The discovery of a strange signal makes a young technician and his uncle question all they know about their utopian refuge. Now, they must solve the biggest mystery of all: Is there life beyond Dome Six?

Dome Six: Book 1 of the Cytocorp Saga is a high-concept, engrossing dystopian adventure with influences from *The Island* to *Logan's Run* and *1984*. Grab your copy today and begin *The Cytocorp Saga*.

Available now at Amazon

ABOUT THE AUTHOR

C.P. James writes cinematic sci-fi with humor and heart. He lives in the magical country of Ecuador. His first novel, *The Perfect Generation*, was published in February 2018. A dystopian trilogy, *The Cytocorp Saga*, was released in 2020. *Reassembly*, a humorous space opera, was launched in April 2021.

- Sign up for my email list (if you haven't already). As a thank-you, you'll get a digital copy of my novella, *Geddy's Gambit,* a prequel to *Reassembly* that will enhance your enjoyment of the series.

- Share your read with friends on social media.
- Email me at cp@cpjames.com with your comments, questions, expressions of concern for my mental welfare, favorite jokes, or unabashed adoration.
- Follow me on Facebook (facebook.com/ authorcpjames) or Twitter (twitter.com/ authorcpjames).
- Extra content at cpjames.com/words

ALSO BY C.P. JAMES

REASSEMBLY

Ship Show

Rocket Repo

Trawler Trash

THE CYTOCORP SAGA

The Technician: A Cytocorp Story

Dome Six: Book 1 of The Cytocorp Saga

Into the Burn: Book 2 of The Cytocorp Saga

Out of the Seam: Book 3 of the Cytocorp Saga

THE PERFECT GENERATION

The Perfect Generation

Clockwatchers

Printed in Great Britain
by Amazon

15010447R00201